THE SWISH

OF THE

CURTAIN

Pamela Brown

Hodder
Children's
Books

a division of Hodder Headline Limited

First published in Great Britain in 1941
Thomas Nelson & Sons Ltd

Published in paperback in Great Britain in 1968 and 1979
by Knight Books

This paperback edition published in Great Britain in 1998
by Hodder Children's Books

A Catalogue record for this book is available
from the British Library

ISBN 0 340 72707 1

Typeset by Avon Dataset Ltd, Bidford-on-Avon, Warks

Printed and bound in Great Britain by
Clays Ltd, St Ives plc

Hodder Children's Books
A Division of Hodder Headline Limited
338 Euston Road
London NW1 3BH

CONTENTS

1

TWO RED HEADS AND

A BLACK ONE

'They've come!' shrieked Lynette, as she ran down the sunlit garden to where Sandra Fayne lay sewing in the hammock.

'Oh, goody! We must go and see them. Hi – Madelaine!' she yelled to her nearly-nine-year-old sister, who was vainly trying to teach Pojo, the puppy, to polka. Pojo was wearing a flowered sunbonnet of Sandra's making, and now she had only the crinoline to finish before his costume was complete.

'Whatyouwant?' asked Madelaine, capering wildly down the path.

'The people have come to the Corner House.'

'What are they like, Lyn? Any children? How many? Girls or boys?'

'Well,' said Lynette breathlessly, 'I was coming up the road and I saw a car stop at the door and a man got out, and as I went past I looked in the back window of the car and I saw two red heads and a black one, and two of them were boys!'

'I'll go and get Jeremy,' said Madelaine, as she squeezed through the gap in the fence into the garden of the next-door house, where Lynette and her brother Jeremy lived.

'Come quick! Something 'citing's happened.'

Jeremy just deigned to lift his fair head from the grass to ask lazily, 'What?'

'They've come to the Corner House.'

'Who have?'

'People.'

'Well, what about it?' Jeremy wanted to know.

'You great lump!' said Maddy, jumping heavily on to him.

'You can't talk about being a lump,' he gasped.

'Well, you are. You lie there all day long reading your stupid ol' books and don't care if anything 'citing happens.'

'Hurry up, Jeremy,' Lynette shouted from the other side of the fence.

'Where am I supposed to be going? Do explain,' he pleaded, as Maddy crammed him through the hole in the fence.

'The people have come to the empty house at last,' said Lynette slowly and deliberately. 'Has that sunk in?'

'Oh, yes,' Jeremy admitted.

'Come on, then.'

'Are we going to call on them?' asked Jeremy, as they passed through the front gate with Pojo frisking at their heels.

'Ooh, I hope not,' said Maddy. 'My shorts are torn just in the wrong place, and my hair is tied up with string.'

'The car's gone,' Sandra remarked.

'Sh,' warned Lyn, as they neared the gate of the house.

'I think there's someone in the garden.'

There was someone in the garden. A girl of about Lyn's age was standing on her hands on the front lawn. As they were walking slowly by she went over and stood up in one neat movement and cried to a boy who was bending over a flower bed, 'This grass is beautifully soft for acrobatics.'

The boy stood up. He was freckled and smiling, and his hair was as red and curly as his sister's. At that moment a tall, dark boy came from behind the house, exclaiming as he came, 'It's a super garage!'

The snoopers were past the house now, and they stopped and looked at each other questioningly.

'Fancy her being able to do that!'

'He's keen on gardening.'

'Gee, what hair!'

'I wonder how old the dark one is?'

'Shall we go past again?' suggested Maddy.

'We'd better not; it's rude,' said Sandra.

'Let's,' said Lyn. 'I don't suppose they noticed us.'

So back they went, but were just in time to hear the front door bang. They stood in a disappointed group, looking up at the tall red brick house, but there were no more signs of life.

'S'pose we'd better go home,' said Maddy sadly.

'Yes.'

They walked slowly back in silent meditation, while each came to the conclusion that they must get to know their new neighbours.

At Sandra's gate Mrs Fayne was bidding good-bye to a voluminous visitor.

'Ow,' groaned Maddy, 'it's Mrs Smither-Pot.'

'Who?' said Jeremy.

'She means Mrs Potter-Smith,' explained Sandra. 'She's that beastly old woman who runs the Ladies' Institute.'

'Oh, I know her; that frightful woman who pats me on the head and calls me "dear laddy",' said Jeremy disgustedly.

Mrs Potter-Smith greeted them gushingly, kissing the three girls and patting Pojo and Jeremy on the head and saying, 'Dear laddy' to Pojo, and 'Sweet doggums' to Jeremy. Mrs Fayne said, 'Mrs Potter-Smith has very kindly invited us to a concert tomorrow given by the Ladies' Institute. You'd like to go, wouldn't you?'

Before the others had time to answer, Sandra replied dutifully, 'Yes, Mummy, we'd love to. Thank you so much, Mrs Potter-Smith. What is it in aid of?'

'It is in aid of the Ladies' Institute summer outing. I hope to take them to Eastbourne this year. Well, I really must be going. I'm such a busy little person, you know, and I've another house to visit. *So* hot for the time of year!' And she bustled off, leaving behind her a strong aroma of eau de Cologne.

'That woman!' said Jeremy, as they walked up the garden path, 'she'll be the death of me.'

' "Dear laddy, sweet little doggums",' chanted Maddy, hopping round him gleefully. 'She's just like a giant panda. Jerry, if a baby giant panda were very large would he be a giant baby giant panda? And if he shrank in the wash would he be a baby giant baby giant panda?'

Jeremy quelled her with a look.

The next day the heat-wave continued, and as they panted down the High Street in their best clothes they cursed Mrs Potter-Smith and her Ladies' Institute.

'I might have been lying in the garden reading,' Jeremy grumbled, running a finger round the inside of his collar.

'There ought to be a law forbidding Ladies' Institutes to give concerts in the Easter holidays,' said Lynette.

'I meant to put my bathing costume on and clean out the goldfish pond, and here I am walking down High Street in squeaky patent shoes and a tickly straw hat,' Maddy groused.

'It may at least prove amusing,' Sandra tried to cheer them up.

'It'll be very amusing if someone tries to play the violin,' Jeremy remarked.

'I suppose you think they ought to come to our house for a lesson from you,' said Lynette bitterly.

'You be quiet,' Maddy joined in; 'he can play Beethoven's silly symphonies like billy-o.' This produced reluctant smiles that turned to giggles and cleared the atmosphere.

After they had reached the Ladies' Institute hall and seated themselves on creaky cane chairs, Maddy produced from her pocket a sticky packet of large pear drops, and proceeded to attack them. Suddenly she pointed excitedly to the entrance. ' 'Ook!' she said, vainly trying to suppress a dribble. The rest turned their heads and met the eyes of the three children from the Corner House.

'That must have been where Mrs Potter-Smith was

going yesterday afternoon,' whispered Lyn, as the three seated themselves in the row in front.

'Shall I offer them a pear drop?'

'Shut up!' hissed Sandra, as the curtain rose in a series of violent jerks, showing the stage empty but for Mrs Potter-Smith's rear view as she bent over arranging some ferns that served as a background. When she realized she was in full view of the audience she gave a frightened squeal and scuttled agitatedly out of sight. The audience, all but Maddy, were polite, and pretended not to have seen her.

The first item was a selection of songs by a Miss Thropple. She was a tall, thin spinster dressed in a violent purple frock with crimson carnations in her black, wispy hair. Maddy remarked that she gargled rather than sang, and they all agreed. Vigorously she warbled 'Cherry Ripe.'

> 'Fule end feah ones,
> Calm end bai.'

The girl with the more auburn of the two red heads turned and gave a delighted snigger. They all returned the smile except Sandra, who, having a good voice herself, was in agony; and when, next, a bespectacled pimply faced boy tried to play a violin, Jeremy felt equally bad. A sugary voice from behind them remarked at the end of the recital, 'That's Mrs Pimmington's dear boy. They're going to have him trained.' Maddy squeezed Jeremy's arm sympathetically, for she knew it was hard for him to hear that this poor specimen would

have the opportunity that he longe~~~
had got to go into his father's office.

The next item was a play calle~~~
Spring', written by Mrs Potter-Smith.

'This sounds good,' remarked Lyn, as t~~~ ~~~ rose
to show what was meant to be a woodland ~~~ade. They
saw the dark boy in front nudge the girl, and heard him
say, 'Just look at the perspective of that tree!'

At this moment some ladies of varying ages and sizes
lumped on to the creaking stage, dressed in floral
creations, and sang:

'We are the flowers of Spring, tra la.'

An answering thud was heard offstage, and Mrs Potter-
Smith puffed on, wearing a Greek tunic, with primroses
in her hair. She flung out her plump arms, declaiming, 'I
am the Spirit of Spring!'

The ginger girl stuffed her hankie into her mouth,
and Maddy whispered confidentially to Sandra, 'Are we
supposed to laugh?'

'No,' replied Sandra, valiantly trying to suppress her
own laughter.

The 'fantasy', as it was called on the programme, wore
on to its dramatic finale, when the flowers of spring, the
birds of spring, the trees of spring, and the clouds of
spring all having performed, Mrs Potter-Smith did a
series of leg wavings, which the audience rightly took
to be a dance. At the fall of the curtain the dark boy
turned round to Sandra and remarked, 'Isn't this just too
priceless for words?' Sandra agreed, and was racking her

ın for a nice conversational remark when the Spirit of Spring appeared in front of the curtains.

'This afternoon, dear audience,' she purred, 'we have a thrilling guest artist, Mr Augustus Wheeley.' The audience nodded politely, as if Augustus Wheeley were a character of world-wide fame. Mrs Potter-Smith beamed sweetly on the audience and departed. The curtain rose. A little man dressed in black with pince-nez greeted them with a squeak, 'Good afternoon, ladies and gentlemen.'

'He speaks as if he's cleaning his teeth,' said Maddy. This remark created so much mirth in her own party that she repeated it to the three in front.

'This afternoon,' continued the little man, 'I am going to sing a selection of Paul Robeson's songs.'

Both parties went into such convulsions that for decency's sake they made a hasty exit. Outside the storm burst, and leaning against the wall they writhed in an agony of giggles.

When at last they had subsided into a weak and bleary-eyed condition the ginger-haired girl said, 'You're the people from next door, aren't you? We saw you in the garden this morning.'

'Oh, we saw you just after you arrived yesterday,' chimed in Maddy. 'You were standing on your hands on the lawn.'

'I hope the view didn't offend you,' remarked the eldest boy.

They all laughed, and Sandra said, 'Hadn't we better introduce ourselves?'

'Well, I'm Vicky,' said the ginger-haired girl.

Her red-haired brother broke in, 'Victoria Jane Halford, she means.'

'And this is my twin,' went on Vicky, 'Percy Turnbull Halford, commonly known as Bulldog.' Percy Turnbull grinned amicably. 'And this,' continued Vicky, 'is our elderly and revered brother, Nigel Murray Halford.'

Nigel bowed politely. 'At your service.'

'What lovely names,' exclaimed Maddy. 'I'm just Madelaine Fayne.'

'I'm Sandra, her sister.'

Sandra shook hands with the three, while they eyed her up and down, Vicky envying her fair hair and unfreckled skin. Lynette, who was next introduced, was Sandra's exact opposite, for her dark hair was straight and smooth and she had solemn brown eyes. Jeremy, the last to be introduced, blushed nervously as he shook hands, saying, 'I'm Jeremy Darwin.'

As they crossed the road they began to compare ages, finding that Nigel, being fifteen, was the eldest; Jeremy and Sandra were a year younger, Lynette and the twins thirteen, and Maddy, who was nearly nine, the baby. They also learnt that Vicky was to go to the local Girls' School that Sandra, Lyn, and Maddy attended; she was already wearing her school blazer with F.G.S. on the pocket, which stood for Fenchester Girls' School. Nigel and Bulldog were to start the summer term at the Boys' School to which Jeremy went.

'That's fine,' said Nigel; 'we shall be able to see a lot of each other.'

'Yes, we must,' they agreed.

'What are you doing tomorrow?' inquired Lyn.

'Nothing, I don't think,' said Bulldog ungrammatically.

'Father will probably want me to help get things in order, but I can skip that,' said Vicky confidently.

'You see,' explained Nigel, 'Mother can't do anything; she has to rest all day.'

'We've got a charwoman coming in,' Vicky went on; 'but father has old-fashioned ideas about a woman's place being in the home.'

'I know,' Sandra suggested; 'we'll cycle to Browcliffe. It's a lovely little bay, and it's only ten miles from here, so we can get there easily in an hour.'

When they had left the three at the Corner House gate Lynette said, 'What do you think of them?'

'They're lovely,' Sandra said.

As they walked up the garden path Vicky asked, 'What do you think of them?'

'Super,' replied her brothers.

2

CASTLES IN THE AIR

In a long line they streamed out on to the main Browcliffe road with a tinkling of bells. Nigel led on his long, low racer. Behind him came Lynette, on a shining Raleigh sports model, a present on her last birthday. Bulldog came next, riding his startling scarlet machine, which he had painted himself. A black flag attached to the front mudguard bore the design of a skull and crossbones. Jeremy followed on *his* bike. There is no adjective to describe it; it was just a *bike*. Sandra rode behind him, her fair hair flying out; her bicycle was very sedate, with no trace of curved handlebars or streamline about it. Vicky, who was next, came with a rattle-crash-bang on an ancient model that made Sandra's look quite daring. Maddy brought up the rear, pink in the face with the exertion of pedalling twice as fast as the others on her tiny bike, which she had long outgrown.

As they sped down Campbell Hill they caught the first glimpse of the sea as it lay sparkling and blue in the sunlit bay.

'Ooh!' gasped Maddy. 'It's warm enough to bathe!'

'Dash! We've forgotten the bathing costumes.'

'Well, we can paddle and dry ourselves on hankies,' suggested Maddy.

'I'm not going to,' said Lyn. 'Paddling's a feeble occupation.'

They dumped their bikes on the grass behind a row of stripey bathing huts and scrunched along the pebbly beach with numerous stops to empty their shoes.

'Is it more painful to get the beach in one's shoes or to take one's shoes off altogether?' asked Vicky.

'I shall have to,' giggled Maddy, guiltily running up from the water's edge. 'My shoes have sprung a leak.' She squelched along in her sopping sandals to demonstrate.

'Why is it,' asked Sandra, exasperated, 'that whenever you go near water you get your feet wet?'

'I suppose my feet are attractive to water.'

'Are the cliffs climbable?' Bulldog wanted to know.

'No!' said Jeremy, definitely.

'You lazy hound,' Lyn accused him. 'They are marvellous for climbing.'

'Do let's go up.'

'Oh, really,' Jeremy sighed, 'you people are too energetic for words.'

'Don't worry,' Maddy comforted him; 'I'll push you from behind.'

With much panting and puffing and slithering and giggling they began to climb, hanging on to tufts of grass, each other, and anything else that came their way.

'Ow!' squealed Maddy suddenly, when they were half-way up, and, letting go, slid bumpily down to the foot.

'That,' she said ruefully, 'was a thistle.'

'We'll wait for you,' said the others as she began to reascend, more cautiously this time.

Having gained the top they flung themselves down on the green springy turf with sighs of relief.

'I'm hungry,' said Bulldog.

Vicky produced three slabs of chocolate, saying, 'Let me see, there are eight squares in one bar, three bars, that makes twenty-four squares all together. That's four bits each.'

Nigel gave an exclamation of disgust at her arithmetic. 'All right,' he said. 'Be polite, help everyone first, and see what *you* get.'

'Don't bother,' interrupted Sandra. 'We've got some food of our own, so has Lyn,' and they produced apples and lollipops. For the next few minutes there was silence.

'Does anyone mind if I do some acrobatics?' asked Vicky, when only apple cores and sticky papers remained.

'Of course not; go on.'

'Do show me how to do something,' asked Maddy, as Vicky did a series of handstands, cartwheels, backbends, and splits.

'Can you stand on your head?' Vicky wanted to know as she crab-walked perilously near the edge of the cliff.

'Sort of,' said Maddy, putting her head on the grass. Kicking her legs up in the air, she came down with a thud on the other side.

'You'll break your neck if you do it that way,' Vicky warned her. 'Go up slowly, put your hands on the ground, and press with them when you feel as if you are going over.' Maddy obeyed and gradually straightened herself in the air.

'If you must wear red knickers,' remarked Jeremy, 'you needn't display them so blatantly.'

'Don't listen to him,' said Vicky, ' 'cause if you laugh you'll wobble.'

Maddy promptly quivered and collapsed. 'You *are* a nit, Jeremy,' she gasped.

They lay on their fronts and gazed out over the sea, where a little white-sailed yacht was tacking idly around in the soft breeze.

'It's one of my ambitions to win a yacht race,' said Nigel, picking grass stalks and dropping them over the edge.

'What's your biggest ambition?' Sandra asked him.

He replied unhesitatingly, 'To be an artist.'

'Would you wear a smock and a beret?'

'No, Maddy, it doesn't pay. I want to go in for commercial art, but Dad wants me to be a barrister.'

'That's like me,' put in Jeremy. 'I want to study music, but I've got to go into father's office.'

'What do you play?' asked Vicky.

'Violin chiefly, piano a bit.'

'What a shame you can't take it up; still, you can play in your spare time.'

'Yes,' said Jeremy cynically, 'I can play "Minuet in G" at Ladies' Institute concerts.'

He was sitting up now, his face pink, and was throwing stones into the sea. Lyn patted him on the shoulder.

'Now, now, don't get het up. You shouldn't have brought up the subject of careers, Vicky; it's our sore point. I want to be an actress, and Sandra wants to have her voice trained, and both our parents object because, they say, we're not good enough and we haven't got a chance.'

'That's silly,' said Nigel; 'you have to start at the beginning some time.'

'I know. But there is some excuse for our parents, because they've never seen what we can do except at a school concert. I'm not saying we're good, 'cause we're not, but we could learn.'

Lyn herself was getting 'het up' now, and her eyes were sparkling as she rolled over on her back.

'Oh, I can imagine it all – Sandra doing her trills to Jeremy's violin accompaniment, and me taking bows in front of the curtain. I think,' she said slowly, 'that my real ambition is for an audience to be so carried away by my acting that they stand up and applaud. I should be dressed in a heavy velvet frock, with long and glittering earrings, and I should curtsey and kiss my hand to the gallery, then I should –'

Here she was interrupted by a giggle from Maddy.

'What are you sniggering about?'

'I was just thinking,' said Maddy gleefully, 'that if I was sitting in the gallery I should flip an orange pip at you.'

'You've no artistic temperament,' Lyn snubbed her.

'All these ambitious people get me down,' said Bulldog, shaking his head pityingly. 'I think it's rot.'

'Haven't you any ambition?' said Lyn condescendingly.

'No; I'm quite happy being what I am at the moment.'

'So am I,' Lyn argued, 'but I should hate to go on being this for ever.'

'I'd love it.'

'But as it's impossible, what do you want to be?'

Bulldog shrugged his shoulders and blinked his hazel eyes at the sun. Lyn still pressed him for an answer.

'Would you like to be a train driver – or – a hairdresser? Tell me what *sort* of thing you would like to do.'

Bulldog was getting uncomfortable under this inquisition. He thought carefully.

'I'd like to invent something,' he decided.

'What?'

'Just something.'

'He's hopeless, leave him alone,' said Vicky.

Nigel reminded her smilingly, 'I've never heard you put forth any very ambitious ideas; at least, not since you told the rector's wife you'd like to be a cannibal.'

'Well, I have got an ambition, so there,' said Vicky, tossing her auburn curls.

'What is it?'

'It's hard to explain. It's an acrobatic feat.' She wrinkled her brow and meditated. 'Well, imagine a bench about two feet high and me standing on top of it with my back to you. Then I put my arms over my head and bend slightly backwards till I'm like this.' She got up and demonstrated. 'Then I give a spring off the bench, land on my hands with my feet in the air, and come down on my feet facing the bench.'

'It sounds lovely,' Sandra said politely.

'It sounds impossible,' corrected Nigel.

'It's not impossible; I've seen it done.'

'Why can't you do it?' Maddy inquired curiously. 'You can do all the positions that come into it.'

'I know. I get as far as the back-bend on the bench, and I daren't give the spring. Time and again I funk it.'

Lyn said comfortingly, 'You only need practice. *You've* just got to pluck up courage once and it's done, but Sandra and Jeremy and I have got tons of things to stop us.'

'And what about you, Maddy?' Nigel asked. 'What's your ambition?'

As he spoke she was burrowing her head into a soft patch of grass; she did not answer, but, pressing her hands on the ground, kicked up her heels, and, straightening her body, stood perfectly still on her head for about a minute. She came down flushed and triumphant, and said, 'Don't clap me; I know I'm good.'

'I was asking,' went on Nigel, 'what your ambition is.'

'It isn't. It was. That was it.' Maddy beamed.

They looked puzzled.

'It was my ambition to stand on my head properly, and I've done it, so I needn't have another one.'

'Don't be so lazy,' said Lyn. 'Find another one.'

'I'd like to see Mrs Potter-Smith with her false teeth out.'

'What a disgusting thought. Try again,' Jeremy advised her.

'I'd like to have my name in the newspaper.'

'Right-o. Let me murder you and it will be.' Jeremy flung himself on her and tickled her into hysterics. She ruffled his hair and pulled his nose until he chased her, and the two other boys joined in.

When they rejoined the girls, with Maddy a kicking, struggling prisoner, Sandra was saying, '. . . and one of the bedrooms will be pink and one blue.'

'Whatever are you talking about?' Nigel asked.

'We're describing what our houses will be like when we are married.'

'*If* you are married,' said Jeremy rudely. 'And anyhow, I thought you wanted careers.'

'I want a career, then a home.'

'You're greedy,' Jeremy told her, 'and I don't think women ought to have careers.' He knew that this always made Lyn see red, and winked at Nigel, who said seriously, 'A woman's place is in the home.'

'The time has gone when women spent their lives being unpaid housekeepers,' replied Lyn cuttingly.

The ensuing argument was heated and furious, and the situation was becoming rather tense when Maddy spotted an ice-cream man on the beach and challenged the others to a race down the cliff to buy some. They also inquired the time, and found that, unless they wished to be late for lunch, they must fly.

As they struggled up Campbell Hill Maddy complained to Jeremy, 'I feel sick, and if I pedal much harder my bike will take to the air and fly.'

'Then your name *would* be in the paper,' replied Jeremy. He put his hand on her carrier and pushed her in front of him.

3

MADDY THROWS A STONE

During the next fortnight the Halfords were shown every nook and cranny of Fenchester, and visited every place of entertainment. In the mornings the seven of them went for bicycle rides or skated on the roller rink, in the afternoons they went to the cinema or saw the sights of the town, and sometimes in the evenings they even blued their pocket-money on supper at a café. Then, one morning, when they assembled as usual outside the Faynes' gate, Bulldog said, 'I'm broke.'

'Same here.'

'And me.'

'So'm I.'

Apart from tenpence that Maddy produced they were completely bankrupt.

'We have been living at rather a pace,' said Nigel. 'I suppose we must calm down a bit.'

They walked disconsolately down the road. Even Pojo's head was hanging dejectedly.

'Where are we going?'

'*Je ne sais pas.*' Lynette aired her French accent.

'Where's that?' Maddy asked innocently.

'Oh, Timbuctoo.'

'We've been everywhere and done everything,'

Jeremy complained, kicking a stone along the gutter.

'Jeremy, walk properly. Here comes Mrs Bell,' Lyn admonished him.

'What's she?' Vicky wanted to know.

'She's the vicar's wife. You saw her in church last Sunday.'

'Is she nice?'

'Yes, and she thinks we are, so we always try to keep up appearances when we see her,' Sandra informed her.

Mrs Bell was overjoyed to see the children.

'Well! If it isn't my young friends. And I've been longing to be introduced to you, my dears.' She addressed the Halfords. 'I'm glad you've made friends so soon. Mrs Potter-Smith was telling me about you. Now, I wonder if you would like to come to tea on Saturday.'

'We'd love to.'

'Very well, come at three, and don't bother about wearing anything special.'

They heaved a sigh of relief, and Sandra, polite as usual, thanked her and asked after the vicar.

'And how is your dear mother? I hear she's an invalid,' Mrs Bell said to Vicky.

'She's a bit better than usual, thank you.'

'Well, I'll just drop in on my way up the road, and ask her about Saturday. Good-bye, dears.'

After they had chorused their farewells Nigel remarked, 'Isn't it funny —'

'I'm laughing like anything,' said Madelaine rudely.

'— that Mrs Bell and Mrs Potter-Smith both gush, but Mrs Bell is a dear, and Mrs P.-S. is a gorgon.'

'Mrs Bell doesn't use any ghastly perfume and

hideous lipstick, and call us "laddies",' Jeremy reminded him.

'She calls us "dears".'

'We may be dears. You never can tell, but we're not laddies.'

'Have you been there before to tea?' Vicky asked.

'Tons of times, and had a marvellous tea, and the garden's super,' replied Lyn enthusiastically.

'What's today? – Wednesday. Goodness! We've been here a fortnight. And what day do we start school?' Bulldog questioned.

'The third of May. That's a week next Tuesday.' Sandra groaned at the thought.

'We start on the second,' said Nigel, 'so let's make the best of our time.'

'Where shall we go?'

'We've seen the ruins of the castle, we've seen the Peckton Art Gallery, we've been in the museum, we've been up the water tower, we've seen all the films, and we've had a boat on the river, and we've explored the barracks.'

'*And* we've no money.'

'Isn't there a quay somewhere? We could go and look at the ships,' suggested Bulldog.

'It's so smelly down by that part of the river,' Sandra demurred.

'I like that smell,' said Maddy, sniffing reminiscently. 'It's like tinned sardines.'

'There's a Dutch ship there that brought a cargo of tulips,' Jeremy informed them.

'Oh, do let's go.' Bulldog, a keen gardener, was

excited at the thought of real Dutch tulips.

'Do you want to go?' Nigel asked Lyn.

Lyn didn't, but she could see that he wanted to, so she shrugged her shoulders.

'I don't mind. Do what you like.'

'What about you, Victoria Jane?'

'I don't want to particularly. Let's vote.' Her suggestion was accepted.

'Hands up for going.' The boys and Maddy raised their hands, the question was settled, and they started for the mercantile part of the river; the boys walked on ahead, talking male sort of talk about cars, and sport, while the three elder girls walked behind, looking in shop windows as they passed. Maddy walked on her own, hopping from the kerb to the gutter, and keeping an eye open for any treasure trove.

In the main street housewives and the élite of Fenchester were crowding the cafés for their eleven o'clock coffee. Maddy stood and gazed longingly until the girls caught her up.

'Mmm, hot chocolate and sticky cakes and Demerara sugar.'

'Come on, you little pig. We've no money.'

They dragged her away.

Gradually the street narrowed into poorer residential quarters, and when they had turned down a little street on the right-hand side they could smell the 'sardine' smell. They went on to the iron bridge, over which heavy lorries were constantly dashing, and looked down into the muddy, oil-patched water.

'Let's play Pooh Sticks,' suggested Maddy.

'What's that?'

'You each find a bit of orange peel' – she picked a piece from the grating of a drain – 'and you throw it over one side.' She dropped it and ran across the road. 'The one whose piece comes out the other side first is the winner.'

They played Pooh Sticks until they had used all the available orange peel, and then went on along the wharf, where there were trawlers and cargo vessels of all nationalities. The Dutch ship was being unloaded when they found it, and a funny little boy with a round tanned face and a red-tasselled cap was carrying immense boxes on his shoulders to a lorry waiting nearby. Nigel spoke to him.

'Good morning. Isn't it a lovely day?'

The boy merely grinned, showing two rows of even, white teeth.

'What have you got there?' Nigel asked, pointing to the box.

The boy understood and shifted the box down on to his knee. Inside it they could just see a flash of colour.

'Are they tulips?'

Still the boy just grinned.

'Try it in French,' advised Sandra.

'*Est-ce qu'ils sont des tulipes?*'

The boy nodded, but did not answer, and a man shouted to him from the boat; he continued his journeys to and fro. They decided that he must be the cabin boy of the Dutch ship.

The heat was terrific for Easter-time, and as they sank down on some large empty oil drums Jeremy said, mopping his brow, 'Thank goodness I'm not carting boxes about.'

When it was time to turn back Maddy begged, 'Do let's go back through the slums.' The dock back streets of Fenchester were unashamedly referred to, even by their inhabitants, as the slums, though their names were celestial enough, such as 'Manna Court', 'Heavensgate Street', and 'Paradise Yard'. The streets were narrow and winding, and great warehouses had sprung up between little cottages that now looked as if choked and struggling for air.

They were walking along in the middle of the road, for the pavement was narrow, and in some places still cobbled, when an errand boy on a bicycle came into sight. Although this was no remarkable occurrence, the seven stared as he approached on a rickety bicycle with an immense basket on the front. His hair was flaming red, more ginger than the twins' hair, or than any other hair in Fenchester. His prominent eyes were pale blue in colour.

As he rode past Maddy remarked, just too loudly, 'Talk about a red herring!'

He heard, and, making a terrifying face, responded with one scathing epithet, 'Fatty!'

There was nothing that annoyed Maddy more than references to her plump little person. She gave a sob of rage, and picking up a large piece of slate that was lying in the road, she threw it at him with all the force she had.

'Don't!' Lyn shouted, but too late. The missile hurtled out of Maddy's hand, but in quite the wrong direction.

There was a crash as the boy turned the corner and disappeared. Maddy gasped and burst into tears. The others swung round.

'What's the matter?'

Maddy sobbed and pointed to the side of the road. They looked and saw, squashed between two warehouses, a little one-storied building of wood. There were two grimy steps up to the front door, which had originally been blue and was now a dirty grey. On the door was a battered notice, 'The All Souls Brethren Chapel. Meetings every Sabbath', and in the left-hand window was a jagged hole where Maddy's stone had found its mark.

'Look what you've done!' said Sandra.

'I didn't mean to,' Maddy sobbed. 'I meant to hit that horrid boy.'

'Well, it hasn't spoilt the look of the place much,' Bulldog remarked.

'What had we better do?' Sandra appealed anxiously to Nigel.

'We must find out who is the rector or minister or whatever they call the boss of a chapel.'

'Don't let anyone see it till we've reported it,' Jeremy advised.

'I'll stand in front of it,' Bulldog offered.

'Right-o, and we'll go into the shop opposite and ask about it.'

Nigel led the way into the cheap eating-house across the road, leaving Bulldog leaning against the creosoted wooden wall with his head in front of the smashed pane. He put his hands in his pockets and whistled innocently, gazing into the sky as if this were his sole vocation in life. The errand boy passed again, and eyed him suspiciously, but apart from a few scraggy cats there was no other life in the road.

Inside the shop Nigel bought a bar of chocolate, borrowing Maddy's last tenpence, and asked the enormous old lady behind the counter 'How's trade?'

She shook her head ponderously. 'Bad, very bad. Not what it used to be.' She sniffed sadly, screwing up her heavy-featured face into a thousand wrinkles and furrows.

'Is the chapel opposite anything to do with the chapel up Forrester Road way?' he asked conversationally. The woman was ready to gossip, for she had taken a liking to this handsome, polite boy, who treated her with such gentlemanly deference.

'No, sir, that it ain't. That ain't been open these three years. The last minister, 'e was 'ad up for forging banknotes. And he was such a nice man. The 'all useter be reg'lar packed, and 'e cured Mrs Cuttleberry, what live across the road o' me; 'e cured 'er rheumatics something wunnerful.'

'Who does the hall belong to now?'

'I couldn't rightly say, sir. Brother Irving, as 'e uster call 'imself, 'e bought the 'all with 'is own money, but being as 'ow 'e's in prison I couldn't rightly say.'

Nigel paid for the chocolate and they trooped out of the shop.

'What news? asked Bulldog, still with his head over the hole.

'It doesn't seem to belong to anyone, as the former

minister has been in prison for three years.'

'But we must do something about the window,' Sandra pointed out.

'Let's see what it's like inside.' Bulldog peered in through the hole. 'It's awfully dark. I can't see much. Yes, I can. There are rows of chairs and a high platform at the other end.'

They each took a turn in looking.

'Thank goodness it's a pretty small pane of glass. We ought to be able to mend it ourselves.' Nigel measured the pane roughly with his fingers. 'Yes, it's about ten inches by six. We could buy a piece of glass that size and easily fix it in with putty. I think I could do it.'

'There's a lump of putty in our shed,' Jeremy observed, 'and if we go round to Blake's workshop we might pick up a bit of glass on the cheap.'

'That's the trouble – money,' Lyn was despondent.

'I,' Maddy exclaimed suddenly, 'have a birthday on Saturday!'

The situation was saved. Maddy would pay for the glass with her birthday money. Nigel marked the length and breadth of the pane on a piece of paper.

'But I shall pay you some, Maddy, when *I* get some,' Vicky told her.

'And I shall pay a little, too,' added Nigel.

'If Nigel pays, I shall,' put in Jeremy.

'So shall I.' This was Bulldog.

'Well I shall, because I ought to have been looking after Maddy better,' said Sandra.

'I shall help if Sandra does,' Lyn remarked; 'so it won't cost anyone much.'

'But what shall we do about it till Saturday? We'll have to mend it in the morning, because we're going to the vicarage in the afternoon.'

'Bulldog will have to stand in front of it day and night,' Maddy suggested.

'Impracticable,' said Bulldog.

'I know,' Vicky exclaimed. In the road there lay a handbill advertising a film appearing at the Palace Cinema. She picked it up. 'Stick this over it and people won't notice anything.'

'Good idea,' applauded Nigel, 'but what shall we stick it with?'

'Sellotape,' Jeremy said, producing some from his pocket.

Carefully they stuck the bill up so that the whole broken pane was covered.

'Super,' was Jeremy's verdict, as he stepped back to see the final effect.

'H'm-h'mm,' Lyn coughed to attract their attention. 'The time,' she said, 'is five past one.'

With squeals of surprise they turned and hurried towards home. Maddy panted along at the rear, occasionally breaking into a trot to keep up.

'Life,' she puffed sadly, 'is just one thing after another.'

4

VICARAGE TEA PARTY

Maddy opened her eyes and wondered why she felt excited. Of course! It was her birthday.

'Fancy me being alive nine years!' she thought, 'and I may live ten times this amount of years.'

She heard the postman come, and bounced up and down with expectation. Then Mrs Fayne shouted up the stairs. 'You awake, Maddy? There are some letters for you.'

'How many?'

'Four and a little parcel.'

She jumped out of bed, and pattered along to the bathroom for a 'lick and a promise'. When she came back Sandra was seated on the bed in a camel-hair dressing-gown.

'Many happy returns, Maddy.'

'Thanks. Have you got a present for me?'

Sandra shook her head sadly but her eyes were merry. 'No. You know I'm broke.'

But when Maddy sat down to breakfast there were five big parcels and a little one and four letters beside her plate. Inside the first parcel, a thin, flat one, was a book of paper dolls with clothes that you painted, then cut out and put on the little cardboard figures. On the outside was written, 'With love from Sandra.' Maddy was delighted, and when she opened the next parcel and found that it contained an enormous paint box from her father she was so delighted that she knocked over her bowl of grapefruit.

'What a good job it's my birthday,' she said, watching the patch of juice spread over the tablecloth. The other presents proved to be a book of animal stories (from her aunt), a money-box shaped like an elephant with a hollow trunk that you put the pennies in (from her uncle), and a large furry lion with a zip down his tummy, where you opened the nightdress case that he held inside him. The last was from her mother.

'I'll christen it Henrietta after you, Mummy,' she said.

'It's not a lady lion, 'cause it's got a mane,' Sandra informed her.

'I'll call it Henry, then.'

She opened one of the envelopes with trembling fingers, assailed by the dreadful thought it *might* contain only a birthday card and no money. Then she heard the crisp crackle of paper. It was a five pound note! Her eyes sparkled, and she tried to kick Sandra under the table.

'Mind my best shoes,' said her father from behind the *Daily Telegraph*.

'Sorry,' Maddy apologized meekly.

The other letters were birthday cards from her friends, and the little parcel which had been put through the door just before the postman's visit, bore the label, 'With love from the Halfords and Darwins.' Inside was a mouth-organ. Maddy blew delighted discords on it. Mr Fayne put his hands over his ears.

'Good heavens! Fancy anyone being so misguided as to give you an instrument of torture like that.' But, all the same, when she offered him a blow he did not refuse.

Directly she had finished her egg she asked, 'Will you excuse Sandra and me, Mummy?'

'Yes, dear, as long as you don't go spending a lot of your money.'

'I think,' put in Mr Fayne, 'that I had better look after some of that for you.'

'Oh no!' Maddy's eyes dilated with horror, and quickly she stuffed it down the elephant's trunk of her money-box. 'There, it's safe now.'

'Yes, as long as you don't lose the box.'

Sandra and Maddy flung on their anoraks, and crawling through the hole in the fence, banged on the Darwins' back door. Jeremy opened it, but with no welcoming words, for his mouth was full. He chewed silently, and when he was able, said, 'Sorry. Bread and marmalade. What do you want?'

'Thanks for your part of the mouth-organ, and look what I've got.' Maddy held up the elephant.

'He's lovely,' said Jeremy uninterestedly.

'It's not the box, it's what's in it,' Sandra explained.

'It's money,' went on Maddy excitedly, 'to pay for the–'

'Sh!' Jeremy, comprehending at last, glanced nervously over his shoulder and drew the door to behind him.

'We want to get it out, and it's the kind you have to take the bottom off.'

'Wait a tick and I'll come and do it for you.'

He went inside, calling, 'Lyn, here are Maddy and Sandra.' They both appeared a few minutes later and in the shed, which smelt of bicycle tyres and blacking, they took the elephant to pieces.

'Let's pretend we're doctors doing an operation for appendicitis,' Maddy suggested. She stuffed her hankie down his trunk. 'Look, I've given him an anaesthetic.'

'The surgeon now applies the knife,' said Jeremy, sliding his penknife under the joining of the base. Gently he levered off the bottom, and the note fluttered out.

'Now we must go round to Blake's and get the glass. Here's the putty.'

They went round the side of the Faynes' house, out at the front gate, and down to the Corner House. Vicky was doing her usual half-hour acrobatic practice in the garden, attired in a blouse under a bathing costume. She was in a back-bend when they scrunched up the gravel path.

'You look funny upside down,' she greeted them.

'No funnier than you do.'

'It's not ten, is it?' This was their usual time for going out.

'No,' Jeremy explained, 'but you know what we've got to do this morning, and Maddy's got the money.'

'Oh, goody.' Vicky got up and ran into the house, calling over her shoulder, 'Take a seat.' They sat down on the grass, and a few minutes later were joined by Nigel and Bulldog.

'Where's Vick?' Lyn asked.

'Making herself look respectable.'

She came out a few minutes later in a green linen frock, looking neat and tidy and altogether as if she had never heard the word 'acrobatic'.

'Now what are we going to do, exactly?' Nigel wanted to know. 'We can't go and mend it quite openly.'

'Why not?'

'Well – we just couldn't.'

'I think we could,' Lyn disagreed. 'If anyone asked what we were up to we should just say we broke the window and were mending it. That's perfect truth, and if we mend it there's no blame on us.'

'True, O King,' said Nigel thoughtfully.

Sandra voiced her opinion, saying, 'I vote we do it openly, because it's no sin to break a window.'

'O.K. Let's go.' Nigel jumped up pulling Sandra after him, and they all started off for Blake's workshop.

'I'll go in,' Jeremy offered, 'because he is a friend of mine.'

Maddy handed over the note that she had been holding tightly screwed in her fist.

'Where's the paper you measured the window by?' he asked Nigel. Nigel produced it.

While they were waiting for him to come out, Maddy found a litter basket attached to a lamp-post.

'Aha!' she thought, 'where there are litter baskets there are usually empty cigarette packets, and where there are cigarette packets there is silver paper.' She plunged both arms into the rubbish it contained. The others, leaning against some railings, talking idly, were startled by a pained yelp. Maddy, with a finger in her mouth, was hopping round in circles.

'I've been stung, I've been stung,' she squealed.

'Oh, you poor little thing,' Sandra swooped on her sympathetically. 'Let's have a look. Oh, it's not very bad. Suck it.'

'However did it happen?' Lyn wanted to know. Maddy explained. 'Well, you must expect wasps in rubbish baskets.'

Jeremy came out of Blake's with a satisfied air, carrying a parcel and jingling coins in his hand.

'A very successful transaction. I've even got some change for you, Maddy!' The others expressed delight. 'Don't clap me, I know I'm good. And furthermore he's given me some hints on putting in panes.'

'Good work!' Nigel commended, and they made their way towards the hall.

They found the bill still covering the hole in the window and the same air of derelict misery over the whole street as on their former visit. Nigel and Jeremy took off their coats and set to work at once, while Maddy modelled little men out of the putty.

'I'm going to explore,' Bulldog decided. 'Do you think I could squeeze round the side and get to the back of the place?'

'I shan't come and lever you out if you stick,' Vicky warned him.

The space between the side of the hall and the next-door building was very narrow, but somehow Bulldog managed to contract his thick, stocky body and squash it into the aperture.

'If I don't come back I leave all to you, Lyn.'

'Delighted, I'm sure.'

'Confound the thing!' said Jeremy savagely as the piece of frosted glass slipped for the third time.

'Shall I play helpful tunes on my mouth-organ?' Maddy offered.

'Please don't.'

'You don't appreciate good music when you hear it,' she mourned.

'Oh, go and find Bulldog.'

With much puffing and blowing she squeezed along the side. When at last she found herself at the back, her dress was black with dirt and her face covered with smuts. She surveyed her hands ruefully and rubbed them down her dress. Bulldog was nowhere to be seen, but the little back door was open, and she walked into a dark, musty atmosphere. Bulldog's voice called to her from the gloom.

'Hi, who's that?'

'Me.'

'Maddy?'

'Yes.'

'Stay there. The lights won't go on, but I've got an electric torch. I've tumbled over three chairs already.' There was a crash. 'That was the fourth.'

The beam of the torch travelled to and fro. Maddy saw that she was standing by the side of a large raised platform, on which stood a chair and a table. There were benches and chairs arranged in rows down the length of the hall, facing the platform, and little blue hassocks in front of them. The windows down each side were of the same frosted glass as the one that was being mended, and as they faced blank walls they let in only a glimmer of daylight. On the other side of the platform was a little door. She went across and poked her nose into the room. It contained a large table with several chairs standing round it, and benches, step-ladders, and brooms stacked in the corners. She was joined by Bulldog.

'Not exactly a cheerful place, is it?'

'No,' she agreed. 'And jolly dirty.'

'So would you be if you were left alone for three years.'

They explored all the corners.

'Here's a little wash basin. I should think when this was a chapel this was the vestry.'

'It's very empty now,' Maddy said. 'I suppose all the vests were taken away when Brother What'sisname was put in jail. May I have the torch? Thank you.'

'H'm. Peculiar place. I found that back door left unlocked, so I walked in. I'll go and fetch the others.'

Left alone, Maddy clambered up on to the platform and wrote her name in the dust that carpeted it. The others arrived, breathless and dishevelled, a few minutes later.

'What a sinister-looking place!' Sandra exclaimed. 'And doesn't it smell horribly. I'd like to get to work on it with a scrubbing-brush.'

'Look, a piano! Spotlight, Maddy!'

Nigel dashed to it and thumped out some jazz with great vigour. Bulldog began to sing in a husky tone, and Vicky did an impromptu dance routine. They only stopped when they were breathless.

'You didn't know we could do that, did you?' Nigel

laughed at the surprised faces of the others.

'It's clever,' Jeremy criticized, 'but it's not beautiful. Whoever taught you to play, Nigel?'

'No one. I picked it up myself.'

'Oh, that explains it!'

'Don't be rude, Jeremy. *You* can't play like that,' Lyn admonished him.

'I think Nigel plays as well as Jeremy, only differently,' said Sandra fairly.

'Let's hear you, Jeremy,' Vicky requested.

He sat down at the piano, stared into space a little, then dreamily his fingers floated into the melody of a Beethoven sonata. The tune changed into 'Barcarolle' from *Tales of Hoffman*.

'Come on, Sandra,' he murmured.

She went and stood by the piano.

> 'Night of stars,
> And night of love . . .'

Her voice was soft but sweet. Lyn got up and danced with her shadow to the slow waltz time. When the last lingering note had died away the others applauded vigorously.

'Why, that's wonderful,' said Nigel appreciatively.

'You know, between us we are quite talented,' Lyn remarked thoughtfully.

'We're infant prodigies,' Nigel agreed lightly.

'Specially me on my mouth-organ.' Maddy produced it again amid groans of despair.

'I think we'd better be going,' said Sandra. 'Bulldog's

torch seems to be fading. Shut the piano lid, someone.'

'Must we squeeze along the wall again?' Lyn asked distastefully, eyeing her pink cotton frock which had been considerably soiled on the former journey.

'I think this back gate will open.'

Jeremy walked over the patch of untidy grass that was strewn with empty tins, newspaper, and refuse of all kinds. He tried the low gate, set in a broken-down fence.

'Yes, we can get out on to a street parallel to the one in front.'

'What's the name of that street?' asked Sandra, latching the gate behind her.

'Pleasant Street,' answered Bulldog. 'It's written up on the wall at one end.'

'The person who christened it must have had a sense of humour,' laughed Nigel; 'I can't think of any street more *un*pleasant.'

As they parted at their gates Sandra reminded them, 'Ten to three this afternoon to go to Mrs Bell's. We must be punctual.'

'Not *too* punctual. It's not etiquette to be waiting on the doorstep on the stroke,' said Nigel.

'You bet we shan't be,' laughed Lyn, 'not with Jeremy and Maddy to be got ready.'

It was half past three when they stood in a row on the vicarage doorstep and Sandra rang the bell. Last minute instructions were whispered.

'Don't say "Gosh", and don't talk with your mouth full,' Sandra warned Maddy.

'And Jeremy, do make polite conversation. Don't sit

like a stuffed giraffe, as you usually do.'

Jeremy was used to being ordered about by his younger sister.

'Remember not to do acrobatics. You're not wearing shorts,' Nigel reminded Vicky, and to Bulldog, 'Don't eat too much.'

However, when Mrs Bell opened the door all their anxiety concerning etiquette was dispelled, for she was the kind of person with whom one felt instantly at home. They hung their coats on the hall-stand, and she led them into the large airy lounge, into which the afternoon sun streamed through the open French windows. They sat down and talked, Mrs Bell asked interested questions about their schools and occupations.

Maddy, who had eaten a large dinner and was now curled up in the sunshine on a divan, found herself growing drowsy. Birds singing in the garden and Sandra's voice telling Mrs Bell about the Domestic Science Department at school were the last things she heard before she drifted into soft rosy dreams. The next thing she knew was a voice, a great distance away, that said, '. . . so perhaps some tea will wake her up.' She opened her eyes and sat up. How awful of her to go to sleep when she was invited out to tea! The others were laughing, but Mrs Bell said comfortingly, 'I don't blame you, Maddy; this room is far too hot, that's what's wrong.' The front door slammed. 'Ah, there's the vicar. I'll make the tea.' She hurried out, and a few minutes later the vicar came in. He was a grave-faced, elderly man with whitening hair.

'He's like a saint,' thought Sandra admiringly, as he shook hands with them. Like his wife, he was a great lover of children, although they had none of their own.

Over the tea-table in the cool old dining-room he began to tell of the book he was writing on the life of St. Paul. They listened with half their attention, the other half being centred on the demolition of the delicious home-made cakes and scones that Mrs Bell had provided for them. One of the dishes was covered with a cardboard box, and when everyone was nearly satisfied she removed it with a flourish. Underneath was a cake coated with white icing and written on it in pink, 'Many happy returns for Madelaine.'

'Ooh,' squealed Maddy rapturously, 'however did you know it was my birthday?'

'Aha, a little bird told me.'

The cake was cut into slices, and Maddy had the piece with the M on it.

'It reminds me of the ones you used to make for the annual sales of work at Maybridge,' the vicar told his wife as he bit into his slice. She blushed as he went on, addressing the children, 'You know, when I first met Mrs Bell she was the daughter of a country rector, and she used to help him run the parish. Then he decided it was too much work for her and advertised for a curate. She was very annoyed at the thought of losing her old position, and made up her mind to hate the new curate, but I was the curate, and you can see what happened.

'What did?' asked Maddy breathlessly.

'They married and lived happily ever after, of course,' said Lyn.

'That's right,' the vicar assented.

'Do you remember those amateur theatricals in the village hall when we used to sing duets?' asked Mrs Bell, her eyes shining.

'Those were great times. If you remember, I proposed to you when you were fitting me for the prince's costume for the Christmas pantomime. *You* were on your knees, not me, because you were pinning up a hem.'

He was addressing his wife now, and they seemed to have forgotten the presence of the children.

'Yes,' went on Mrs Bell, 'let me see, wasn't it one of the doctor's daughters who played Cinderella, and you had to kiss her? It used to make me feel so jealous!' They both laughed.

'And do you remember how we all used to bring peppermints to suck during rehearsals, and old Mr – oh, what was his name? – he was the choirmaster–'

'Rawlins?' Mr Bell suggested.

'Mr Rawlins. Yes, he used to get into such tempers and tear up the script.'

'It sounds as if you had a lot of fun,' said Lyn enviously. 'I wish there were a dramatic company I could join.'

'Well, my dear, where there's a will there's a way. I think you children ought to start one of your own. You're all quite clever. I've heard you, Lynette, and Sandra, at that end-of-term concert, and Jeremy, I know, plays a violin, and you three can do things in the acting line, can't you?' she asked the Halfords.

'Oh yes, they can. Vicky dances, Nigel plays the

piano, and Percy' – Lyn giggled – 'he sings.'

'I thought your voice was beginning to break.' Mrs Bell seemed surprised.

'Oh, it's not that sort of singing,' Bulldog explained hastily, wincing at the use of his first name. 'It's a sort of tenor.'

'I see. Well, with all that talent I'm sure you could get up a very nice little show.'

'Why ever didn't we think of that before?'

'What a good idea!'

'Oh, wouldn't it be fun!'

'Do let's, then I can play my mouth-organ!'

The children were excited by the idea.

'The only thing is, where should we give the show?' Nigel asked, frowning thoughtfully.

'I could let you use the Ladies' Institute hall, but I'm sure Mrs Potter-Smith would be offended,' said Mrs Bell apologetically. 'Though really I thought that dance she did was almost indecent.'

The children giggled at the remembrance of it. Maddy, who was drinking her tea, spluttered suddenly and choked. She coughed violently and tried to say something.

'Got – idea . . .' She struggled for breath and her eyes streamed. 'That place!' Here she was interrupted by a more violent fit than ever.

'Maddy, don't try to talk. Hold your breath,' Sandra urged.

But Vicky realized what she was trying to say.

'Don't you realize what Maddy's thought of?' she asked excitedly.

'That hall – in Pleasant Street.' Nigel banged his fist triumphantly on the table.

'Of course, the perfect place!'

There was an excited babel of chatter. The vicar and his wife looked bewildered until Sandra explained how they had found the All Souls Brethren Chapel.

'Ah, yes,' said the vicar, leaning back in his chair, 'I know the place, and I heard something about the fellow who ran it. You say the place is not being used at all?'

'That's right, sir.'

'Well,' said the vicar knitting his brow, 'I think I will have a little talk with the local authorities and see if it can be arranged for you to use it.'

The children were seething with delight.

'But I thought the man paid for it himself; therefore it still belongs to him,' said Mrs Bell anxiously.

'Not if the notes were forged. It's a difficult legal situation, but I'm sure it can be cleared up.'

'How glorious!' exclaimed Lyn. 'A theatre of our own! Oh, it's a dream come true.'

'It'll need a lot of cleaning up,' said Sandra, 'outside and in.'

'I'll turn that back-yard into a garden,' Bulldog offered enthusiastically.

'And I'll paint the outside,' said Nigel.

'We can use that vestry place for a dressing-room as there's a wash basin. And there's the piano, that'll be useful, and oh – what about curtains?' Vicky was stumped.

Mrs Bell got up suddenly. 'Follow me,' she ordered mysteriously.

They mounted two flights of stairs after her and found themselves in the attics. She entered one and opened a chest that stood in the corner. There was a layer of newspapers and mothballs on top, and underneath lay some heavy blue material. She unfolded it.

'Curtains. Stage curtains. They're what we used in Maybridge. And here,' she patted the chest, 'are a lot of our costumes and properties.'

She delved into the box and brought out armfuls of dresses, swords, hats, and all the most thrilling junk imaginable.

'All this, dears, is at your disposal if you care to use it,' she told them kindly.

'Thank you, oh, thank you, *dear* Mrs Bell,' they cried ecstatically. 'However can we repay you?'

'By giving a really enjoyable play and working at it very hard,' she replied. 'Now, I expect you'd like to be discussing it among yourselves, so I'll leave you.'

She disappeared, and over the open costume box they wildly and enthusiastically discussed the future.

5

THE BLUE DOOR THEATRE

It was Monday morning and they sat round the table in
the little room of the hall, armed with pencil and paper.
Silence reigned for the first time since the decision at
the vicarage tea-table had been made. Realizing that
before it was attempted to get up a show they must give
the appearance of the place a lot of attention, they were
now each engaged in making a list of necessary
alterations and the cost it would involve. The vicar had
arranged the turning on of light and water.

'I've finished.' Vicky banged down her pencil.

'Tell me some,' begged Maddy.

'Don't be silly. This isn't a parlour game.'

'Youngest read first,' ordered Nigel, who, as eldest,
had been appointed chairman of the meeting. Maddy
stood up and coughed importantly.

'Unaccustomed as I am to public speaking–'

'Don't fool about!'

Maddy read her list.

'Number one – remove peculiar smell. Cost – all
depends. Number two – get something to muffle the
loud pedal of the piano in case Nigel plays it. Cost –
don't know.'

She sat down, and Nigel glared.

'Is that all? We'll only consider the first point. That is – the peculiar smell. Now, what does it consist of?'

They sniffed earnestly.

'I think it's just general dust and cobwebs and dampness,' said Sandra.

'With a touch of bad drains,' added Jeremy.

'Well, how do we remedy it? Come on, Sandra, this is in your line.'

'It needs all the floors scrubbed, all the windows cleaned, and a good dusting.'

'Right, we'll put that on the list.' He took a fresh piece of paper. 'Number one – cleaning of interior. Cost?'

'Nothing. We can do it ourselves,' Sandra told him.

'Now you can cross off anything to do with cleaning that you have on your lists. Next, please. Which of the twins is the younger?'

'Bulldog. Half an hour.'

Bulldog read his list.

'Number one – plant marigolds in the garden. Number two – put up stage curtains. Number three – paint door. Cost – nothing.'

'Good list. Now, about the first. We presume that you mean to do up the back-yard?'

'Yes.'

'Can we leave that to you? And what will it cost?'

'Nothing. I can get some seeds and plants from home. And the path to the back gate must be scrubbed.'

'About the curtains,' went on Nigel, 'I should think we boys could manage that if the girls sewed on curtain rings and things. But what about the paint for the door?'

'There's some blue paint in our shed,' said Jeremy.

'Fine. The door was blue originally. Well, that won't cost anything. We can put those down on the final list. Yours, Vick?'

'Number one – whiten the front steps. No cost. Number two – wait for a wet day and see if the roof leaks. Number three – mend all broken chairs and possibly paint them.'

'Good idea,' applauded Nigel. 'I'll put down about whitening the steps. We can do that ourselves; and, Jeremy, is there enough blue paint to do the back fence and gate too?'

'Yes, and the roof as well. It would look rather good.'

'We'll have to wait for a wet day to see about leaks; and couldn't we paint the chairs and benches blue too?'

'Rather gaudy!' Sandra objected.

'Gayer the better. Let's vote on it.'

Sandra was the only one against it.

'Sorry, old girl. Lyn, you next.'

'One – re-creosote the exterior walls. Two – scrub the interior walls. Three – divide this room into two with a curtain, for dressing-rooms. Four – wash the electric-light shades.'

'The creosote will cost something, but we'll try and do it ourselves. We can also scrub the walls and we'll have to find a curtain or something for this room, and we can easily scrub those light shades.' He added to the steadily growing list. 'Jeremy?'

'One – have piano tuned. Two – have chimney in this room swept. Three – clean up the wash basin. And four

– see if there is anything wrong with the drains and the lavatory.'

'You and your piano. It does need tuning though; and I admit a chimney sweep would be a good idea. How much does one cost?'

'It's a question of finding one, these days,' supplied Sandra, gloomily.

'Wash basin, drains, and lavatory we can manage ourselves, unless there is anything radically wrong. Your list, Sandra?'

'One – wash the little flat hassocks and use them as cushions for people who sit at the back and can't see too well. Two – make curtains for the windows. Three – paint a signboard with the name of the theatre to hang over the door.'

'Super idea about the cushions. What about the curtain material?'

'Get something very cheap. Total cost, about' – she added up on her fingers – 'very little if we have two at each window, even less if we only have one.'

'Only one,' was the unanimous decision.

'I can paint a sign-board,' offered Nigel, 'if Jeremy supplies the paint; can you get enough, by the way?'

'Daddy deals in paints and varnishes,' Lyn explained.

'Good for us. Well, the question now arises, what shall we call ourselves? And the theatre?'

'Before we start that, have you any left on your list, Nigel?' Sandra asked him.

'Only one. Scrub the pavement outside. And we must remember we have only a week to do everything in.

This time next week we shall have our hands to the plough again.'

'Do let's make up our minds what we're going to be called,' urged Lyn.

'What sort of name do we want?' Vicky asked.

'It must be short, it must roll easily off the tongue, it must explain what sort of people we are, and it must be attractive,' tabulated Nigel.

They thought in silence, then Sandra asked, 'Shall we be the Something-or-other Company, or the Something-or-other Club, or what?'

'Not "club",' stipulated Lyn; 'we want to sound as professional as possible.'

'What about the "Fenchester Repertory Company"?' suggested Vicky.

Nigel shook his head. 'No, we're not a proper repertory, and we can't call ourselves "Fenchester" because we're not important enough – *yet*,' he added optimistically.

'What about the "Something-or-other Players",' suggested Sandra.

Lyn screwed up her nose. 'Sounds like cigarettes.'

'Let's decide what we're going to call the theatre itself, then call ourselves the Something-or-other Theatre Company,' was Jeremy's suggestion.

'Yes, "Theatre Company" sounds good, doesn't it?' appealed the chairman.

They all assented.

'But what theatre company?'

'We could call it the Blue Theatre,' suggested someone.

Bulldog pounced on the suggestion. 'Yes, but not just "Blue" – what about "Blue Door"? 'Cos we are going to paint it blue.'

'Blue Door Theatre Company.' They all tried it over to see how it sounded, and Nigel wrote it down and studied it from every angle.

'We'll vote on it,' he said, and every hand went up.

They looked at each other excitedly across the table, now that the decision was made.

'The Blue Door Theatre Company,' announced Maddy in B.B.C. accents, 'now present to you *Uncle Tom's Cabin*, with Madelaine Fayne as Little Eva, and Jeremy Darwin as Uncle Tom Cobley and all.'

One afternoon during the next week Mrs Fayne ran into her next-door neighbour, Mrs Darwin, who asked, 'I suppose you can't tell me where those children of ours get to all day and every day? I am sure they are up to some mischief.' Her dark eyes, so like Lyn's, were anxious.

'Sandra only told me last night,' said Mrs Fayne, smiling.

'Well, what is it?'

'There's no need to be anxious, because the vicar and Mrs Bell know all about it. You see, the children broke a window of a little chapel or mission hall down Pleasant Street. Do you know the place? It's a dilapidated wooden building. It's empty now,' went on Mrs Fayne, 'and they mended the window themselves, and at the same time explored the place. Well, when they were at Mrs Bell's, Lyn was saying how much she wanted to go on the stage.'

'I know all about that,' groaned Mrs Darwin. 'I hear nothing but that subject morning, noon, and night, and Jerry is just as bad over his music.'

'Evidently Mrs Bell suggested their starting a little dramatic company of their own, and the vicar said they could have the hall, and he would make it all right with the authorities. So that's where they go every day.'

Light dawned on Mrs Darwin.

'Now I understand why my scrubbing brush disappeared, and why Jeremy's been coming home with blue paint on his hands. Well, well, what will they get up to next?'

'It's better than going round the town in a gang and squandering their money right and left, as they were doing up to a few days ago,' said Mrs Fayne. 'And I don't suppose this concert or whatever it is will ever come off.'

'And then there's school next week.' Mrs Darwin heaved a sigh of relief. 'They'll soon forget this stunt.'

And they parted to continue their shopping.

At the All Souls Brethren Chapel there was great activity, for today was Thursday, and on Saturday the Clean-up Campaign must be finished. There was a small gathering of dirty little children standing on the pavement gazing up at the roof where Nigel and Jeremy, in filthy overalls, were slamming on blue paint with lavish brushes. This was the third coat it had been given, as the paint ran in little rivulets down the grooves of the corrugated iron and dripped to the ground; this time it looked as if it were going to stay on.

Jeremy rubbed a hand across his brow, left a blue

smudge, and sighed heavily as he squatted in a perilous position with his heels dug into the troughing.

'I shall dream of blue paint tonight,' he moaned, 'lakes of it, oceans of it, all dripping down on to my feet.' He made a final tour of inspection along his side, then shouted to Nigel, who was in a similar position on the other side of the roof.

'I'm finished, and I'm getting off this awful perch if I can.'

'You can't,' Nigel answered him; 'the girls have taken the step-ladder.'

'Whatever for?' wailed Jeremy.

'To put up the window curtains, I think.'

Inside the hall Sandra was seated on the platform, sewing on hooks and rings, while, at one side, Lyn had just arranged the vivid blue curtain. She stood back and admired it.

'Looks good, doesn't it? The ironing made all the difference.'

Sandra broke off the thread. 'Here you are, the last one. And now we shan't see that awful frosted glass.'

'But think what we shall burn in electric light!'

'The vicar said he'd see to that. He's a kind fairy in disguise.'

'Now, what's next on the list?'

Lyn produced a piece of paper from the pocket of her jeans.

'Maddy's washing the hassocks, Bulldog's painting the back railings, the boys are painting the roof, and Vicky is mending chairs.'

A sound of hammering from the little room confirmed this fact. Vicky was never happier than when armed with a hammer and a few nails. Whenever she finished a chair she would call to Maddy, who was standing at the wash-basin up to her eyes in soapsuds, and Maddy would come and jump up and down on the chair to test its safety.

'Soapsuds, soapsuds,
Oh, the pretty flowers,'

sang Maddy, wringing out another flat blue hassock.

'Come and try this one,' she was invited.

She mounted the chair and bounced vigorously; there was a splintering sound, and she was precipitated to the floor.

'I must say you're a bad carpenter,' she grumbled, rubbing the part of her anatomy that had suffered most damage.

Vicky was not perturbed. 'Oh, I can easily mend it, and our audiences won't jump on them, we hope.'

'Unless they applaud very hard,' said Maddy. 'Didn't Lyn say it was her ambition for an audience to jump on their chairs?'

'No. She said she wanted them to stand up and clap.'

Maddy mused in silence for a while.

'Lyn's a peculiar person, isn't she, Vicky?'

'What do you mean?'

'Well, if she wasn't Lyn she'd be stuck up and silly and bossy, but, as she is Lyn, she's not.'

'I think I see what you mean,' said Vicky, tentatively

tapping a nail. 'I've never met anyone so – so – like she is, before.'

There was a furious commotion on the ceiling above them.

'What a row those boys are making on the roof,' remarked Maddy.

Jeremy's voice reached them faintly. 'Bring us that ladder. We've finished.'

Lyn and Sandra evidently obeyed, for a few minutes later the two roof painters came in, peeling off their filthy overalls.

'You look like a clown, Nigel,' giggled Maddy.

Nigel dipped his blue-patched face under the tap and rubbed it with his hands.

'Don't bother to wash, Nigel,' said Lyn, entering. 'The next job on the list is creosoting the outside walls.'

Nigel groaned. 'Who would be a painter?'

'You said you wanted to be an artist,' Maddy reminded him.

'I'm getting sick of flat washes. Where's the creosote?' he asked wearily.

'Bulldog's just finishing the back fence. You'd better start on the back, then you can use the same pail.'

The next day the creosoting was finished, the stage curtains that Mrs Bell had given them were hung, and the interior walls, which were of wood, given a good scrubbing. On Saturday morning they went over every inch of the building and found it to their satisfaction, and Nigel painted a very tasteful sign to put over the door. 'The Blue Door Theatre', it said, in bold, saxe-blue lettering on a brown background. They fetched the ladder, and Nigel fixed up the sign; then he stepped back and regarded it critically with his head on one side.

'How's that?' he asked.

'Wonderful!' breathed Lyn. Already she could imagine appreciative audiences, colourful costumes, and a lighted stage.

They stood and stared at it, hypnotized by the adventure it promised. The woman from the little café opposite came to the shop door and looked out.

'The – Blue – Door – The-*a*-ter,' she spelt out laboriously. 'Well, I never, what will them children do next?'

6

REHEARSAL TONIGHT

Miss Mollings' voice droned on, and Form Lower Five A were mentally dozing. Sandra felt Lyn's foot nudging her from behind. With the ease born of long practice, she stretched her hand down by the side of her chair, found the foot, and extricated a note slipped under the strap of the shoe. She smoothed it out and read it.

'Rehearsal tonight,' it read. 'Don't forget. Pass to Vicky.' She obeyed, employing the same method as Lyn, and a few seconds later an answer came back. It was one single word, 'Where?' Sandra wrote, 'At the theatre?' and passed it back to Lyn, who leant forward and whispered, 'I expect so.' At this moment the bell rang, signifying the end of school for the first day of term.

'Oh, help!' groaned Sandra, as they packed their homework into their satchels. 'Think how many times we've got to go through a day like this before end of term!'

'Just look at all this,' Lyn held up a pile of books; 'and as there's a rehearsal I can't see it getting done till tomorrow night.'

'We shan't rehearse every night, shall we?' asked Vicky anxiously, 'because I've got lots of things to catch up in. You're far more advanced than I was at my old school.'

'How do you like being a new girl?' Lyn inquired.

'Quite well, but I should hate it if you two weren't here.'

'Come on. Do hurry. We'll go and meet the boys,' said Sandra, from the doorway.

In the cloakroom of the Fenchester Boys' School Bulldog was sitting on a bench suffering from what he termed to himself 'New-boy-itis.' He wished Jeremy and Nigel would hurry up. They were in a higher form than he, and he only saw them on the way to and from school. Nigel was lucky to have someone he knew in his form.

A boy came up to him, grinning, and said, 'Halford, your young lady is waiting for you.'

Bulldog blinked. 'My – what?'

'Your girl friend. She's outside, and she asked me to hurry you up.'

'What's she like?'

'Blonde.'

Bulldog's heart described an arabesque; surely Sandra had not deigned to come and meet him!

'How old?' he asked eagerly.

'Oh, just a kid – got a sort of pony-tail.'

Bulldog ground his teeth. That little idiot Maddy! He would be the laughing-stock of the school now. The boy who had brought the message was shouting gleefully to the rest of the people in the cloakroom, 'I say, chaps, the new boy's sweetheart has come to meet him.' Bulldog blushed till he could blush no redder, while facetious remarks were passed that made him itch to start a fight. He was much relieved when Nigel and Jeremy appeared and said, 'Sorry we're late, and we must hurry 'cos the girls are waiting.'

'The girls?' questioned someone.

'Our sisters,' stated Jeremy, and the joke of Bulldog's 'young lady' was dropped.

When the girls found that Maddy had preceded them and already sent a message to Bulldog they were annoyed.

'You shouldn't have done that,' scolded Sandra; 'you might have got him into a row.'

But when Bulldog arrived it was Maddy that got into the row. He was in a temper, and Maddy, whose intentions had been of the very best, was nearly in tears when Nigel intervened.

'That's enough, Bulldog. You meant quite well, didn't you, Maddy?'

'Yes,' gulped Maddy.

'Well, don't do it again. And really, girls, if you don't mind, please let this be the last time you come to meet us,' begged Jeremy.

'Some boys would be pleased to have us to meet them,' said Lyn haughtily.

'We'll come to meet *you*, if you like,' offered Nigel.

The girls were secretly pleased at this suggestion, but they did not reply and the matter dropped.

At their gates Nigel said: 'First rehearsal tonight, but we can't rehearse because there's nothing *to* rehearse; we've got to decide on a programme. I hope people have some ideas?'

'Brimming with them,' Lyn replied. 'See you at six.'

They scrambled through their teas, dashed through their homework in a way that made their parents say, 'When I was at school . . .' and at quarter past six were seated round the dressing-room table.

'How different it looks and smells from last time we sat round like this,' remarked Sandra.

'And how shiny the table is! You can see your reflection in it,' said Lyn.

'And lovely blue chairs.' Maddy patted them appreciatively.

They made another tour of inspection, gloating over their handiwork.

'See how beautifully the stage curtains hang.'

'Doesn't the floor look spotless?'

'And the piano has cleaned up well.'

Lyn pulled back one of the stage curtains. 'It doesn't *swish*, does it? It sort of rattles. A real curtain should swish.'

'These don't, because they only draw back instead of going up,' explained Nigel.

'Of course! I wondered what was wrong.'

'One day we'll be able to afford real ones,' he promised, 'with wings and side-flaps, and what-not. And now, to business.'

They reluctantly returned to the dressing-room and sat down again.

'It's nearly half past six,' he said, 'and we must be home by nine; but we're not leaving this hall until the programme is settled, so if we don't concentrate we shall get in a row for being late home.'

The others put on earnest, business-like expressions. Nigel brought out a notebook and pencil, and the meeting began.

'I propose,' he said, 'that we each take a special job that we can do. F'rinstance, Vicky had better be ballet mistress.'

'Gosh!' exclaimed Bulldog, alarmed. 'We've not got to ballet dance, have we?' The idea of Bulldog the jazz fiend, ballet dancing, amused them highly, but Nigel comforted him by saying, 'I vote the girls stick to that side of the affair.'

'What shall I be?' Maddy was anxious to know.

'Call boy, prompter, scene-shifter, messenger, in fact, bottle-washer-in-chief,' Nigel informed her.

'Can I be wardrobe-mistress?' asked Sandra.

'Sure you can. And Jeremy must be musical director, and Bulldog can be in charge of lighting, properties, etc.'

'I'm scenic artist and stage manager, and Lyn's going to produce; and everyone must stick to their own job and not interfere with other people. In a book I've been reading on amateur acting – '

'Have you been reading it up? So've I,' said Lyn.

'She made me wade through it, too,' grumbled Jeremy.

'Vicky and I read it, and you lent it to Sandra, didn't you, Vick?'

'Yes, Maddy and I read it,' said Sandra. 'We did the exercises in acting, too. Maddy got quite good at bursting into tears.'

'Shall I show you?' asked Maddy.

'Go on.'

She turned her back for a minute, they saw her shoulders heave, and when she faced them again tears were streaming down her plump cheeks, and she sobbed very realistically.

'Bravo! Jolly fine,' commented Lyn. 'I tried, and after a bit I got it, but I know I couldn't do it now.'

'It's all right to start, but I can't stop,' sobbed Maddy miserably.

She continued to cry for the next ten minutes, despite their united efforts to calm her.

'It's no good,' she wailed. 'I'm not unhappy at all – I just can't stop!'

'Try standing on your head,' suggested Vicky.

Maddy obeyed, and instantly her sobs ceased. They drew sighs of relief, and Maddy grinned.

'Funny, aren't I?'

'You're a little nuisance,' said Nigel good-humouredly. 'And now to business once more. What is the programme to consist of?'

'There must be one straight play,' said Lyn firmly.

Nigel made a note of it.

'And something musical,' Jeremy stipulated.

Nigel put this down.

'And something funny,' demanded Maddy.

Nigel scribbled again.

'And something exciting,' said Bulldog.

'That will come under the play.'

'And something with picturesque costumes,' suggested Sandra.

'That'll be the musical thing or the play.'

'Some dancing,' was Vicky's suggesteion.

'In the "musical", too. Now, let's decide on the play. What's it to be?'

'*Romeo and Juliet.*' This, of course, was from Lyn.

'Shakespeare's quite impossible with our small stage and equipment and lighting and experience,' Nigel decided.

'Too many characters, too,' added Sandra.

'We ought to make up our own,' said Vicky, 'because no one writes decent plays for children.'

'But can we?' Nigel asked doubtfully. 'Anyone offer to take it on?'

No one did, and things had come to a deadlock when Sandra suggested, 'Couldn't we make up the plot together, and then write the dialogue, each person saying what they think the character they are playing would say?'

'We could try it that way, of course,' agreed Nigel and the others.

'Jeremy blushed and said uncertainly, 'I'll write the musical sketch if you like. That is – I mean, if no one else . . . you see, I . . .' but his nervousness was overwhelmed by the rejoicing at this suggestion.

'Good old Jerry.'

'I never knew you wrote songs,' said Nigel with interest.

'The top of the piano is covered with manuscripts, but he hardly ever finishes one,' explained Lyn.

'What sort of accompaniment shall we have?' asked Sandra. 'Jeremy plays the piano, and so do I, and he plays the violin.'

'And I play the mouth-organ,' added Maddy.

'It all depends in what setting the "musical" is. If it's in a drawing-room we can have the piano on the stage; if it's gipsies, or something like that, Jeremy can play his violin; and if it's a slum Maddy can play her harmonica.'

The mouth-organist stuck out her tongue.

'Let's have gipsies,' said Lyn eagerly.

'Gipsies are overdone,' Jeremy disagreed, 'and people are tired of them, because I hear the last item on Mrs Potter-Smith's programme was a gipsies' camp-fire.'

'I'd like to see Mrs Potter-Smith kicking a tambourine,' giggled Maddy.

'Let's have peasants of some kind,' Sandra begged, 'because they're so picturesque.'

'Italian, French, or Spanish peasants?'

'Spanish,' said Lyn definitely, 'because in the box that Mrs Bell gave us there's a pair of castanets.'

'I've got an idea.'

Jeremy ran out on to the stage and began to play the piano; the others followed him. He was improvising a wild, rhythmic tune.

'Enter some Spanish muleteers and sing this. It's something about going to an inn to dance, and señoritas and cypress groves.' The notes changed to a slow provocative little tune. 'Enter the aforesaid señoritas singing this and introducing themselves; then one of the men sings a song something like this,' he played a few mournful, wailing chords. Then suddenly he stopped, blushing. 'Sorry, I didn't mean to go on. It was just an idea – forget it.'

But they were all enthusiastic. Nigel thumped him on the back.

'Why, boy, that was wonderful! I've never heard such music. Where did you get it from?'

'I saw one of the performances of a touring Spanish company in London, and I tried to make it like that.'

Vicky's eyes were shining. 'If you can get a tune like that for me to dance to I shall love you for ever after.'

'We'd better each decide what we want to do in the musical, and give our orders to Jeremy and he'll write it up,' said Nigel.

Jeremy found a piece of paper and wrote down, 'Opening Chorus'. 'That had better be men, I think.' He put Nigel's, Bulldog's, and his own name down. 'Now what on earth shall we do with Maddy? She can't possibly be a señorita, she's not glamorous enough, and she's too fat.'

'And I can't make eyes!' added Maddy, casting a nasty look at Lyn.

'I think she'd better be a man,' said Sandra; 'but I can't *think* what she can do.'

'I could teach her an easy little character dance,' offered Vicky, 'if Jeremy concocted a tune first.'

'Now the señoritas – that's Lyn, Sandra, and Vicky. A song for them. Now a solo of some kind. Any offers? Come on, Nigel, you'll sing, won't you?' urged Jeremy.

'No, I will not. Once and for all – no!'

'Well, one boy has got to sing, because that last tune can't be wasted, and I've already thought of some words for it.'

'Sing it yourself,' suggested Vicky.

'Lor' no! I've got a voice like a squeaking brake now.'

'He used to look sweet when he was in the choir before his voice broke. Mrs Bell told his mother he looked like an angel,' teased Maddy, and received a kick under the table.

Bulldog was looking apprehensive. He could feel it coming, and it came.

'Well, Bulldog must sing,' Jeremy decided.

Bulldog searched for words with which to express himself, but only succeeded in making vaguely appalled noises.

'Yes, of course he must. He was in the choir at our old school,' Nigel told them.

'Right-o, I'll get a song for him, and one for Sandra. Would you prefer a happy one or a sad one?'

'Sad, please, and nice and soprano.'

'What's your compass?'

'Middle C to high G.'

Jeremy made a note of it, and then wrote 'Dances'. 'Now who will dance? Vicky for one. Solo?'

'If you think I'm good enough.' She looked inquiringly at Nigel, and he nodded.

'Then a duet dance for Lyn and Sandra, I presume?' went on Jeremy.

'What about you? What are you doing?' Vicky wanted to know.

'Oh, I'll be accompanying.'

'But you must have a solo. Do a violin solo.'

He agreed, and it was arranged that, for the songs, the accompaniment would be violin, and he would have to go off-stage and play the piano for the dancing.

'Where is this affair set, by the way?' asked Bulldog.

'At an inn at the foot of some mountains, I should think,' said Jeremy.

'In the garden,' suggested Nigel; 'then I can draw a moon and some cypress trees on the backcloth.'

'We'll end it with a song all together.' Jeremy completed his notes.

'Now, has anyone anything else to say before we pass on to the next item,' said the chairman.

Sandra had been making rough sketches of costumes, and now said, 'I should be glad of any old lengths of brightly coloured materials, and anything to make frills of.'

'Isn't it rather early to start thinking about clothes?' demurred Lyn. 'When are we going to give the concert?'

'I thought the evening of the day we break up for the summer hols. would be the best time,' said Nigel, 'because no one will have gone away then. But we can't decide on a date until we see how things are going.'

Maddy bounced up and down on her chair. 'Isn't it all exciting! I keep on having trickly feelings down my spine.'

'Now for the next item, which I have got down as "Something Funny".'

'It'll probably all be screamingly funny, especially the serious parts,' said Lyn pessimistically.

'Can anyone think of anything funny?'

'Yes, Bulldog ballet dancing, and Maddy playing the mouth-organ,' suggested Jeremy.

'That,' said Maddy haughtily, 'would only appeal to some senses of humour.'

'Couldn't someone recite a poem, and the others act it?' suggested Lyn. 'It could be a cautionary tale or a nonsense rhyme.'

'We ought to keep to writing our own stuff, because aren't there acting fees or something, if you use other people's plays?' said Nigel.

'Yes, I believe there are, and we can't afford that.'

Bulldog had been looking thoughtful. 'You know you said I should be funny ballet dancing? Well, why shouldn't I, just to make people laugh?'

'That's an idea,' agreed Nigel eagerly; 'a humorous dancing-class. Lyn could be Madame Popoffski or some peculiar name like that, we three boys could be new pupils, little girls brought by Maddy, our nurse, and Sandra could be the meek lady pianist with a cold in her head.'

'Good idea.'

'It ought to be funny.'

'But what about me? What part shall I play?' asked Vicky.

'You're the drawback. You dance too well to be funny.' Nigel wrinkled his brow.

'Could she *not* be in this, but have a separate solo of her own in between this item and the next, to give us time to dress?' suggested Sandra.

It was decided that Vicky should do a ballet solo and Jeremy should accompany her on the piano.

'And now,' said Nigel, 'the big event. The play, which has got to be exciting.'

'And serious,' added Vicky.

'And colourful,' put in Sandra.

'And emotional,' said Lyn.

'But not sloppy,' urged Bulldog.

'What do you mean by sloppy?' asked Lyn, laughing.

'Not a lot of falling in love.'

'Don't be silly. You can't have a play without some love interest. But anyhow, no one will have to fall in love with you, mercifully, because you're too short,' replied Lyn scathingly.

Bulldog was mystified. 'What's height got to do with it?'

'A heroine can't be kissed by the hero if he has to stand on tiptoe to do it.'

'Golly! Are we going to have kissing in it?' Bulldog looked shocked.

'Of course,' said Lyn scornfully. 'Have you ever seen a play or a film that hasn't any?'

Bulldog scowled.

'The question is: who's going to have the chief part?' said Vicky.

'Lyn,' said Sandra and Nigel together.

'Well, it's all right, then. Jeremy can be the hero, and it'll be quite normal for him to kiss her.'

They were all relieved except Jeremy. 'Have I got to kiss her in front of all those people? S'posing they don't realize she's my sister?'

'They oughtn't to be thinking about Lynette and Jeremy Darwin, but about the hero and the heroine,' Lyn reminded him.

'Now we must decide on what kind of characters

we're to be. Everyone write down what character they'd like to play. Remember it's not to be modern.'

This idea was not a success. Maddy wrote down *a dragon like St. George's,* Bulldog wrote *a cave man,* Vicky wrote *a Roman soldier,* Lyn wanted to be an Egyptian princess, Sandra a Victorian dowager, Jeremy wrote *a troubadour,* and Nigel *a highwayman.*

When the papers were read there was a howl of laughter.

'It would need Bernard Shaw to write a play bringing in this assortment of characters,' remarked Jeremy.

'I think the hero and heroine ought to choose the period,' said Nigel.

'It's all the same to me,' said the hero carelessly. 'I'll probably have to be dressed up in a lot of "tat" whatever period it is.'

'I think Cavalier and Roundhead,' decided Lyn, 'then Nigel can be the Roundhead villain. Jeremy will look lovely in a plumed hat and silk knee-breeches. Now let's decide on the plot.'

They gazed at the beams across the ceiling and let loose their imaginations.

'I am the beautiful daughter of a Royalist soldier,' Lyn announced dreamily.

'Your father is very rich, and you live in a marvellous mansion,' added Vicky.

'You're in love with me, the gardener, who, in the first act, brings you the news that war is declared between Parliament and the King. I go away to fight on Cromwell's side (because I don't think a plumed hat would suit me), and you hate me,' said Jeremy.

Sandra went on, 'Lyn's father goes to fight for the king. He comes home wounded and followed by Cromwell's men, under the command of the gardener, now a captain. That is Act II.'

'In Act III, Scene I, the gardener, because of his love for Lyn, lets the father go free, and provides the whole family with passes and money, to get to Holland.' This was Nigel's contribution.

'The last scene is the gardener arriving in Holland, having given up the chance of being a general in Cromwell's army, to come and marry me, and we live happily ever after!' ended Lyn triumphantly.

They were pleased and surprised at the ease with which they had evolved a plot.

'That's smashing!' said Nigel. 'Now for characters. Lyn – the girl, Jeremy – the gardener, me – the father, Sandra – the mother. That leaves Vicky, Bulldog, and Maddy. Bulldog can be the brutal Roundhead sergeant. Vicky – Lyn's maid, and Maddy – another soldier, and any other odd characters we may have to bring in.'

Maddy sighed. 'Why do I always have to play odd people?'

'Obvious reasons!' Jeremy told her.

Nigel looked at his watch. 'We've got some time before we need start for home, so let's begin to write the play. Who writes quickly?'

'Sandra does.'

He handed her a pencil and an exercise book which he had brought in anticipation.

'What is it to be called?' she asked.

'We'll decide that afterwards. Put Act I, and we'll fire away.'

Sandra said slowly as she wrote, 'Act I. The scene is laid – where is it laid?' she asked.

'In the garden of Sir Someone's estate.'

'Sir William Whitney,' suggested Jeremy.

'In the garden of Sir William Whitney's estate. Someone Whitney – what's your name going to be, Lyn?'

'Julia.'

'Julia Whitney, his daughter, is sitting in a sunny arbour with her mother. They are embroidering.'

'Don't bother to put much except the dialogue,' advised Nigel, 'because all the little etceteras will come as we rehearse.'

They finished the first act before they went home, and on the way home they discussed the second. There was no rehearsal the next night, but in all three houses, when prep. was finished, work was being done for the concert. Jeremy sat at the piano with a manuscript book on the rack, and ran his fingers through his fair hair until it stood up like a cockatoo's crest. Lyn was in the next room with the exercise book containing the first act of the play, and was learning her part. Sandra, up in her bedroom, was going through the chest that Mrs Bell had given them, and laying aside all the garments she thought would be useful. Downstairs, Maddy with her tongue out, was copying people's parts for them into separate exercise books. In the Halfords' house Bulldog was at the piano giving his voice a little exercise. The thought of that solo to be sung in the Spanish musical play hung like a heavy load on his heart. In her bedroom, Vicky was in her ballet shoes going through a rigorous routine of exercises that she had learnt at the dancing-lessons she attended at her last school. Nigel was lying on his front on the lawn, sketching scenery on a drawing block.

And when the sky over Goldenwood Avenue lost its sunset splendour they went to sleep and dreamed muddled dreams of the concert.

At the next rehearsal Jeremy had finished the musical sketch.

'I think *Spanish Inn* would be quite a good name for it,' he said as he sat down at the piano to play it to them. 'Excuse my voice, won't you. Enter the muleteers. This song will be accompanied by the violin.'

He sang his way right through the operetta which, though very slight in theme, had an attractive opening chorus, a duet very suitable for Lyn and Sandra, Vicky's solo being a wild tarantella. Maddy's dance, however, was a funny little joggy tune with an easy rhythm. Bulldog quailed at the sentiment of the words of his solo, but the closing number, 'Goodnight, Spanish Inn', pleased the entire company.

'Did you write all that by yourself?' asked Vicky wonderingly, when at last Jeremy sat back and mopped his brow, moist from the effort of singing a whole operetta by himself. The others were staring at him wide-eyed.

'Yes; last night. Mother and Dad went out, and I started at seven and went on until I had finished, at half past eleven. I heard the front gate open, so I switched on the wireless, and just dashed upstairs in time. I heard Dad say, "It wasn't the piano, it was the wireless". Well, does it meet with your approval?'

'Approval! It's glorious! If only we can do it as well as you did, it will be an immense success.'

They spent the rest of the evening learning the songs that they were all to sing together.

It was arranged that rehearsals would be on Mondays, Wednesdays, and Fridays, and once, either morning, afternoon, or evening, on Saturdays. By the following Saturday both *With Madame Popoffski* – as the sketch was called – and *Red as the Rose*, the three-act play, had been written, and Lyn said at the Saturday evening rehearsal, 'We shan't start rehearsing on the stage till Monday week, by which time everyone must know their parts absolutely word perfectly. Don't bother about acting, but just get your lines parrot fashion and know the words of your songs.'

The other inhabitants of Goldenwood Avenue were rather surprised by the behaviour of their young neighbours during the following week. They were used to seeing them walking briskly up the hill, laughing and chattering so they could be heard the length of the road; but now they walked silently, generally in single file, with red exercise books in their hands, either with their eyes glued intently on the contents, or staring into space and muttering quickly under their breath. They carried their parts with them all day at school, snatching at every possible moment; nearly every evening they went up into fields near-by that were not yet built on, and sprawled in the long grass to continue their study.

'*Goodnight, Spanish inn and garden – Goodnight, till next we meet –*' Maddy would mutter as she undressed for bed, while Sandra said rapidly, '*Oh my poor husband would to heaven these dastardly rebels were struck down what time is it daughter?*'

One night as Mrs Darwin went upstairs to bed at eleven o'clock she heard someone speaking in the back bedroom. She looked in. The moon was shining through the window on to Lyn, who sat up in bed, her hair tousled, going through her longest speech. It was her vituperation of the ex-gardener captain.

'O you serpent!' she was declaiming bitterly. 'We have treated you as an equal, you have professed your love for me, and now you return to scorn us, to treat us as we might have treated you had we not been so kind-hearted, oh, so foolishly kind-hearted –' Here Mrs Darwin shook her gently by the shoulder and she woke up, alarmed.

'What's the matter?' she asked.

'Nothing, dear, but you were snoring.'

Her mother kissed her and went out. Lyn soon fell into the heavy sleep that only an overworked brain produces.

7

THE VICAR APPROVES

Mrs Bell was a constant attender at rehearsals, and a useful critic. Her gentle advice on puzzling subjects was always followed by the children.

Every Saturday evening she sat on one of the blue chairs at the back of the hall, and they went through the whole programme. She made it her rule not to speak until the end, and then her words were pearls of tact.

'Maddy, dear,' she would say, 'when you are the soldier in *Red as the Rose*, you might stand up in a more military manner. Roundheads didn't stick their tummies out!' And Maddy, who had objected when Lyn had told her she looked more like a piglet than a soldier, beamed and said yes, she'd try.

It was Mrs Bell who told Nigel that he might look a bit more dashing when Lyn was flirting with him in the Spanish play, and informed Sandra that her top G was too loud. All these points had been noted by the producer at rehearsals during the week, but Lyn got so worked up under the strain of controlling a stage full of people that her tongue was apt to run away with her.

The first few rehearsals were hilarious affairs. They were excited and could not concentrate on the work in hand, but after that boredom and slackness set in.

Bulldog would excuse himself from rehearsals on the ground that he had to stay at school for a cricket practice, and had his homework to do. Maddy would feel tired and go to bed early, and Lyn very often had to go out with her mother. After one particularly bad rehearsal, when Lyn had slapped Jeremy's face because he had laughed at a too melodramatic rendering of Julia Whitney, and Maddy was sulking because she could not remember the routine of her dance, Mrs Bell decided to have it out with them. She walked up to the lighted stage and said mildly:

'Well, and when are you going to give the concert?'

They looked blank. Rehearsals had become so much a part of their lives that it seemed as if this state of things would last for ever, with the programme getting no better and no worse. Also, exams. had begun, and naturally they were busy revising. They had acquired numerous little slovenly habits, such as not bothering to pull the curtains at the beginning and end of items, and hurrying over long speeches and saying, 'Oh, well, I did that bit properly last rehearsal.'

'There are three weeks before the end of term,' went on Mrs Bell, 'and the vicar and I are going away the first week in August, so . . .' She left the sentence expressively unfinished. 'I really can't spend my time at rehearsals like this, so I won't come again until a fortnight tonight, when the vicar will come too. If he approves, the concert ought to come off the next week. Good night, dears, and work hard, won't you?'

When she was gone they were strangely subdued.

'Sorry, Jerry,' said Lyn; 'I hope I didn't hurt.'

Jeremy grunted his acceptance of the apology.

Nigel said, 'Look here, everyone; we're absolute parasites.'

'Hear, hear,' seconded Lyn. 'Through Mr Bell's kindness we have a marvellous theatre; through Mrs Bell's kindness some good costumes, and then we don't work to please them.'

'I think it's a mistake to rehearse during term,' said Sandra thoughtfully. 'It's a case of trying to do two things at once, and doing them both badly.'

'In future,' decided Nigel, 'we'll keep our dramatic attempts for the holidays. Personally, I feel dead beat all day with exams. and rehearsals.'

'In three weeks' time we've got to do it!' Vicky reminded them, with horrified eyes.

'We can do it,' said Nigel, with his face set determinedly. 'Next week exams. are over, and we shall have no homework, and we shan't do any work at school, and we've jolly well *got* to do it.'

Lyn said suddenly, as the thought struck her, 'I know what it is that's wrong; why we get so fed up with plays.'

'Why?'

'Because we've gone on too long without properties and costumes. We knew everything properly after the first fortnight of rehearsing, but now it's gone dull and stagnant. Sandra, put us into costumes, and Nigel and Bulldog, get the scenery and properties fixed, and we'll make it come to life again.'

Lyn's eloquence was approved, and in Sandra's home during the next week the prevailing noise was the whir of the sewing machine. Round at the theatre Nigel, in his dungarees, was slashing poster colours on to immense sheets of brown paper. Bulldog was getting himself all mixed up with electric light flexes in the attempt to arrange the footlights.

'It's no good, Nigel,' he said despondently one evening, 'I shall never fix up these wretched lights. I'm a darned bad electrician if I can't, though.' He scratched his head thoughtfully.

'Well, if you can't, no one else can,' Nigel soothed him.

'And if we make a good lot out of this concert, we may be able to have a proper electrician to fix them up for us.'

They had several rehearsals with properties and scenery, to get used to timing their actions, and there were some amusing muddles. Lyn took too long over eating a piece of bread which was supposed to be some supper in *Red as the Rose*, and when Jeremy, as Anthony, walked in she could not exclaim her appointed lines because her mouth was full. In *Spanish Inn* Vicky inadvertently leaned up against the backcloth that Nigel had painted – representing a long low tavern with mountains behind – and smudged the roof.

As the weather was gradually getting hotter they wore as little as possible at the rehearsals.

'Whatever shall I do when I have to wear that great heavy skirt for Julia?' groaned Lyn.

'What about me, then, in a plumed hat and hair hanging all over my face?' groaned Nigel.

Nigel's hair was a standing joke. Sandra had been at her wits' end, wondering how she was going to provide him with long curling hair, as the Cavalier gentleman, Lyn's father. Then she had seen a photo of Mrs Darwin when a girl, with long black ringlets.

'Lyn,' she exclaimed, 'what's happened to your mother's ringlets?'

Lyn looked at her in surprise.

'They've been cut off, of course. Have you only just noticed?'

'Can she possibly have kept them?' asked Sandra eagerly.

'I believe she has.' Lyn called up the stairs, 'Mum, have you got your hair stowed away anywhere?'

'My what?'

'Your hair. The lot you had cut off.'

'It's up in my wardrobe in a box. What do you want it for?'

'Sandra has an idea.'

A few moments later Mrs Darwin descended carrying a little wooden casket. 'Here it is. Next you'll be wanting the hair off my head for that concert of yours.'

Sandra held up one black tress after another. 'It's lovely. You ought to grow *your* hair, Lyn. But don't you see my idea? This is just the colour of Nigel's hair, and if I fix it on to a length of black tape, we can clip it on to his hair with slides.'

'Good idea, but won't he hate it? And what about a moustache?'

'There's a lovely wooffly one in Mrs Bell's box. He ought to look smashing!'

And he did. Sandra insisted on having a dress parade

at the hall, and they all put on their costumes for each item in turn, while she made copious lists of strings to be sewn on, tucks to be taken, and holes to be mended. Lyn, in her Spanish dress, looked a picture of exotic beauty with her black hair built up at the back of her head, scarlet lips and cheeks, and her eyes, already striking, heavily mascara'd. Sandra also practised the make-up, using ordinary cosmetics scrounged from their mothers.

As they had no footlights, Sandra considered grease paint unnecessary, except for the muleteers, who appeared in a healthy tan.

The dresses for *Spanish Inn* were a success, and had cost nothing at all. The girls had begged old dance frocks from their aunts and mothers, and trimmed them with zigzag frills; their velvet bodices were found in Mrs Bell's box, where they belonged to Dutch costumes; Sandra had embroidered these with bright silks. Vicky, whose father had been in India during the war, produced three fine lacy silk shawls bought in Calcutta; one was white, one blue, and one orange. They draped these shawls over combs Sandra had cunningly contrived from cardboard, to hang loosely round their shoulders.

The boys wore tight-fitting black or navy blue slacks widening just above the ankle; the girls had supplied them with string beach sandals, except Nigel, who took eights in shoes, and had to have some specially manufactured from cardboard and raffia. The wardrobe mistress had made them embroidered boleros, and in Mrs Bell's box they found a silk Russian shirt with a high neckline and full baggy sleeves caught in at the wrists. This fitted Jeremy perfectly, but he refused it, as it impeded his playing the violin; so Nigel, on whom it was slightly tight, had to wear it. Jeremy wore a silk blouse of his mother's with slightly full sleeves, and Maddy and Bulldog had to be content with school blouses turned back to front, with more embroidery. The muleteers' hats were the real masterpiece. Sandra had bought some black, shiny paper, glued it on cardboard, and made broad-brimmed toreador hats. Black cloaks, lined with the brightest lengths of material to be found, completed their outfit.

For *With Madame Popoffski* the costumes were most outlandish. Vicky had found three of her discarded tutus that the boys could squeeze into, and they wore old gym shoes with the insteps removed and ribbons attached and tied round their ankles. Large white bows adorned their hair, which was parted in the middle and fluffed out for the occasion. The final result, when cheeks were rouged and lips painted into cupid's bows, was devastating. Sandra, as the pianist, wore an Edwardian dress in an offensive sandy check, with leg o' mutton sleeves and a high collar; her hair was drawn back into a straggling bun, and she wore large horn-rimmed spectacles. Madame Popoffski had an ashen face, scarlet lips, and her hair drawn back in the ballerina style. Lyn had practised a broken accent until she found herself using it at school, to her mistresses' amazement. She wore a peculiar green garment reaching to her ankles, a cross between a dressing-gown and a surplice. Maddy's outfit was the sanest, and she made a ridiculously small nurse for her elephantine charges. When they had all got into these clothes and seen the effect, they roared with hysterical laughter.

'Oh, you don't know what you look like,' gurgled Vicky, as her twin did a series of eccentric arabesques round the hall. When they had recovered they returned again to their separate sides of the dressing-room curtain and put on their clothes for *Red as the Rose*.

Nigel asked, 'I suppose you haven't got any hair for me, Sandra? It doesn't really matter if you haven't; I'd much rather go without.'

But Sandra said mysteriously, 'Aha, you shall see what you shall see! May I come through?'

'No, Bulldog is half naked.'

'Hurry up, Bulldog, and don't forget your doublet goes on before your breeches.'

'You can come through now.'

Sandra said, 'Close your eyes.' And when Nigel had done so she fixed on his curly hair, and holding the mirror in front of him said, 'Open them.'

'What an idiot I look!' grumbled Nigel ungratefully, gazing at his reflection, then, seeing her face fall, added, 'But it's a jolly good idea. Now the moustache.'

He smeared gum on his upper lip, and adjusted the coal-black moustache.

'You look a very noble creature!' Sandra complimented him.

'Now let me make your eyebrows more bushy.' She ruffled them up and painted them with mascara. 'Now frown.' He did so and she painted in the furrows with a moistened black pencil. 'You look more elderly now.'

He put on his broad, plume-bedecked hat and made a sweeping bow.

'How do I look, mistress mine?'

'Fine, husband; but take off your hat when you bow. Now I must go and dress Lyn.'

In a few minutes the heroine was wearing her demure pink fichu'd dress.

'Don't forget to curl your hair up every night,' Sandra reminded her, 'between now and the concert, will you?'

'Don't be silly. How can I have curly hair in the last item if I have to have it sleek in the one before?'

The wardrobe-mistress frowned. 'That's a teaser.' She pondered. 'Don't bother to curl it, then. I'll just have to twist it in ringlets as best I can.'

Maddy and Bulldog appeared, looking very military in aluminium-painted cardboard armour. They carried their helmets in their hands, as they looked rather peculiar when worn. Their pikes were curtain rods with silver-paper heads. Jeremy, wearing his gardener clothes, brown breeches, shirt, and hose and an old flat straw hat, managed to look very attractive, and when he put on his armour Lyn said his dashing appearance made her feel quite jittery. His dress for the last act, when he arrived in Holland, was the same black cloak as he wore in *Spanish Inn*, with a slouch hat. Lyn wore a more sober dress of mauve silk.

In the last act Maddy was the little Dutch servant, and wore the complete outfit from Mrs Bell's box. Sandra wore grey all the time, and Vicky, as Lyn's maid, had a neat black and green dress, also found in the invaluable box.

'Sandra,' said Nigel, as she made more lists, 'you're a witch with clothes. How much has all this cost?'

She counted up on her fingers.

'Only five pounds or so – you'd be surprised.'

'Jolly good, my girl. You're the soul of thrift and prosperity.'

'I shall be the soul of bad temper when I start to do all the little alterations on the list.'

'You see that the other girls help you. Vicky is quite capable of sewing on buttons, but she hates it.'

'Oh, I quite like it, really,' replied Sandra good-naturedly; 'and I must remember to iron the clothes before the dress rehearsal, and before the actual night. That means there must be one free night between them.'

'Yes, definitely there must. There are sure to be tons of last-minute jobs to be done. Listen, everyone,' Nigel yelled, to be heard above the noise in the dressing-room. 'Today is Friday; tomorrow, Saturday, we do it to Mrs Bell and the vicar. They must approve. On Monday we go to the printers and get the programmes done; on Wednesday we have a rehearsal –'

'Property rehearsal,' put in Lyn.

'And on Saturday another rehearsal –'

'For words and acting,' announced the producer.

'On the next Tuesday is the dress rehearsal, and the Thursday is –'

'The Concert!' they yelled in varying pitches of excitement.

'Suit you?' asked Nigel.

'Fine!' they answered, struggling into their everyday clothes.

The next day they performed to their audience of two, and it was the best performance they had yet given. The only fault that the vicar could find was that the waits in between were too long. They got excited and lost their clothes, and while Sandra was endeavouring to dress herself they would shout, 'Sandra, where are my shoes?' 'Have you got my hair-grips, or have I, Sandra?' until the poor wardrobe-mistress was frenzied. At the end the dressing-rooms looked like two badly kept secondhand shops.

'This can't go on,' Sandra told them sternly. 'Look at your lovely pink dress, Lyn, thrown on the floor like a dish-cloth; and Nigel's moustache all muddled up in it.'

'I've torn my Spanish dress,' confessed Vicky sadly, 'but it's only a seam.'

Sandra had to make another list of things to be done before the dress rehearsal. When they were dressed they went to hear the vicar's verdict. The vicar approved.

'Well, young people, I must say I'm proud of you. It's a very good show, and you have made it funny without vulgarity, gay without rowdiness, and sad without sentimentality. An excellent entertainment. Excellent.'

'It'll be all right for us to give it on Thursday week, sir?' asked Nigel. 'You're free, I hope, that night?'

The vicar looked through his diary and said he was.

'And to what charity shall we give the collection?' Sandra wanted to know.

'You are having a collection, not admission tickets, I understand?'

'That's right, vicar.'

'You see, someone might put five pounds in a collection, but tickets would only cost ten pence,' explained Maddy.

'But, on the other hand,' the vicar laughed, 'there are people who will put in a penny.'

'Or a button,' suggested Bulldog.

'You would be well advised to pass round a plate, to avoid *that*, not a bag,' said Mrs Bell. 'Who will you have to pass the plates? Some of your friends?'

'I should think two of our fathers would.'

The vicar suggested the fund for the new church organ as being the most suitable cause.

'And who is seeing to the curtains?'

'Our fathers are,' said Lyn firmly. 'We're not having outsiders back-stage; they'd put us off.'

'And will you need help in the dressing-room?' offered Mrs Bell.

'No, I think I can manage, thank you,' replied Sandra, although she knew it would be a terrific tax upon her temper and patience.

'Well, good night and good luck, and we'll be here on Thursday week.'

When they were gone the children walked slowly back to the dressing-room and faced the disorder therein.

At the printer's Nigel asked: 'How much would you charge to print a hundred and fifty copies of this programme?' He handed over a sheet of paper. It read:

THE BLUE DOOR THEATRE COMPANY

NIGEL, VICTORIA, AND PERCY HALFORD; SANDRA
AND MADELAINE FAYNE; AND LYNETTE AND JEREMY
DARWIN

Invite you to an entertainment in aid of St.
Michael's Organ Fund. Come and bring your
friends to the Blue Door Theatre, Pleasant Street, at
7 o'clock, Thursday, July 28th.

The programme will be as follows:

SPANISH INN

A musical Play in one act, written and produced by
Jeremy Darwin.

SCENE: The garden of an inn in Spain.

Interval

WITH MADAME POPOFFSKI

A sketch in one act, written by the entire company,
and produced by Lynette Darwin.

SCENE: A Dancing School.

Ballet Solo by Victoria Halford.

A three-act drama, written by the entire company,
and produced by Lynette Darwin.

Act I: The garden of Sir William Whitney's
mansion.

Act II: The drawing-room of Sir William's
mansion.

An afternoon three months later.

Act III, SCENE 1: The same, next morning.

SCENE 2: A cottage in Rotterdam, evening.

There will be a collection during the interval.

Costumes: Sandra Fayne.
Scenery: Nigel Halford.
Lighting: Percy Halford.

The girl looked at it doubtfully. 'It's rather long, but we could stencil off a hundred and fifty for two pounds.'

'Thank you. That will be fine. When will they be ready?'

'Tomorrow, or the day after.'

That evening they made a list of people to whom they must send invitations.

'Now, what about old Miss Jones?' asked Lyn.

'No, she wouldn't approve of some of the jokes in *Madame Popoffski*.'

'But she'd love *Red as the Rose*. I'm sure she's romantic at heart.'

'O.K. We'll invite her. Now what about our various daily helps?'

'If our Bertha comes she'll want to bring her old man.'

'Oh, he can come.'

'And don't forget all the Sunday School teachers,' Jeremy reminded her.

And so it went on. Lyn and Sandra had invited all their form from school, and there were numerous friends of their parents to be invited. When they counted up they found two-hundred-and-nine names, and instead of cutting down the list, they decided to send one programme between two people, where this was possible. As the programmes were ready by Tuesday, they spent the evening on their bicycles delivering them, and there were many houses in Fenchester that evening in which somebody exclaimed, 'Just look! Why, it's from those Darwin (or Fayne) children. We must go and see this.'

In the children's homes there was great perturbation. Their parents were beginning to realize that the impossible idea of the past months had taken concrete shape. Mrs Fayne talked to Mrs Darwin over the fence.

'Well, what do you think about this concert affair?'

'Frankly, I'm surprised. I didn't think they had such sticking power. They're working far too hard.'

'I know. Sandra's been up till ten o'clock every night this week over the costumes. Do you think their schoolwork is suffering?'

'Jeremy's exam results were awful. But there, I'm afraid they always are, because he's so lazy. He'll only work at things he likes. I can't really grumble, because he got honours in his last music exam.'

'Sandra's results weren't quite as good as usual, and she's got her G.C.E. in two years' time.'

'Same for Jeremy; and I think Nigel takes his next year.'

'He's a nice, well-mannered boy.'

'It's he that's kept them up to scratch, I think, and Mrs Bell, of course. She told me at church last night that they've got up a very nice little show.'

'I suppose you've seen the programme? It makes me laugh, the serious way they're taking it.'

'Do you know they've invited over two hundred people?'

'No! Supposing something goes wrong!'

Mrs Fayne's gentle face was horrified, but Mrs Darwin shrugged her shoulders.

'Well, it'll be their own fault. I told them at first it was to big an undertaking. Just fancy, a theatre of their own! I'm sure it's in a filthy condition.'

'I shall feel terrible on the night, won't you? Just as bad as if I were running it.'

'I offered Lyn my help behind scenes, but she thanked me politely by saying that no outsiders were to be allowed behind.'

Mrs Fayne laughed. 'They're rather sweet, aren't they? If I don't see you again before the concert, will you call for me? Then we can go together.'

'And watch our infant prodigies disporting themselves.'

When the infant prodigies returned from school that day they went down to the theatre laden with properties. Nigel carried a rustic chair for the arbour scene in *Red as the Rose*, Jeremy a card table that was to be draped to cover its modernity for the drawing-room scene. Sandra had several carefully ironed dresses over her arm to prevent them from being crushed, and Maddy had a large case containing crockery, and several tins of raspberries. When Bulldog first saw this he gaped. 'What are the raspberries for?'

'Wine, scarlet wine; alcoholic liquor, of course,' answered Jeremy.

'What a good idea. I adore tinned raspberry juice.'

But he was damped when Nigel said, 'We shall use water for the rehearsals.'

On their way to the theatre, which they made

through all possible back streets to avoid the amused and curious glances of passers-by, they noticed an antique shop. Maddy could not resist second-hand goods of any kind; she was sensitive to smells, and fascinated by the fusty, mysterious odour that hung about Smallgood and Whittlecock's. She fell behind the others and gazed into the dark interior. It was then that she saw the spinning-wheel. It was small and made of dark brown wood with a scrolled stand. She put out her hand and touched it; the wheel turned slowly and silently.

'Sandra,' she yelled, 'come here!'

Sandra walked back to her. 'Do come on,' she scolded. 'You're always bringing up the rear.'

'But do look!' urged Maddy. 'Do you think Mummy would let me have a spinning-wheel?'

Sandra looked at it without interest, then her eyes gleamed. It was just the thing for the Dutch cottage scene. She pulled Maddy away from the shop front and whispered, 'It's sure to be an old man in that shop, and you know old men like you. You go in and beg him to lend us that for the last scene of *Red as the Rose*.' She drew out a programme from her pocket. 'And give him this.'

Maddy nodded and went inside. It seemed empty until she saw a little grey, elderly man, who was so much the colour of most of the stock that he seemed to merge into the junk piled in the corners.

'Well, my dear,' he asked in a crackly voice.

Maddy put her hands behind her back and said, 'Do you like concerts, Mr Smallgood and Whittlecock?'

'Er – yes – yes.' Mr Smallgood and Whittlecock seemed surprised.

'Very much?'

'It all depends who is giving the concert,' he hedged.

'I am.' Maddy waited for him to say something.

'I'm sure it will be a nice one,' the little man said at length.

Was this child mentally deficient or was he?

'Would you like to come?'

'Very much, I'm sure.'

'How much?'

The antique seller was stumped. Never a man of many words, his vocabulary did not run to such fine points as this.

'Enough to lend me that spinning-wheel?' questioned Maddy eagerly, her end in view.

Anything to get rid of this peculiar child, thought her victim.

'Yes, yes, certainly, for as long as you like.'

'Oh, thank you, *dear* Mr Smallgood and Whittlecock.'

Maddy thrust the programme into his hand, picked up the cumbersome spinning-wheel, and staggered off towards the theatre. He wiped his brow.

On Tuesday of the next week the girls broke up. Vicky, Lyn, and Sandra sat next to each other on wooden chairs in the suffocatingly hot assembly hall, while the headmistress read out tedious lists of order marks, untidy marks, and exam. results. A few rows in front of them sat Maddy, a vacant stare on her face. She was mentally going through her dance routine. Tonight it was the dress rehearsal, and she must not make a mistake. Last time she had done it well, and Nigel had said, 'We'll have our Maddy a dancing-star yet.'

'. . . And the essay prize goes to Madelaine Fayne in the Junior School,' said Miss Maclowrie.

'Stamp – shuffle – hop – turn,' Maddy was thinking.

'The subject was a description of scenery typical of some country. Madelaine chose Spain, and her essay, although untidy, was the most interesting one received.'

'Stamp right – stamp left – shout,' muttered Maddy.

Her next door neighbour poked her.

'Go on, Maddy,' she whispered.

Maddy awoke from her reverie with a start and gazed wildly round her. Go where? Then she saw Miss Maclowrie smiling down at her and holding out a book. She got up, pink with confusion, and received the prize. It was a book on *Peoples and Homes of Many Lands*. She sat down, still wondering how she got it, and looked on the fly leaf. In her headmistress's neat script was written, 'Madelaine Fayne. Prize for Essay on "A Typical Scene in Spain".' Then she remembered how she had dashed it off one night before rehearsal, just by describing the scene of *Spanish Inn*. 'What a bit of luck,' she thought. 'If only my luck will hold.' And it did.

The dress rehearsal that night was, as Sandra said, 'Too good to be true,' and Maddy's dance was the star turn. The little staccato tune just suited her personality, and tonight her steps were neater and more carefully executed. To make contrast with the other dances it did not speed up towards the end, but slowed down and became firm and measured. There was a long wait before the last beat, and Maddy was supposed to stand on one leg with the other held in the air at the side, and at the final chord, which was heavy and crashing, to bring it down with a stamp. Usually she giggled, and could not balance enough, but tonight she held it, beaming wickedly at her non-existent audience, and finished with a stamp and a flourish of her broad, black hat. The rest of the rehearsal went as splendidly as *Spanish Inn*. Lyn managed real tears when she broke her engagement with Jeremy, and Nigel's moustache did not come off. Vicky's dance was not as good as usual, as she had practised so hard before coming out that she twisted her ankle, and it still hurt. Sandra told her she must not dance another single step until Thursday night.

It was nearly ten when they left the theatre, and they were so tired that they left their make-up on. They walked home through the dark streets, arm in arm and in an uplifted mood. The stars were out, and there was a shaving of a moon. Lyn gazed up into the sky.

'Please God,' she prayed, 'make me an actress!'

8

APPLAUSE

The day after the dress rehearsal was nerve-racking. There were several little jobs to be done at the theatre, but not enough to keep them busy, consequently they were round there all day, fidgeting and getting bad attacks of nerves. Sandra developed a sore throat, mostly brought on by worry, and Vicky's ankle got steadily worse. Maddy made herself a nuisance, and Jeremy, who had nothing to do, teased her and made her lose her temper.

When they left the theatre in the evening there was not a single job waiting to be done the next day. Everywhere was dusted and swept, the chairs were set out, blue hassocks neatly placed on back rows to add extra height to the seats, and all the clothes re-ironed and hung in the neat dressing-room. The table, which was half on one side of the curtain and half on the other, was laid out with mirrors, cosmetics, and brushes and combs. Sandra had sensibly collected as many of these as possible, knowing that in the rush many would get lost. Nigel had pinned up all the backcloths on top of each other. The *Spanish Inn* was on top; then the window, showing a view of roof-tops for *Madame Popoffski*; then the arbour, then the French windows; then the cottage fireplace for *Red as the Rose*. In this way scene-shifter Bulldog had only to take out several drawing-pins each time to change the backcloth.

Pinned on the dressing-room door was a list of furniture for each scene, and the kind of floor covering to be used. For *Spanish Inn* they had green baize to represent grass, but this was only at the back of the stage, to allow enough bare boards for dancing. This baize was removed for the dancing-class sketch, but laid down again for the arbour. The same rug did for Sir William Whitney's mansion as for the Dutch cottage. In the dressing-room Sandra had procured bowls for each person, so that make-up could be removed easily, and everyone had a jar of cold cream to help with their ablutions.

No detail had been forgotten, so that when they woke on Thursday morning they had the whole day before them with nothing to do. Nigel rounded them up at about eleven o'clock and said, 'Put on something decent and we'll go into town and have something to celebrate with, at the coffee bar.'

A lot of people in Fenchester turned that morning to take a second look at the little group of boys and girls strolling down the High Street. They looked so neat and cool and tidy. But, although their outward appearance was cool, they were in a ferment inwardly, each one feeling his or her own particular brand of excitement. In the coffee bar they sat on high stools and drank pink milk shakes in tall glasses. Nigel proposed the toast.

'To us, the Blue Door Theatre Company; may we make a name for ourselves and never lose it.' Solemnly they clinked glasses, to the amusement of the waitress. Out in the sunshine again they made their usual round – Woolworth's, Marks and Spencer's, the public library, the park, and the market.

At dinner Mrs Fayne said firmly, 'Now, this afternoon, Maddy is going to rest.' Maddy said, equally firmly, 'No. Please, Mummy, I must go out with the others.'

'You're staying in this house on your bed.'

Maddy turned down the corners of her mouth preparatory to crying, but Sandra put in, 'We're all going to rest, Mummy, but not indoors; in the fields.'

'That's very silly of you. It's much hotter up there.'

'But we're going under the big tree in the top field.'

Mrs Fayne shrugged her shoulders. 'If Maddy is too tired to act tonight don't blame me.'

All afternoon they lay on their backs staring up at the tree and the sky, playing lazy, futile games of their own invention.

About half past three they began to get restless and giggly, and Maddy started fighting with Jeremy, so they retired to different corners of the field to get some real rest. Maddy fell asleep. Bulldog chewed grass stems and wondered whether his song would be all right. Vicky massaged her ankle, Lyn had a long and intimate talk with herself, and came to the conclusion that the rest of her life depended on whether she did well in the evening. Sandra dozed and tried to think of a new way to keep Nigel's moustache on. Jeremy had a most awful fit of nerves; he gritted his teeth, clenched his hands, and turned hot and cold all over. Nigel was the only one who could, and did, turn off his thoughts and drift in a relaxed state of coma without sleeping. At half past four they went home, and Nigel ordered everyone to eat enough tea to keep them from feeling faint during the evening.

On the walk to the theatre they discussed how they felt. Maddy said she felt just ordinary, but this was only bravado, for she was shivering violently, though the evening was anything but cold. Lyn said she felt excited and 'wound up inside'. To herself she was pretending that it was her first 'first night' on a West End stage. Sandra, when asked, could only reply, 'I feel worried,' and did not disclose her physical feelings. The boys said they felt 'a bit het up', and judging from the pinkness of Bulldog's complexion he suffered most.

Outside the theatre they looked up at the sign.

'Tons of people will be seeing this for the first time tonight,' remarked Sandra. 'I wonder what they'll say?'

Their footsteps echoed as they walked up the side of the hall, that had an expectant, waiting look, with the chairs facing the drawn curtains. They went into the dressing-room, neat and tidy at the moment.

'How different it will look at ten o'clock tonight,' said Lyn.

'But not *too* different,' warned Sandra, 'or you'll hear about it. Now start getting dressed, and this is the only time you'll be able to dawdle tonight.'

They got themselves into their Spanish clothes and Sandra made them up. Maddy screwed up her face.

'It feels all stiff and cracky,' she grumbled.

'You look sweet. Now go and sit quietly somewhere.'

Maddy found a chair and sat down on it. Her stomach seemed to be making violent efforts to escape. When Bulldog was ready he went out on to the stage and tested the curtains, then arranged the properties – low benches and a barrel supposed to contain wine. Jeremy, white underneath his tan make-up, came across to the piano, which stood on the opposite side of the stage covered by the curtains, and arranged his music and tuned his violin. The familiar feel of it under his chin restored his confidence. Lyn was gazing at her face in the mirror with a haunted look in her eyes; she now knew what stage fright was. Sandra, her hands clasped under her chin, was pacing up and down like a caged lion. Although none of the audience had arrived they spoke in whispers.

There was a knock on the back door, which was in the corner by the piano. It was Mr Fayne, stoutish and jovial, and Mr Darwin, an elder edition of Jeremy, who had been roped in as 'sidesmen'. Bulldog explained the lights to them.

'Now, when I give the signal, a rattle of the tambourine, one of you switch off the hall lights, which are at the back by the main door, and when I give it again switch on the stage light. The switch is on the other side of the door all by itself. When the curtains are drawn to, you put on the auditorium lights and the stage one off.'

'And what about the boxes and the circle and the gallery?' asked Mr Fayne facetiously, trying to break the nervous tension in the air.

They laughed longer and louder than the joke deserved, but felt better for it.

Through the blue door waddled little old Miss Jones, always a first-comer wherever she went. She planted herself on the middle chair of the front row.

'Go and tell her gently but firmly that the front row is reserved for relations and Mr and Mrs Bell,' Jeremy told the stewards.

Miss Jones moved into the second row, and a few more of the audience began to trickle in. They sat down and started to talk in subdued voices, unaware of the seven pairs of eyes that peered through gaps in the curtains at them. At a quarter to seven the hall began to be quite full of people studying the white programmes in their hands and looking at their wrist watches. At ten to seven Mr and Mrs Bell arrived, and with them a tall, thin, clerical figure in gaiters.

'Who is it?' hissed Maddy to Nigel, who occupied the gap next to her.

Nigel's eyes were goggling.

'It's the bishop; the Bishop of Fenchester. Come into the dressing-room!' He pulled them away from the curtains. 'Listen, we must do it well, the bishop is here!'

'The bishop? Do you think he'll like *Madame Popoffski*?' asked Vicky doubtfully.

'He'll have to. We can't cut out anything now.'

Mr Fayne came in holding a slip of paper. 'A note for you from the vicar. Do you know the bishop's here?'

'Yes, isn't it extraordinary?'

They read the note. The vicar had written: 'The bishop wishes to say a few words afterwards.'

'Wait a minute, please, sir,' said Nigel, 'while we think of a suitable reply.'

'Just say "Thank you",' advised Sandra.

'How does one address a bishop?' Nigel was puzzled. 'Your highness or your lordship?'

Mr Fayne told him.

'We thank your lordship very much,' wrote Nigel.

The hands of the clock pointed to two minutes to seven.

'If you forget your exact words, say something that means the same thing, but above all *act*,' urged Lyn.

'We go on in one minute!'

Maddy clutched hold of Jeremy's hand. 'I can't!' she whispered. 'I shall be sick!'

Jeremy gulped and squeezed her hand reassuringly. 'I feel like that, too, Maddy, but we'll be all right after the first few minutes.'

'Our parents have arrived,' Vicky informed them, and they crowded out on to the stage to have a peep at them as they filed into the front row. Mrs Halford sat at the end in her wheel chair looking frail but excited; her hair was the same colour as Vicky's. Her husband, a grave, dark man, sat next to her. Bulldog decided that he must put up a good show for his mother's sake, as she had been looking forward to the concert for weeks.

Mr Fayne said, 'Seven o'clock.' Vicky squeaked, 'My castanets!' and dived back into the dressing-room for them.

The boys lined themselves up on the front of the stage for the opening chorus. Jeremy played the first few bars and someone rattled a tambourine. Instantly the hall was in darkness. The boys stepped in front of the curtain. Vicky rattled the tambourine, and on went the stage lights.

The children's parents received yet another shock on this evening of surprises. They had arrived at the theatre expecting to find a little dilapidated room with some of their children's friends as the audience, and found instead a smart new theatre, with quite important people about, including the bishop. And now, when the lights went up, expecting to see characters dressed as in charades at a family party, they saw four dashing, gaily dressed Spanish men singing a swinging tune to an excellent violin accompaniment. At the end of each verse the muleteers clapped their hands and stamped, off-stage castanets were rattled and tambourines crashed. During the last verse, Maddy and Bulldog pulled aside the curtains and rejoined the others, in time for the final shout,

'Come to the Inn.'

They then stepped aside and sat on the benches, but Jeremy stood, still playing while the audience craned their necks to see the scenery better.

Bulldog had put blue paper round the electric light bulb to give an effect of dusk, and in this light the inn and the mountains made a silhouette in the background. Maddy, sitting astride her bench, felt happier. They had got through the song all right, and she had struck the right note at the end, where she usually went wrong. She allowed herself to smile.

'Doesn't Maddy look sweet?' whispered a fond aunt to a less fond uncle.

Lyn and Vicky entered, tapping their high-heeled shoes on the boards, and sang their Dolores and Marquita song with many coquettish glances at the muleteers. Neither voice was good, but they managed to give a southern impression.

'Never knew Darwin's sister was such a beauty!' whispered one of Jeremy's friends to his companion.

Bulldog beckoned to Lyn at the end of the song, and she went and sat by him, spreading out her full skirt around her. Jeremy was at the piano. Vicky began her tarantella.

Up till now the audience had been merely politely appreciative, but when this red-haired señorita, with flying skirts and snaking body, whirled into her dance they sat up and drank it in. Vicky responded to Jeremy's playing as if there were a link between their brains. Her heels stamped faster, her castanets clapped, and she was a coloured spinning-top. Her audience on the stage stamped in time to the music and shouted encouragement in words gleaned from a Spanish dictionary. With the final chord she stopped dead still, one toe pointed to the side of the stage, one arm curved over her head, the other behind her back, smiling over her shoulder at the applauding audience. Flushed, and trying not to gasp, she sank on to a bench, and Maddy handed her a glass of raspberry juice. She held it up to the light and it flashed ruby-red, then she swallowed it thankfully down.

The clapping of the audience ceased as Sandra entered, dejected and drooping.

Nigel said, 'Carmina looks sad tonight.'

'And I can tell you why,' announced Jeremy.

He stood up and sang in a husky voice unaccompanied, of how he had heard Carmina bemoaning her fate. Then he tucked his violin under his chin and played, while Sandra sang, 'I once used to dance for you, Juan.'

Her voice suited the song, as it was soft and clear, but she gave it no expression until the end, when she seemed to listen and hear the twang of his guitar in the distance. She reached her top G on the 'ar' of 'guitar' quite without effort. Then her face, which had brightened for the last few lines, fell again, and, as the audience applauded, she went slowly to the back of the stage and sat down apart from the others. She drank several wine-glasses of raspberry juice, and the audience waited eagerly for the next turn.

Jeremy nearly forgot to go out to the piano, and Maddy was left standing in front of the stage while he got there. But she just grinned naïvely down at her mother, and, quite on the spur of the moment, as Jeremy played the opening chords, she spat on her hands and rubbed them together. The audience were delighted. She jogged through her little dance, the others shouting the tune and banging tambourines as it got slower and jerkier and slower and jerkier – until it left her standing on one foot waiting for the last crash of chords, which, when it came, was almost drowned by the audience's vociferous applause.

Next came Lyn and Sandra's tambourine dance, and then Bulldog's solo. He started before the piano, and when Jeremy skipped a few notes to catch up with him, he started again. Then they both stopped and there was a horrible silence. Bulldog saw his mother's anxious, pained expression, and tried again. He picked up the accompaniment, and struggled through the first verse. He had a peculiar voice; it had just finished breaking, and was not soprano, nor was it bass, and hardly tenor. The general effect of the song was comical, after the unlucky beginning, and the audience got ready to laugh, but finding it was not supposed to be funny, they tried not to appear amused. In the second verse there was a rattling of the door, and a late-comer walked in through the darkness. Bulldog could discern Mrs Potter-Smith's bulk as she shuffled and whispered her way along a row of chairs to a spare seat in the middle of the line. He faltered and struck a wrong note, forgot the words, and continued with the words of the last verse. He turned appealingly to the others. Nigel whispered to Sandra, and they started to sing the last verse all together, in a melancholy chant, as Bulldog tossed down glass after glass of raspberry juice.

Then Jeremy played his violin solo, putting all his heart and soul into it, and the musical members of the audience appreciated it highly, the bishop among them, who whispered to Mr Bell, 'What a fine musician that boy is!'

The whole company came to the front of the stage and sang the closing chorus, the girls taking the soprano part, the boys the alto. Bulldog and Maddy, who were at each end of the line, pulled the curtains across in front of them, the stage lights went out, and the auditorium lit up. They scuttled back to the dressing-room to change. Bulldog unpinned the backcloth with set teeth. What a fool he had made of himself with that awful song! And if he wasn't funny but only silly in *Madame Popoffski* . . .

He removed the benches and erected the practice bar for the dancing-class, and arranged the side curtain so that it hung behind the piano and the pianist could be seen by the audience. Then he hurried into the dressing-room and flung off his Spanish clothes. No one mentioned the conspicuous failure of his song. Their dressing was accompanied by the rattle of coins being dropped into the plate.

'There's a 50p piece just going in,' prophesied Maddy, pinning her white handkerchief behind her head; but at that moment a thin hand wearing a bishop's ring was placing a pound note on the heap of previously collected coppers and silver.

Mrs Halford squeezed her husband's arm. 'Murray, what did you think of Vicky's dance?'

'Very good,' replied her husband. 'And I remember when someone else with red hair used to dance just as madly as that.'

He referred to the time before their marriage, when she had been training as a dancer, and he, a young barrister, had knocked her over while driving his car carelessly through a London street. She had been injured in both legs, but this did not prevent her from falling in love with the driver of the car and they were married as soon as she came out of hospital.

'I wonder why Vicky said she didn't want to go on learning dancing?' mused Mrs Halford, 'because it is obvious that she loves it.'

'I told her it was too expensive,' Mr Halford confessed.

'You wicked man!' she flared up. 'Of course it's not too expensive. You're trying to save up to send me abroad, aren't you? Now, tell me the truth.'

Under the searching stare of his wife's hazel eyes he was forced to admit that he had that idea in mind.

'Well, I'm not going!' she declared. 'Not if it means Vicky giving up her dancing.'

Mr Halford knew when he was beaten.

Farther along the front row Mrs Fayne and Mrs Darwin discussed *Spanish Inn*.

'And didn't the clothes look nice? Sandra is a good needlewoman.'

Mrs Fayne smiled, pleased at the compliment to her daughter, and hastened to reply that Jeremy was an equally good musician.

'What a very attractive little girl the one with the ponytail is!' remarked the bishop, crossing his gaitered legs and leaning back on the blue chair. 'And how comfortable these seats are!'

A general air of satisfaction lay over the audience. They had enjoyed the first item, subscribed generously to the collection, and now the greater part of the programme was to come.

In the boys' dressing-room Mr Fane and Mr Darwin, counted the collection.

'Fifty-nine pounds and sixty pence,' announced Mr Fayne at last.

'I'll make it up to sixty pounds,' offered Mr Darwin, bringing out some coins from his pocket.

'Sixty pounds! How lovely!'

They were surprised at the amount.

'I have counted the people and there are roughly two hundred,' announced one of the stewards.

'Hurry up, don't keep them waiting, then,' urged Sandra, daubing lipstick on Nigel's mouth.

She ran on to the stage and sat down at the piano and laboriously thumbed out 'The Blue Danube'. A titter of laughter ran through the audience when the curtains were drawn, to show her sitting on the piano stool, shoulders hunched up, with her usually brilliant hair dragged back to a bun, and the tip of her nose a violent pink. Then on came Lyn, with her remarkable Russian make up and long gown.

'Ah, Miss Smith,' she exclaimed, throwing up her hands in a gesture of despair, 'you Eenglish have no soul. You play one-two-*three*, one-two-*three*, but it is *one*-two-three, *one*-two-three. Again, please.'

'I'b sorry, Badabe Boboffski,' replied Miss Smith, dabbing at her nose with a tiny handkerchief, 'id's the code id by head.' And she thumped harder still.

'No, no!' screamed Madame Popoffski, waving her arms excitedly, and she let loose a string of words in what was supposed to be Russian.

Miss Smith sniffed mournfully. 'Oh, Badabe Boboffski, dode speak lige thad to the dew pubils; they're Lady de Swoffle's children, you dow.'

There was a ring off-stage and Madame Popoffski sailed away to answer it. She came back and whispered to Miss Smith, 'Those de Swoffle children, they change into ballet dresses – they are the baby elephants. The legs – ah, they have the knees like the gooseberry. And I who must make them to dance! . . . But they come now.'

Her expression changed to a sweet, simpering smile as the three boys and Maddy entered. The audience roared. Bulldog had a suspender dangling below his ballet skirt, and Nigel's white socks were rucked round his ankles.

'Jeremy makes rather a sweet little girl,' remarked Mrs Fayne.

Jeremy was acting shyly and trying to hide behind Maddy.

'Now, my dears,' purred Lyn, 'I wish you to come forward and curtsey and say to me your names.'

The three little girls giggled, and Maddy went round tidying them up, straightening Jeremy's bow, pulling up Nigel's socks, and attempting to hide Bulldog's suspender. She pushed him forward; he squatted down, steadying himself with his hands, and simpered 'Oxslip.'

'You say your name is Oxslip?' repeated Madame, astounded.

'Yes, miss. They call me Oxo, because I'm beefy,' giggled Bulldog, still squatting on the floor.

'Oxslip!' groaned Madame Popoffski to the pianist. She shuddered, then forced back her sweet smile and patted him on the head.

'I see, Oxslip, that I must instruct you to make the

curtsey.' She did an exaggerated curtsey. 'So, with the toe pointed; and you will please call me Madame.'

Bulldog tried again, this time putting his legs into such knots that he fell sprawling, catching hold of Madame's ankles and pulling her down as well.

'Oh, Oxo!' reproved Maddy, shaking her finger at him.

Madame got up in as dignified a way as possible, and cooed, 'Now, my next little pupil.'

Nigel curtsied and said coyly, 'Velia, Madame. They call me Vealy for short, because I'm not so beefy as Oxo.'

Madame told them that she would teach them a few steps, then they must do a little dance introducing them.

'Arabesque,' said Madame, with one leg raised behind her and her fingertips lightly touching her chin.

'Arabesque,' repeated Oxslip, clasping her bottom jaw tightly in both hands and kicking out behind, catching the part of Miss Smith that was sitting on the piano stool.

'*Entrechat*,' said Madame, jumping high into the air and clicking her feet several times.

'*Entrechat*,' repeated the pupils, jumping with their legs flying out at all angles, and landing with a thud that shook the stage.

'*Pas de bourrée.*' Madame glided across the stage on her points, with small steps and a rapt expression.

'*Pas de bourrée.*' Bulldog followed her, stumbling about on the tips of his gym shoes, which were stuffed with cotton wool.

'Now, Oxslip, you will dance,' Madame ordered him. 'Miss Smith, you will play some tune that suits this young dancer of such grace, such emotion.'

Sandra banged out, 'Pop-eye, the Sailor Man', and Bulldog, wobbling perilously, did a series of laboured pirouettes on bowed legs.

'But that is too heavy, too like the Donald Duck,' screamed Madame.

Miss Smith returned to the 'Blue Danube', and Bulldog did a coy fluttering dance that made the audience rock in their chairs. Whenever he raised his right leg the suspender flapped; he ended up in a final curtsey just as Madame had taught him, with his toes pointing outwards and holding up the frill of his skirt at the back. The only mistake was that he was facing the wrong way, and the view received by the audience was an expanse of red flannel drawers. The bishop mopped his streaming eyes and tried to control himself. Mrs Bell giggled unrestrainedly. The two friends of Jeremy laughed till they nearly fell off their chairs, and one of them managed to gasp, 'Never knew that chap could be so amusing. He's new this term.'

At the end of the sketch, the applause was feeble as the audience were still laughing.

'Isn't Bulldog a scream?' giggled Mrs Halford, her usually pale cheeks flushed with laughter. She glanced at her programme. 'Vicky's dancing,' she remarked.

The lights went off and the curtains were drawn by Mr Fayne on one side and Bulldog on the other. The stage was bare but for the backcloth, a beautifully drawn rose arbour. Jeremy was at the piano, which was, once again, hidden by the curtains; he played a soft valse from Les Sylphides.

Vicky, in a crisp snow-white ballet dress, twirled gracefully on to the stage. Coming directly after her brother's attempt, her entry made a remarkable contrast, and the audience was spell-bound. She was a different being from the fiery señorita who had danced the tarantella; she was some vague wood sprite, here for a moment, gone the next. The light had on its blue shade, which gave the slim, white-clad figure an appearance of transparency. She finished up with a series of slow *fouettées*, and sank on to the ground in a billow of tarlatan. The applause was magnificent, and she was called before the curtain time after time. This gave Jeremy opportunity to remove his little girl make-up and get dressed to play his part as Anthony. Lyn, fastening up her dress at the side, was quivering with excitement. Her chance was coming, she *must* act it well; up till now she had just been average, and had made no hit at all, but as Julia she *must*, oh, she *must*. Sandra put on the final touches of make-up.

'You look lovely, Lyn,' she told her, 'and if Jeremy won't woo you properly just force him to.'

'He'll hear about it afterwards,' said the heroine grimly, 'if he doesn't!'

'What's that about me,' asked Jeremy, from the other side of the curtain.

'We were just saying we didn't suppose you'd woo Lyn properly.'

'You just watch me! I'll be an absolute Don Juan. You ready?'

He picked up his rake and went on to the side of the stage. Bulldog was arranging the arbour, a rustic bench and a chair and table. Lyn as Julia and Sandra as Lady Whitney came on and sat down with their embroidery, and the curtains parted. It made a pretty picture to the eyes of the audience; the arbour looked its best under the heavy light, and its occupants appeared dainty and calm. They sewed in silence till Lady Whitney's head dropped and she snored slightly. Julia ran to the edge of the stage, peering across the sunlit garden. She beckoned to Anthony, who came on attractively dishevelled in his gardener's breaches and hose, and doffed his straw hat.

They moved over to the other side and conversed in whispers.

'My darling,' said Julia, 'I must speak with you. After our talk in the garden last night . . .' she looked down, unable to go on.

'It was – it was the moon – and the darkness – and seeing you so suddenly as I did. Otherwise, not for the world would I have professed my love for you.'

'But, Anthony, I am glad – glad. It had to happen.'

Anthony expressed his doubts for the future.

'By the morning light I recognize our folly. It would grieve your father, Sir William, to know that you love a worthless working man such as I. You must marry some rich and noble gentleman, worthy of your grace and beauty.'

'Do you remember what you said last night, Anthony?' Julia smiled reminiscently. 'You said my eyes were twin stars, and my lips red as the rose. Were you lying?'

'I' faith, no! Your lips are so, as red as the rose on

yonder bush. It is a plant I have cultivated myself, and I call it the "Lady Julia".'

Vexed by his timid behaviour, Julia taunted him with cowardice, until he caught her to him. The embrace, awkward and clumsy at rehearsals, went off perfectly. Nigel, as Sir William, entered, complete with curling locks and beard. He held a letter.

Speaking in a deep bass voice he cried, "Ecod!' not noticing the pair, who sprang apart. 'Wake, wife! I have ill news. This day the rascally Parliamentarians have rebelled against the King. I must go at once down to the village and muster a force to prepare to fight for him.'

Lady Whitney collapsed into tears at once, and Sir William led her off-stage, back to the house. Terrified, Julia turned to Anthony, but when she understood that he was a Parliamentarian, she rebuffed him with a stony face.

She watched him go, bewildered and stunned, then walked across the stage, and in the wings Bulldog handed her a rose, the one already used in *Spanish Inn*. She walked back across the stage, clasping the rose to her, then she burst into tears, and to her joy they were real ones. The curtains closed.

For the second time that evening the bishop wiped his eyes, but not for the same reason.

'What an excellent little actress. She certainly has a real talent.'

There were bangings and thumpings from behind the curtains as Bulldog moved the furniture for the drawing-room scene.

Lyn went to the wash basin and had a drink of water.

She was happy now, as she knew the last scene had been a success, and that the next scene would be better. She slipped on to the stage before the others were ready, and sat down on the chair by the backcloth, representing the open french windows, and worked herself up into the strained state of mind she was supposed to be in, as her father had not been heard of for a month. Lady Whitney, with face powdered and lines under her eyes to make her look worried, and Vicky as Ursula the servant girl, joined Julia a few moments later. They all sat staring into space as the curtains were pulled. Bulldog, in the wings, hit a tin tray four times with a spoon. Lady Whitney jumped up.

'Four o'clock after noon,' she cried, hysterically. 'I shall go mad. We have sat like this for years, for centuries, waiting and listening for what? I want to know – for what? He's dead! I know it! He's killed!'

Julia and the maid calmed her, and they sat again in their former attitudes talking of the battles lost and won. Off-stage, Bulldog clapped castanets to resemble horse's hooves, faint at first, and then gradually getting louder. The three women ran to the window.

'It's William!'

'Oh, it's father!' cried Lady Whitney and Julia simultaneously, and they hurried out to meet him. They came in with him a few seconds later; he was limping and pale. As they gave him food and bathed his wounded leg he told them of his adventures. To Nigel's annoyance, Sir William's moustache, as usual, dropped off. The audience were delighted, if unsympathetic, when he moistened it with the water used to bathe his wound, and stuck it on again. Bulldog set to work again with the castanets – two pairs this time – and Sir William sprang to his feet, alarmed.

'The Roundheads – they are following me. I must hide.'

Sir William picked up his things, kissed his wife, and hurried from the room. Lady Whitney, tearing off her shoes and stockings, began to bathe her feet in the water prepared for her husband, and Julia sat down at the table and began to eat the meal.

In came Bulldog and Maddy as soldiers. Their appearance was singular, to say the least of it, and the audience laughed heartily. Maddy's pony-tail and cheerful face were incongruous, combined with a pike and armour, and Bulldog they expected to be funny, after *Madame Popoffski*.

The women clung together terrified, then Julia stepped forward. 'May I ask, good sirs, to what bad fortune we owe this intrusion?'

Bulldog explained that they were looking for Sir William Whitney, and that they had orders to search the house. Their captain was coming to question the household.

'I will see the captain, mother. You and Ursula go with these soldiers. Show them that we have no fugitives here.'

They went, and Lyn, left alone, knelt by her chair and moved her lips in a murmured prayer. Anthony, in armour, entered and stood behind her.

'Julia,' he said softly.

She sprang up, recognized him, and her eyes flashed.

'You!' she cried angrily. 'So you have come back to gloat over your victory. Just what one expects from a common gardener! But you may search, you may question, you may threaten, and much good may it do you.'

Anthony told her gently that he wanted only to help them, but she rejected his offer with furious disdain.

Here a scream rang through the hall, and Lady Whitney ran in, throwing herself at the captain's feet. She had seen her husband captured, and she begged for mercy for him. Anthony signed to Julia to take her away. With a look of hatred she obeyed. Anthony called to Bulldog and told him to take all the men back to their camp, and he would follow the next day with the prisoner. The curtains drew together, but only to denote passage of time, as the next scene took place in the same setting.

It was the next morning, and Anthony was interviewing Sir William, who had only just recognized him as his former gardener. Anthony told him that he was going to give him his freedom and take the consequences, and gave him a paper that would enable him to get to Holland with his family.

'But why are you doing all this for me?' Sir William wanted to know.

'I love your daughter.'

Sir William asked cautiously, 'And what do you want in return for your kindness?'

'Nothing, Sir William, but the assurance of her safety, which is dearer to me than life itself.'

Here Sir William shook Anthony by the hand.

'My man, although you are a Roundhead, you have the instincts of a Cavalier. Never shall I forget your kindness!'

Anthony went away, and Sir William informed his family of their good luck.

'Anthony did this?' asked Julia.

'He did. And he told me why.'

The curtains swung together as Julia looked down.

The clock in the dressing-room said half past nine as they changed for the last act. When the curtains were next pulled, the backcloth represented a large fireplace, and on one side of it sat Sir William smoking a pipe, and on the other Lady Whitney, embroidering. In the corner, Maddy, as Gretel, in the Dutch costume, sat at the spinning-wheel teaching Julia to spin. They talked of how safe and comfortable they felt so far away from the war, and of how good Anthony had been to them. There was a knock at the door.

'Answer it please, Gretel.'

Gretel went to the door. A figure in a black cloak stepped in, pulling off his slouch hat. It was Anthony. Julia gave a little cry. After welcoming him, the parents excused themselves, saying that they would prepare a bedroom for him. Gretel was sent out to see that the chickens were shut up for the night.

'I am sorry for all I said to you at our last meeting,' apologized Julia.

'You are lovely when you are angry,' Anthony told her.

'And now that Parliament has won the war, you will be a gardener no longer?'

'I have been offered the position of general.'

'So you will have to return to England.'

'If I accept it.'

'But you would not be so foolish as to refuse?'

'I am tired of military life. I should like to live here, in Holland. A little cottage by the canal with white steps and a red-tiled roof, and chickens in the back garden, and a wife in front of the fire.'

Julia sat very still. He went across and took her in his arms.

'Does that sound a happy life to you, my sweet?'

'Very happy,' she murmured against his shoulder.

Gretel came bustling in. 'The chickens are quite safe and happy.'

'And so are we, Gretel.'

The curtains closed as Gretel stood gaping in wide-mouthed amazement at the contented couple.

The entire company grouped themselves on the stage and bowed to vigorous applause. Maddy squeezed Jeremy's hand to attract his attention.

'Do you think they liked it?' she asked.

'It seems like it,' said Jeremy, nodding towards the bishop, whose hands were clapping their fastest.

The bishop stood up and the applause ceased. 'Ladies and gentlemen,' he began, 'what I am going to say may not be very coherent, but you will have to put it down to the way in which these young people have played havoc with my emotions. I have been laughing at one moment, crying the next. I am sure none of us will forget this evening, and the very good entertainment given by the Blue Door Theatre Company. But I feel it is more than good entertainment we have enjoyed tonight; it is an example of cultivation of talents for reasons which are not egotistical.'

'Oh, quite, I agree,' murmured Maddy.

'So I am sure you will join me in wishing these young players many successes and much happiness.'

The audience clapped loudly till Nigel, stepping forward, held up his hand for silence.

'As the eldest of the Blue Door Theatre Company, I want to thank you all on their behalf for coming tonight, and the bishop for his kind speech. The collection for the new organ fund came to sixty pounds, which, when a few expenses have been deducted, we shall have pleasure in handing over to Mr Bell. We want to thank Mrs Bell for her kindness and good advice, and the people who helped with the curtains, lights, and collecting. We must now say goodnight, and we hope you have enjoyed yourselves as much as we have.'

At the piano Jeremy struck up the National Anthem, and they stood up straight and stiff and sang it wholeheartedly.

The next half-hour was a whirl of congratulations and compliments. Relations and friends surged into the dressing-room to chat and gossip, and the children were patted on the back until they were sore. Lyn's performance as Julia was highly praised, and the compliment that pleased her most was from the bishop.

'You will make a fine actress one day, if you work hard,' he told her.

Bulldog was hailed as the comedian of the company, and Vicky's dancing put down as wonderful. Jeremy's music master told him that he had not made such a fool of himself as he had expected. Jeremy knew this to be one of the highest forms of praise his master could give. At last the audience trickled out and they were left alone, but for their parents.

'Don't you bother to wait for us; we may be ages,' Nigel told them.

They took the hint and went home, and at half-past ten the Blue Door Company trailed along the dark streets, carrying all the things that had to be returned immediately. They were silent but happy. Maddy went to sleep walking along, a feat which was only possible to her. Jeremy and Sandra lugged her along between them. At the gate she woke up and said, 'Have I got to go on now?' imagining herself still at the concert.

'No,' replied Sandra, 'you've got to go to bed.'

' "Good night till next we meet," ' quoted Nigel, as he closed the front gate.

The Fayne children and the Darwins sat in the drawing-room of the Corner House waiting for the Halfords, who had overslept. It was a hot sultry morning with no sun, and everyone was inclined to be bad tempered. Jeremy sat on the piano stool, idly touching the keys.

'Stop fidgeting, for goodness' sake,' snapped Lyn, who was pale and heavy-lidded.

Jeremy perversely thumped out 'The Sound of your Guitar', until Sandra said, with an air of martyrdom, 'I know it's a very nice tune, Jeremy, and of course if you want me to be sick . . .'

Jeremy banged down the lid, dug his hands into his pockets, and striding into the hall shouted up the stairs, 'Aren't you ready yet, Nigel?'

Vicky's voice floated down in reply, 'He's only just got up!' A few minutes later they appeared, looking as languid as the others.

'Where's Maddy?' asked Bulldog, noting her absence.

'She's got a headache.'

'So've I,' groaned Nigel. 'Don't let's do anything energetic.'

'Let's saunter down town,' suggested Lyn.

'No,' disagreed Nigel. 'We shall only have tons of people congratulating us!'

'Well, don't you think that's rather enjoyable?' asked Lyn.

'No, I don't. I hate people gushing over me.'

'That's only a pose,' said Lyn scornfully. 'You positively glowed when my mother told you she never thought her ringlets would adorn such a handsome Cavalier!'

'Stop bickering and get a move on.' Sandra was impatient.

They walked into town, occasionally exchanging a remark about the concert. Outside the public library they met a school friend of Sandra, who had been at the concert.

'Hullo,' she cried boisterously, 'congrats!' She patted Sandra vigorously on the back. Sandra's head throbbed. 'I thought you were all wonderful last night. And as for that dancing-class thing!' She giggled loudly at the thought of it.

'What an awful female!' muttered Bulldog to Jeremy.

'I was wondering,' went on the girl, 'if you'd like me to join your company. I can't act or anything, but it would be fun.'

The Blue Door Theatre Company were dumb-founded. They searched wildly for some suitable excuse.

'Well, it's like this,' began Nigel, then stopped.

'You see,' Lyn faltered.

Although they had not spoken of it, each could feel that the rest did not like the idea of a stranger in their midst. Sandra struck on the right excuse.

'You go to chapel, don't you?'

'That's right.'

'Well, we all go to Mr Bell's church, and it was he who gave us the theatre, so—'

'Oh, I see,' she responded regretfully. 'Well, good-bye.'

They heaved a sigh of relief as she went on her way. This was only the first time that morning that they had to refuse offers of recruits for the company, and each time it became more difficult.

About eleven o'clock they were joined by Maddy.

'Hullo,' she greeted them, 'I'm a drug fiend!'

'A what?'

'I've taken two aspirins,' she announced proudly, 'and now I feel grand. I saw one of Jeremy's school friends, and he gave me this.' She held up an envelope, and Jeremy would have taken it, but she snatched it away. 'No, it's not for you. Look!'

On the outside was written 'Miss L. Darwin.' Lyn blinked. 'For me?' She opened it, blushing, and read it out to them:

★ ★ ★

DEAR LYNETTE, – I was at the concert last night, and
I think you are the most wonderful actress I have
ever seen. Why has your brother never told me
about you, I wonder? I hope you don't think it
colossal cheek of me to write to you. You must ask
Jeremy to introduce us. – Yours very sincerely,

JOHN FLANDERS.

Jeremy gave a hoot of laughter. 'My goodness, fancy old
Flanders falling for you. Well I never!'

Nigel said cruelly, 'There you are, Lyn, you have all
you want in that letter of gushing admiration.'

Lyn turned on him furiously. 'You'll take that back.'

'I shall not. It's exactly what you confessed a liking for.'

'There's thunder in the air,' remarked Maddy
ambiguously.

Lyn stalked on ahead with Sandra at her side. Nigel
sighed, and said a bit too loudly, 'Girls are more trouble
than they're worth.'

Lyn turned sharply and retorted, 'Some boys don't
know when they're lucky.'

'Meaning, I suppose, that if John Flanders had the
pleasure of your company he would be as sweet as
honey to you.'

Lyn tossed her head.

Jeremy and Vicky sighed, looking anxiously at each
other, and wondering what their respective brother and
sister would say next.

'Please remember we're in the High Street,' implored
Sandra.

'Aha,' Jeremy crowed, looking ahead of them down the street, 'who is this that heaves in sight?'

Two of his school friends were sauntering along, their hands in their pockets. One of them was John Flanders.

'Would you like us to leave you, Lyn?' asked Nigel sarcastically.

This goaded Lyn further. 'Yes,' she replied, 'all except Jeremy.'

They all turned and walked off in the opposite direction.

'Hullo, you,' said Jeremy, with a grin as they met. 'Meet my sister, Lynette. Lyn, this is John Flanders and Gregory Macmillan.'

They shook hands. Jeremy looked at his watch. 'Goodness, it's past eleven. I shan't get there in time. Cheerio! You don't mind me leaving you, Lyn, do you?'

Lyn said she did not.

'Where are you off to?' Macmillan wanted to know.

'One of those thingummy-jig affairs,' said Jeremy vaguely, as he hurried off to find the others.

Lyn spent the rest of the morning walking round the town with Macmillan and Flanders. She found them congenial company, as they treated her most politely and admiringly, as if she were some fragile piece of Dresden china. John Flanders bought her a little spray of roses from a flower seller and presented them, quoting from Jeremy's part in *Red as the Rose*. By the entrance to Woolworth's they ran into the others, and Lyn said, 'Hullo, Nigel. Hullo, Sandra. Hullo, Maddy. Hullo, Vicky, Hullo, Bulldog. Hullo, Jerry,' with a suavity that was most annoying. In Woolworth's Mrs Potter-

Smith met the greater part of the Blue Door Theatre Company.

'Oh, my clever darlings,' she cooed, 'I want to tell you how I loved your perfectly divine concert. Of course, it's such a shame you've never been trained. I mean, one can always tell the difference. And how sweet of the dear bishop to come; but there, I know he makes an absolute martyr of himself.'

The 'clever darlings' were not in a mood to listen to veiled insults.

'Of course you didn't see the beginning part of the programme,' said Nigel smoothly, alluding to her late entrance, 'so you didn't see Vicky's dance. I know you are interested in dancing.'

'I thought it was a very lovely show, and even though the person sitting next to me said that she thought that the dancing-class play was rather vulgar, I stuck up for you. Yes, I stuck up for you. "They're very young," I said. "Too young to quite understand what is what." And when she said that the last play about the Wars of the Roses' – here Nigel winced – 'when she said that was a bit too full of love-making, I said, "But they're so young, so very young," I said, "to attempt a play like that." ' The children seethed. Mrs Potter-Smith went on. 'You know, I am thinking of getting up another of my little concerts. People do appreciate them so, and I thought I would ask the dear vicar to lend me the hall you used.'

'But Mrs Potter-Smith,' Sandra gasped, 'that isn't his hall; it's ours.'

'Yes, dear girlie, but the vicar must have first say in the matter.'

Nigel said firmly, 'I don't think it would quite meet your requirements.'

'No,' Maddy backed him up, 'the stage is very fragile, it won't bear too much. Time and again I have gone through, and they've had to wait for me to get thin enough to squeeze out! And then there are rats in the dressing-room. They eat the cosmetics: that's why Nigel's moustache fell off. You see, he had put the gum all ready on it, and while his back was turned a rat came and licked it off!'

Mrs Potter-Smith goggled.

'And if you really want permission to use it, you have to go and ask the chaplain it belonged to last. His name is Brother Irving, and he's in prison for murder. We went to see him to get his permission, and it was a good job Vicky had her hockey stick. D'you know, he's so strong he can bend the bars on the door with his hand; and he stretched out . . .' Maddy shot out her hand with fingers spread towards Mrs Potter-Smith's fleshy throat. She moved a few paces backward. 'He stretched out and caught me by the neck, and if Vicky hadn't banged his hands with her hockey stick' – she shrugged – 'it would have been the end of me.'

The others tried to stop this flow of cheerful lies, but once she was in full swing Maddy went from length to length.

'And he told us,' she lowered her voice mysteriously, 'that there is the body of one of his victims buried in the back yard of the hall. We had noticed a peculiar smell, certainly, but we thought it was the marigolds that

Bulldog had planted. P'r'aps that's why they've grown so well.'

Mrs Potter-Smith was scarlet with rage. 'Goodbye,' she snapped and hurried off.

'You little liar,' chuckled Nigel, patting her on the back. 'You've certainly done the trick.'

'Whatever made you say all that?' the shocked Sandra wanted to know.

'It just came. Inspiration, you know. It's quite easy when you've practised a bit.'

On the way home they met several people who told them how much they enjoyed the concert and how they hoped that another would be forthcoming. As they walked up Goldenwood Avenue they could see Lyn talking to her two new friends.

'That girl makes me sick,' seethed Nigel.

'You're bad-tempered today, that's what's the matter with you,' said Sandra, sticking up for her friend.

'Take an aspirin,' advised Maddy.

Nigel kicked his gate open. 'Oh well, cheerio. I'm going to bed this afternoon.'

'I'm going out with Mummy,' said Sandra, 'and we're buying Maddy a new coat.'

'Does that mean I have to come too?' asked Maddy suspiciously.

'It does. And we're going to visit Aunty Beth.'

Maddy groaned. 'Life is going to be awful, now that we can't make rehearsals our excuse for everything.'

'It's terrible to have nothing to do,' grumbled Bulldog, who all last term had grumbled that he had too much to do.

'I can't see us doing any more plays till next Christmas hols,' said Nigel, 'because I shall be working for G.C.E. next year, and so I shan't be able to rehearse during term time.'

'And we couldn't possibly do anything without you,' added Maddy loyally.

'Things are rather broken up,' sighed Sandra. 'We're going to Bristol to stay with our grandparents next week, and then we're going to the seaside for a fortnight.'

'We're going to Scotland,' Nigel told her.

'You're lucky,' Jeremy said; 'we're not going away at all. I shall have a pretty mouldy time if Lyn's going to play around with those' – he jerked his head up the hill to where Lyn stood with Macmillan and Flanders, and he searched for a word – 'those stage-door johnnies.'

By the end of the holidays Lyn was sick of the sight of the two boys. They haunted her wherever she went, and she soon tired of their excellent manners and pretty speeches. Most mornings they walked in the park and made feeble conversation. Lyn found that the only subject on which they could talk intelligently was themselves. After long doses of Macmillan's descriptions of his father's horses, and how he himself had nearly won a point-to-point, Lyn longed to hear Nigel and Bulldog talking their usual nonsense; and when John Flanders told her in minute detail of how he did the hat-trick in last season's cricket, she felt she would give anything for the light banter and cross-talk of the Blue Door Theatre Company.

Jeremy spent all his holidays practising his violin, for

he had an exam. to take in October. In Scotland the Halfords fished and rode and climbed, while the Faynes swam and sunbathed on the beaches of Bournemouth. Only Lyn was bored and miserable.

One day, towards the end of the seven weeks' holiday, John and Gregory received a surprise when they knocked at the door of number seventeen Goldenwood Avenue at the usual time. Instead of Lyn appearing, dainty and smiling, Jeremy, violin in hand, greeted them.

'Hullo, Lyn's not coming out this morning; we're going down to meet the Halfords at the station.'

The two boys were crestfallen.

Nigel and the twins, leaning out of the carriage windows as far as they dared, were surprised to see Lyn waiting eagerly with Jeremy on the platform. From his letters they had gathered that Lyn was quite inseparable from Macmillan and Flanders. She greeted them effusively, kissing Vicky in her excitement.

'Oh, it's lovely to have you back!' she sighed contentedly. 'You don't know what an awful time I've been having.'

No one mentioned her two cavaliers, but Nigel treated her with a new coolness that lasted many weeks.

The next day when Macmillan and Flanders called, Jeremy told them, 'She's not coming out this morning 'cos the Faynes are arriving some time today, and we're waiting in for them.'

The morning after that, as they reached the bottom of Goldenwood Avenue they heard a tinkling of many bicycle bells, and the seven swept by with cheerful shouts of greeting.

'This,' said John Flanders, 'is the end.'

'She's jilted us,' agreed Gregory.

But they were not destitute for long, as the next day John's cousin, a pretty, aristocratic-looking little blonde, came to stay with him. When she was sitting in the milk bar with them one day she asked, 'Who are those people over there, with that dark girl dressed in red?'

'Those,' replied John scornfully, 'are not fit people for you to know, Clarys; they're the scum of Fenchester.'

Lyn, draining a raspberry shake, and giggling over a particularly ridiculous sally of Bulldog's, did not notice her acquaintances in the corner.

9

THE SWAN OF AVON

Time passed quickly for the Blue Door Theatre Company. Once they were into the autumn term, there was Christmas to be thought about. They were invited to perform a Nativity Play for the Kindergarten Sunday School party, which was a great success, then there was Christmas Day and Boxing Day to celebrate, and to their delight, early in January it snowed, and they were able to go tobogganing.

Returning to school was rather an anti-climax, and by the time the Easter holidays were approaching they were feeling the need for a little excitement. It came about in an unexpected fashion. One night, Lyn could not sleep. It was eleven o'clock, and she had been in bed for two hours, tossing and turning and shaking up her pillow in an effort to get comfortable. It was a welcome diversion when the front-doorbell rang. She jumped out of bed, ran along the landing, and peered over the banisters as her mother opened the door.

'Why, Bishop!' Lyn heard her exclaim in astonishment. 'How nice to see you!'

'I hope I've not called at too late an hour,' said the bishop, in his cool, cultured voice.

'Of course not. Do come in.'

The bishop was ushered into the drawing-room. Lyn heard him greet her father, then the door was closed, but not shut. She crept a little farther down the stairs, and strained her ears; they were exchanging pleasantries. Then the bishop said, 'The real object of my visit tonight was to make a request. Can you spare your children for two days?'

'Why, yes,' replied Mrs Darwin, in a puzzled tone. 'I suppose so.'

'I am planning a little trip on the twenty-second of April, and I have just been to see Mr and Mrs Halford and Mr and Mrs Fayne who have given their permission for the children to come, so I'm sure Jeremy and Lynette would like to join us.'

'Where do you propose to go?' asked Mr Darwin.

Lyn crept down a few more steps, to hear the bishop say:

'To Stratford-on-Avon. I always attend the Shakespeare Festival on the twenty-third of April, and I should like to take the Blue Door Theatre Company, knowing how interested they are in acting.'

'How kind of you, Bishop. I'm sure they'll be thrilled.'

'Thrilled isn't the word,' thought Lyn, gripping the stair on which she sat. *Shakespeare Festival. Stratford-on-Avon.* The words drummed in her brain, carried by a rush of overpowering excitement. Her first impulse was to go and tell Jeremy; then she heard the bishop speak again.

'We shall start on the Wednesday afternoon, and get back on Friday, after seeing two plays. It will be *Romeo and Juliet* in the evening and *Twelfth Night* in the afternoon.'

Lyn nearly fell down the stairs with delight. This was just the kind of pretence game that she and Sandra used to have when they were younger. They would pretend that all sorts of wonderful adventures happened to them, and they usually began by some kind person taking them somewhere. It was cold sitting on the stairs, and her nightie was thin, but she stayed to try to hear more about the expedition.

'They will only need night-clothes and tooth-brushes,' the bishop said, and Lyn added mentally 'and an autograph album.'

Sitting on the prickly stair carpet she was lost in day-dreams; suddenly the door opened and her parents and the bishop came out. Luckily there was no light on the stairs, so she kept as still as she could. Her parents did not notice her as they ushered the bishop out. Directly the drawingroom door was shut she ran into Jeremy's bedroom and jumped on to his bed, shaking him by the shoulder.

'Wake up, Jeremy, do you hear? Wake up!'

'Wazzermatter?' grumbled Jeremy, burrowing his head further into the pillows.

'The most wonderful thing! Do wake up and listen!'

But Jeremy was asleep again. She pulled his ears hard and he sat up, furious.

'Leave me alone, girl.'

'Jeremy, do listen! The bishop has just called.'

'Who?'

'The bishop. He wants to take us to Stratford-on-

Avon. All of us. The Faynes and the Halfords too.'

'Whaffor?' asked Jeremy, preparing to go to sleep again.

'To see two Shakespeare plays and the Festival. Now, are you awake?'

'Lor', yes! How super!'

There was a flow of excited chatter.

When Lyn at last got back to bed she fell asleep and dreamed that she was playing Juliet, sitting on the top stair of the stair-case, while the bishop, as Romeo, occupied the bottom one.

The seven of them lived in a state of continual excitement during the following week. They could talk and think of nothing but the Festival, and they read *Twelfth Night* and *Romeo and Juliet* most carefully, each giving their opinions on how the plays ought to be produced.

Sandra's mother bought her a new blue dress for the occasion, and Lyn had a new travelling case.

The afternoon of 22nd April found them awaiting the bishop at the station. For the first time in her life Maddy was carrying a handbag. She was wearing her grey kilted skirt and blazer, and her handbag matched her red jumper. Jeremy and Bulldog wore grey flannel suits, but Nigel had a blue sports coat. As it was true April weather they all carried mackintoshes. At last they saw the gaunt figure of the bishop coming towards them.

'So you're all here?' He counted them carefully. 'I mustn't lose any of you on the way, or your mothers would never let me take you out again.' He hurried them into a compartment.

'How nice,' remarked Maddy, after she had dived for a corner seat, 'we all fit in. Four on each side. And if the bishop sits on the same side as Bulldog they will cancel out each other's size.'

Sandra made the warning face that means, 'If you don't shut up you'll hear about this afterwards,' but the others, who were in holiday mood, only laughed. The train started up and pulled out of the station.

'What time shall we get there?' asked Nigel.

'About ten o'clock,' was the reply; 'and we have to change trains three times.'

'I love train journeys,' confided Maddy; 'and this will be the longest I have ever been.'

'You won't like it much at about nine o'clock this evening,' the bishop warned her.

'I expect she'll go to sleep. She generally does in the car,' said Sandra.

'That's because I have such a boring person sitting next to me,' Maddy told her rudely. 'But I shan't today.'

The bishop, who sat next to her, bowed. 'Thank you, Maddy. A very nice compliment.'

'I'm good at compliments.'

'What do we do? Clap?' asked Jeremy sarcastically.

They bickered for a while; then the bishop retired behind a copy of the *Diocesan Mail*, and they played 'Coffee Pots' until it was time for their first change.

'Here we are,' said the bishop.

They reached up and got their suitcases from the rack, and stepped out on to the platform.

'I've been sitting down so long,' complained Maddy, 'that I feel drunk now that I'm standing.' She staggered round in circles, till Sandra made her behave properly.

'We have twenty minutes to wait,' said the bishop, 'so what about a spot of tea?'

'What about it?' repeated Maddy appreciatively. 'Lead me to it!'

They had some very dish-watery tea and doughnuts in the dowdy station buffet, then went back to the platform, where quite a number of people were waiting for the train. When it came in it was very full with people returning from market in a neighbouring town, and there was not an empty carriage to be found.

'We shall simply have to split up,' the Bishop told them, 'and find a seat wherever we can. Luckily we change again in about half an hour at Gloucester, so keep your eyes open for the names of the stations.'

When they assembled at Gloucester station Bulldog was missing, so Nigel was sent back on to the train to find him. He discovered him standing on the seat in an empty carriage holding his suitcase up in the air.

'Come on, kid, do,' Nigel hurried him.

'I can't,' gasped Bulldog; 'I'm attached to the communication cord, and if I move I shall pull it, and have to pay a fine.'

'You silly chump, however do you mean you're attached?'

Nigel, jumping up on to the seat beside him, saw that the keys of the case, which were attached to the handle by a short piece of yellow string, had got wrapped tightly round the cord.

'We must hurry, Bulldog,' he said, 'the train goes in a few seconds. You are an idiot!' Nigel pulled the cord roughly and instantly disentangled the keys. 'Don't you know the cord is pulled to stop the train? How can you stop it once it's standing still? Come on, get a move on.'

They jumped out on to the platform just as the station-master was blowing his whistle. Jeremy alone was waiting for them, a worried look on his face.

'Come on, you two, we've simply got to fly. The bishop's just discovered our train goes immediately, so he's rushed off with the girls. We've got to get right down to the other end of the platform.'

They ran for all they were worth, and Lyn, seeing them coming, stuck her head out and yelled, 'Hurry up, train's moving.' They jumped into the compartment and collapsed panting on the seat.

The journey seemed to go on for ever, but at last a porter shouted the magic words 'Stratford-on-Avon,' and they got out.

'Well, we're here,' said Lyn to Sandra, in a satisfied tone. 'I was afraid we should have a crash on the way and never actually arrive.'

'I expect you would all like a wash,' said the bishop, 'if you feel as grubby as I do.'

'They made their way to the cloakrooms. Washing her hands in the shiny white basin with the hot water sending shivers of delight over her body, Lyn smiled at her own reflection in the mirror.

'Isn't all this absolutely super?' she said. 'We've never been anywhere like this alone together, with no grown-ups. The bishop doesn't really count; he leaves us alone so much.'

'And he doesn't make a lot of boring plans, he just lets things happen, which is what I like,' said Vicky, dragging a comb through her burnished hair.

'You look tired, Maddy. Feel it?' asked Sandra.

The lines under Maddy's round blue eyes belied her stout denials. Feeling much fresher than before, they went out to find the boys.

'Here you are, then,' the bishop greeted them, pleased at the renewal of their neat appearances. 'I certainly shall be proud if people take me for the father of you all.'

They walked through the main street of the gaily lit town, which was crowded with people.

'It's always like this on the eve of the Festival. Shakespeare lovers come from all over the world,' said the bishop.

'How wonderful to think that one man's writings can make an international understanding,' reflected Lyn.

'And think what it's done for the town itself,' remarked the more commercially minded Nigel. 'I should say one could make a fortune out of a shop in this street, or a hotel.'

'Where are we going to stay?' Sandra was anxious to know.

'At the "Swan". I stay there every year when I come for the Festival. It's just along there, in front of us, look. A timbered place.'

They arrived in front of the Elizabethan inn and looked up at the sign, a white swan on a black background. The curtains were drawn behind the latticed windows and the light shone through.

'Doesn't it look cosy?' remarked Vicky, and yawned. 'I feel ready for bed.'

'I feel ready for something to eat,' muttered Maddy as they went into the vestibule.

The boots showed them up the winding, carpeted staircase to their rooms. The boys had a big room with one double-bed and a single bed, over which they all quarrelled. In the end Nigel got the single bed by sheer survival of the fittest. In the girls' room were two double beds.

'I'll sleep with the infant, as I'm more used to it,' Sandra said with an air of martyrdom.

Then the bishop knocked on the door.

'We'll hurry down to the dining-room,' he said, 'as our dinner is waiting for us.'

They sat at a large table in the low-raftered room and ate an enormous meal. First came chestnut soup, then fried sole and chips, then guinea-fowl, then jelly and cream; and when the bishop said at the end of all this, 'Who is having coffee?' Sandra laughed.

'It's obvious you're not used to taking children out.'

'What makes you say that, Sandra?'

'Well, you'd know, if you were used to it, that we shall say *yes* to everything, unless you put your foot down.'

'Perhaps I ought to say, "Who can take coffee without being ill tonight?"'

'I shall be, anyhow,' said Maddy resignedly, 'so I might as well be hanged for a sheep as for a lamb.'

Afterwards Sandra told the bishop, 'I don't think we ought to go to bed yet, on top of this big dinner. Do you think we could go for a tiny walk, for the sake of our digestion?'

The bishop looked doubtfully at his watch.

'It's nearly half past ten, so mind you're in by quarter to eleven and in bed by eleven. The earlier we're about tomorrow morning the more we shall be able to see.'

They ran upstairs for their coats and went out into the crowded streets again. All the passers-by were in a very merry mood.

'Not the "merry" that people are at Fenchester in Carnival Week, when all the pubs are drunk dry, but a more intelligent kind of merriment,' differentiated Lyn.

'It's quite a small town, really,' remarked Vicky, as they found themselves at the end of the main street.

'We'd better turn back now,' decided Sandra. 'That is, if anyone feels capable of going to bed yet.'

'I'm not a bit full now,' Maddy told them, as she carefully walked along a narrow strip of cobbles. 'It's amazing how much one can eat without suffering for it.'

They reached the 'Swan', and said good night on the warm brightly lit landing.

The girls' room was in the front of the hotel, just over the sign, and for a long time they sat on the broad window seat, in their dressing-gowns, listening to the people going by and the clock striking the passing quarter hours. When they at last got into their soft, cold beds the time was after midnight. They lay in the darkness listening to the silence, which was now broken only by the bishop's snores coming from the next room.

'He's driving his pigs to market,' remarked Maddy

vulgarly, and intoxicated by the strangeness of their surroundings and the lateness of the hour, they had to stifle their laughter in the pillows. One giggle led to another, and once Vicky gave such a hoot of laughter that the bishop lost his pigs altogether, and they lay in petrified silence.

In the boys' room they were swapping yarns made up on the spur of the moment, but as Bulldog fell asleep just as the hero was rescuing the heroine the other two abandoned this and soon joined Bulldog.

'I'm so excited,' confessed Lyn, 'that I simply can't sleep. Whatever sort of wreck shall I be tomorrow morning, I wonder.'

Until the small hours of the morning they talked and talked, then, as the clocks struck three, they began to get drowsy. Vicky's last waking thought was, 'Bother! We've forgotten to say our prayers.'

The maid knocking on the door of the girls' room was not surprised to receive no answer, as she had previously taken tea into the boys' room, and all that had been visible of them were three humps under the bedclothes. She walked in and banged the tray down on the table that stood between the two beds, on one of which lay a red head and a black one, and on the other two fair ones.

'Your tea, missies,' she announced loudly, but was only answered by grunts. She banged the door behind her, and Lyn stirred slightly. For a minute she thought she was at home and turned over to go to sleep again, thinking through a haze of slumber that she need not get up till she heard Jeremy let the bath-water out; then she felt Vicky's feet at the bottom of the bed and remembered, and was out of bed in a moment.

'Wake up!' she cried. 'It's today!'

She flung off her nightdress and danced madly round the room in her birthday suit, then began to hurry her clothes on. Vicky was wakened by the cold draught caused in the bed by Lyn's exit, and she got up. Maddy and Sandra continued to slumber until the other two snatched their pillows from under them. The tea, rapidly getting cold, soon disappeared.

'We can't all bath, but I should think two of us could if we hurried. Anyone want to particularly?'

'I do,' cried Lyn, and ran into the adjoining bathroom, where they heard her splashing and singing opera. The unmistakable aroma of bacon and eggs met them as they went down to breakfast. The bishop and the boys had preceded them, and Jeremy's greeting to them was, 'We're waiting for the women, as usual.'

'Trust men to be on the scene if there's food about,' rejoined Maddy with spirit.

The dining-room was very full of other visitors, and they were all staring at the peculiar party that sat at the centre table, making a considerable amount of noise, and evidently in charge of the elderly clerical gentleman. Two spinsters at the next table were overjoyed when the chance came to satisfy their curiosity. Maddy, who, though a slow eater, was a thorough one, was left behind at the table to finish her egg, while the others went to tidy their rooms. Instantly the two spinsters, who both wore pince-nez and had faded mousy hair, came and sat one on each side of her.

'So you've come here for the Festival?' said the thinner one, in her reedy voice.

Maddy, her mouth full, nodded an affirmative.

'With your father, I suppose?' asked the plumper one, who, when Maddy nodded again, shot a triumphant glance at her companion. When Maddy's mouth was empty she told them, 'My father's a bishop.'

'So we noticed. And what a large family he has.' The thin one was pumping her scientifically.

'Yes, there are six of us. But, of course, Sandra is his third wife.'

'Sandra?'

'Yes. The fair girl that sat at the end of the table. She's only our stepmother, so we call her by name.'

'But surely she's very young?' said the plumper spinster.

'Yes. She's just eighteen. This is really their honeymoon. They were married on Easter Monday.'

The spinsters were thrilled. Here was a nice piece of romance!

'I suppose your real mother is dead?' asked the skinny spinster.

'Yes.' Maddy made her voice break pathetically. 'She died of dyspepsia.'

'How sad!' breathed her audience eagerly.

'It was father's fault. He was so fond of curry that he wanted it every day, and it was poison to Mummy. Her last words were, "Never let Maddy eat curry." I'm Maddy. Jeremy, that's the fair one, is my real brother, and the other ones are stepbrothers and stepsisters.'

'You never knew your first stepmother, of course?' inquired the thin spinster.

'No. But I expect you've heard of her. Her name was Anna Pavlova.'

Somewhere in the musty depths of these ladies' minds the name struck a chord. 'The dancer?'

'That's right. And that's where Vicky, the red-haired one gets her talent from. She's danced at Covent Garden already.'

'Well, well.' The plump one clicked her false teeth. 'What an interesting life you must have had!'

'It's all right,' acknowledged Maddy, 'when father's sober. But when he's not – my goodness! Sandra doesn't know that yet, though, so we try to keep him out of her way when he's drunk. Only last night he came home tight, so the boys put him in the bath and turned the tap on. That's the only way to cure him, we've found. And he went to Sandra as sober as anything.'

The spinsters' eyes goggled, and Maddy chuckled to herself. This would teach these horrible old women not to pry into other people's business. She had finished the egg, so excusing herself, she ran upstairs to the bedroom, and lying on the bed heaved with silent laughter.

'Whatever's up with you?' Vicky asked.

'I'm just 'cited,' replied Maddy.

'Hurry up and clean your teeth. We're going to the church to see Shakespeare's monument.'

'Would he mind very much if I didn't clean my teeth? I bet he didn't always remember.'

The eight of them walked across the bridge over the Avon and to the little grey church where the Greatest Poet's remains are laid. It was a fragile April morning, and the trees seemed to have awakened with a start to find their bright new coverings of green leaves. The elms in the stone-scattered graveyard stood protectingly round the church, plainly showing their jealousy of the stream of tourists who entered, staring and touching and talking. The interior was packed, and the bishop and his party had to fight their way to the monument on the north wall of the chancel, where a professional guide was holding forth.

'A thousand-word-a-minute Oxford accent,' murmured Jeremy bitterly.

They stared up at the bust set in a cherubim-surrounded grotto.

'What do you think of it?' asked the bishop, in a neutral sort of voice.

No one answered. Secretly they were disappointed at this gaudy piece of sculpture.

'The skull on the top is the best part,' allowed Maddy.

Lyn at last spoke her mind. 'I think it's one of the ugliest things I've seen.'

The bishop heaved a sigh of relief. 'I was afraid you were going to say you liked it, because you thought it the right thing to say.'

'He's too fat,' criticized Vicky. 'I'm sure he had a more ascetic face than that.'

'There is no actual proof that this was meant to be a bust of Shakespeare,' the bishop told them. 'In fact, there is no real proof that Shakespeare was more than a pseudonym.'

'How funny,' chuckled Bulldog, 'if all these people here are taking all this trouble over someone that isn't anyone.'

They read the lines that are inscribed on the plate let into the floor of the chancel above his grave:

> Good frend, for Jesus' sake forbeare
> To dig the dust encloased heare.
> Bleste be ye man yt spares thes stones,
> And curst be he yt moves my bones.

'These words may have been written by him, or again they may not,' the bishop said. As they went out into the sunlight again he asked, 'And now you would like to look round the shops a bit, no doubt?'

'Please!' replied the girls.

'Well, I won't come with you as I've seen them many times before. I will go and visit a friend of mine. If you meet me at the hotel at ten to eleven we shall have time to find somewhere to stand and watch the procession.'

For the next hour they poked about the numerous second-hand shops in the side streets. They were packed with Shakespeare souvenirs of every kind. Lyn bought a minute copy of *Romeo and Juliet*, the size of a postage stamp, but very thick. Sandra bought a handkerchief with 'Stratford-on-Avon' worked across it. The others contented themselves with bars of toffee with 'Shakespeare Festival' written on the toffee with white sugar. Crowds were collecting in the main street, and ladies were selling sprigs of rosemary tied up with black and yellow ribbon, to help some local cause. They found the bishop and went out to procure a stance from which to watch the procession. In the middle of the road important-looking people of every nationality were gathering under their own particular flags, which were rolled round the flag-poles.

'Look at that lovely Chinese lady! Isn't she fat?' remarked Maddy loudly, as an apparition in a fur coat, with almond eyes sunk in rolls of yellow fat, passed by. She had taken it for granted that the lady spoke only Chinese, but by the way she turned and glowered, Maddy felt that her assumption was incorrect.

A lot of speeches were made, and then at a given signal the representatives pulled a cord and the flags fluttered triumphantly in the fresh April breeze. The crowd let out a roar of cheers, in which the bishop joined no less heartily than the Blue Door Theatre Company. The procession surged by, and they cried excitedly to one another, 'Look! there's a Frenchman; I can hear him talking.'

'There's an African!'

'Gosh! Look at that Indian's turban.'

Lyn disappeared into the crowd with her fountain-pen and autograph album, and came back with page after page of scrawly signatures.

'And now,' suggested the bishop, 'shall we hurry back for lunch? The play starts at two o'clock, and I have booked seats in the circle.'

During lunch the two spinsters got up and came purposefully across to the bishop.

'We want to congratulate you, Bishop,' said the thin one.

The bishop's lean, dark face was puzzled. 'Er – thank you very much.'

'We think you have a most creditable family,' the plumper one said, insinuatingly.

The bishop threw back his head and laughed. 'Thank you very much,' he said again. 'I'm rather proud of them myself.'

The ladies walked out, and Maddy breathed once again.

'So it was true,' the spinsters concluded.

They got to the Memorial Theatre, square and modern in contrast to the genuine and imitation Elizabethan buildings that crowded the town. Their seats were in the front row of the circle, where they had a good view of the stage, now covered with a safety curtain, and of the auditorium and the tiers of seats behind them. It was fascinating to watch the various types of person that filed in.

'There are two schoolmarms,' pointed out Jeremy. 'Look, they've got flat heels and tweed suits.'

'So've I,' remarked Vicky, 'but I'm not one.'

'You don't look so dried up and soured.'

'Thank you for the compliment, and here comes a schoolmaster. He's wearing pince-nez and carrying a copy of Shakespeare.'

'Look, those two ladies have come because it is fashionable.'

'That man has come because his wife made him.' Lyn pointed to a bald, meagre little man with a bowler hat.

'There are some schoolgirls just come in. They've got some nuns with them, so they must be from a convent.'

'Look, there's the orchestra.'

They took their instruments, and as they tuned up

Maddy remarked, to Jeremy's disgust, 'I don't like the tune they're playing.'

To Lyn the merry overture seemed a waste of time, and she was not happy until Orsini, Duke of Illyria, could be seen in his sumptuous apartment, giving way to his varied emotions and extolling the virtues and charms of the fair Olivia. Then the scene changed and the front part of the stage, now the sea coast, was occupied by the shipwrecked sailors and Viola.

'Gosh, she's good!' murmured Lyn to Sandra, before Viola had spoken a dozen words, and it became obvious as the play progressed that she was an actress of great ability, although of no great age.

Maddy enjoyed more than anything the fooling of Sir Toby Belch and Sir Andrew Aguecheek, and of all the laughs that echoed in the rafters of the Memorial Theatre that afternoon hers was the loudest.

'Good legs,' remarked Nigel to Lyn, as Viola appeared in her male attire.

'This isn't a musical comedy,' Lyn told him cuttingly.

After Viola, the clown was the best of the company. He had a whimsical, twisted face, and was very small and agile; his rendering of 'Come away, Death' was very clever.

During the interval between Acts Two and Three the bishop and his party went out on the flat roof-top for a breath of air. They were quite weak from laughing at the scene in the garden where the foolish knights and Fabian had watched Malvolio reading the letter that he supposes to be from Olivia.

They returned to their seats, and nearly split their

sides over the duel scene and the taunting of Malvolio in his cell. The man who played this part seemed to have been specially manufactured for it, as he was tall and thin and long-faced, and had the skinniest legs that the children had ever seen. During the last scene Maddy heaved a sigh of relief and confided in the bishop, 'I thought they'd never be able to untangle the plot and live happily ever after.'

'So you see how "the whirligig of time has brought about its revenges",' quoted the bishop.

Lyn made her way round to the stage door, where there was already a crowd of other autograph hunters, and when the actress who played Viola appeared she was surrounded with a sea of albums and fountain pens. Long before she had reached Lyn she glanced at her watch.

'I've no more time now. Sorry,' she told her admirers and walked away.

Lyn waited a second while the disappointed crowd dispersed, then she ran as fast as she could down the road after the slim figure in a camel-hair coat.

'Please,' she panted, catching her up, 'couldn't you sign just one more?'

'Sorry, I'm in a hurry.' She did not slacken her pace.

'But you don't know how much this means to me.' Lyn's eyes filled with tears, and the actress's heart melted.

'All right. Give me your album.'

As she wrote her name, 'Felicity Warren', Lyn told her, 'I'm coming to the performance tonight.'

'Are you? I'm Juliet. First time I shall have played it

professionally.' She handed back the pen.

'I wish you luck, then,' smiled Lyn. 'Are you feeling nervous?'

'A bit. Look here, like to walk a little way with me?'

'I'd love it.' Lyn forgot the others, who were waiting for her by the main theatre entrance.

As they walked 'Viola' repeated, 'Yes, it's my first time, but I'm not particularly nervous. That always comes while I'm dressing.'

'Same here,' agreed Lyn eagerly; 'and you can't stand still enough to do up fasteners, and your face sweats so that make-up won't stay on.'

The actress looked at her in surprise. 'Are you on the stage?'

Lyn blushed and stammered, 'Oh, no. I was only – I mean –'

'Amateur?' was the question.

'That's right,' and Lyn told her about the Blue Door.

'You're certainly enterprising people,' commended the actress, when Lyn had finished. 'I suppose you all want to go on the stage eventually?'

'I do,' Lyn told her earnestly; 'it's my only ambition. And I'd prefer Shakespeare to any other kind.'

'It's hard work, but it's a wonderful life, if you're fond of it. I adore it. I feel I could never give it up, but I shall have to make the wrench one day, and I'm saving so I can buy a nice little villa and settle down to a dull, sober life.' Her intelligent face clouded, then she laughed and went on. 'Still, when one has been shipwrecked, married a duke, eloped, and committed suicide, all in one day, for several years, perhaps one tires of excitement.' She stopped at the gate of a boarding-house. 'Here are my digs, so we'd better say good-bye.'

They shook hands.

'It's been glorious talking to you,' Lyn told her, her eyes shining. 'And good luck to you tonight.'

Lyn ran all the way back to the hotel, bubbling with excitement. She had seen *Twelfth Night*, and chatted intimately with a real actress, and was going to see *Romeo and Juliet* in the evening! She found the others halfway through a high tea of eggs and chips, and before she had finished recounting her adventure, word for word, the bishop said:

'Now calm down, Lyn, and eat up your tea; you won't get another meal till you get home in the early hours of tomorrow morning.'

They were back in the same seats in the circle at half past five for the rise of the curtain. Lyn was imagining Felicity's face in the mirror as she made up, and she felt a twinge of sympathetic stage fright. She was not particularly interested in the first scene, but the boys were thrilled with the duelling. At Romeo's entry she thought, 'But he's far too old. He was only supposed to be nineteen or so.'

The bishop was thinking, 'What nice children these are to take to the theatre; they don't eat sweets, or laugh in the wrong place, or talk to each other during the scenes.'

When Juliet entered, in the third scene, Lyn sat up eagerly and strained across the edge of the balcony. Felicity was wearing a shimmering green satin dress and a sparkling sequin cap. She certainly looked no more than Juliet's fourteen years. Her first few words were not quite audible, but presently she began to act with a charm and vigour which greatly excelled her performance as Viola.

The ball scene was beautiful, with the music and the flowing pattern of the dancers making a colourful background for the first meeting of the lovers. But, as usual, the outstanding part of the play was the balcony scene. Nigel was in raptures over the artistic scenery, contrasts of white walls and dark blue sky, green trees and a silver moon. Romeo climbed over the wall, shrinking against it as his merry friends passed by; then, standing under the balcony of Juliet's window, he soliloquized. Juliet appeared, radiant yet dreamy, leaning against the pillar.

To the bishop the lines gave the pleasure of familiar and beautiful words, but to the children it was a new revelation of every romantic story they had heard. When the curtain fell, Lyn found herself squeezing Sandra's hand with all her might, but Sandra had not noticed. They flopped back in their seats, smiling happily at one another, and the curtain rose on the scene in Friar Lawrence's cell. After more duelling, and the stormings of old Capulet because his daughter refused to marry Paris, there came the scene in which Juliet drugs herself. Lyn noticed that the audience was becoming most appreciative of Felicity's acting, and the applause that followed her exits was deafening.

'One day,' Lyn told herself, 'it's going to be *me* acting Juliet on that stage.'

The tragedy drew to an end all too soon, and the

nerve-racking suicide scene in the vault was enacted.
Felicity, in her shimmering white wedding dress,
surpassed herself; as she fell dead across Romeo there
were audible sobs from many parts of the theatre. Lyn
could hear Sandra sniffing; she herself was not at all near
tears, but merely worked up. She sat straight in her seat,
every nerve tingling to catch the emotion of the scene.
The eventual discovery of the bodies seemed feeble and
superfluous, and her eyes were glued on the motionless
corpses, who in their very immobility still retained the
characters of their parts. The players, after taking their
bows, stood to attention for the National Anthem, then
everybody made for the exits.

'It seems funny to have no curtains,' remarked
Maddy. 'What a marvellous swish they would have
made as they came down! Think of the rattle-scrape of
our curtains!'

'I'm going to invent something for those curtains,'
vowed Bulldog as they descended the stairs.

They discussed the play from every angle, and there
was a heated argument between Nigel and Lyn as to
whether or not Juliet were too happy in the balcony
scene.

'Don't you see how it spoilt the tragedy of the play?'
asked Nigel, getting exasperated. 'Why, the girl was
almost flippant at times.'

'So she ought to be,' argued Lyn. 'My goodness, a girl
who is not flippant when flirting with an admirer on a
hot summer evening isn't human.'

'But think of the danger he was in. He was an enemy
of her family, and you know what a brute old man

Capulet was. Don't you think she'd be more urgent and nervous?'

'No, I don't. She was only fourteen, and it was the first time she had been in love.'

'All the more reason for her to be a bit afraid.'

'I think Juliet was perfect,' said Lyn stubbornly, 'and you know I'm hard to please.'

Here the bishop interposed, more sternly than they had ever heard him speak before. 'As neither of you knows anything about love, or how Shakespeare meant his plays to be acted, don't you consider this argument rather futile?'

'Sorry, Bishop,' smiled Lyn. 'We didn't mean to be ungrateful. It's been the most perfect day of my life.'

They collected their cases from the 'Swan' and went to catch the train.

'We have only to change twice this time,' the bishop told them, 'so I advise you to try to get some sleep.'

For the first part of the journey they talked Shakespeare, but when they were settled on the train that would take them to Fenchester, conversation ceased. Lyn, her cheek bumping against the cool window pane, looked out into the starry night, and phrases from the plays ran through her mind in rhythm with the wheels. Maddy was smiling in her sleep, living through the scenes with Sir Toby and Sir Andrew. Sandra, putting her arm round her small sister, thought sleepily, 'I could go on dozing in this train, wedged between Maddy and Vicky, for ever and ever.'

Nigel, with his head sunk on his chest, was building colossal stage sets of white marble, that stretched round him for miles, and finally enveloped him. Vicky was trying to read a paper-backed novel, but the print was dancing a tarantella in front of her aching eyes, and she was not awake to notice when the book rustled to the ground. Jeremy was asleep, dreaming music as always, but the tunes so vivid in sleep were elusive in the light of day.

The bishop snored, slightly out of time with the throb of the engine, but happily and steadily, while Bulldog was mentally making the engine miss half a beat and coincide with the bishop. The bishop sneezed, and when he resumed his snores – joys of joys – they were in perfect unison with the other predominant vibration. Bulldog sighed and slept, while the carriage of slumber sped over the green fields of England.

10

STORMS AND SHAKESPEARE

After the Festival expedition there were very few excitements during the term that the Blue Door Theatre Company could enjoy all together, but they each had their own pursuits. Vicky was in the display given by the school of dancing which she attended. It was at St. George's Hall, the biggest assembly room in the town, and there were three performances, one on the Friday evening, a matinée on Saturday, and a final evening performance.

The Blue Doors turned up at all three and clapped Vicky's solo with great enthusiasm. It came in a number called 'Dancing through the Ages', and she represented the medieval travelling tumbler. She wore a pied costume of yellow and green, consisting of hooded tunic, tights, and odd stockings to do a clever acrobatic dance. She also appeared in several of the *corps de ballets* and the chorus, and had a *pas de deux* with another girl in a ballet called '*Le petit chaperon rouge*'. On the last night she had two bouquets, one from the Blue Doors and one from the Bells. The dancing-mistress was pleased to see such a new pupil excel herself, and offered her a free extra lesson each week, on the condition that she worked for some exams. Vicky accepted with alacrity, and her mother was overjoyed, though Mr Halford was dubious.

'You know she'll be wanting to take up dancing as a career if she studies it too hard,' he warned her.

'And why shouldn't she? You didn't have such an aversion to dancers when you met me, now did you?'

Mr Halford frowned and hunted for words, but couldn't find any.

Vicky, however, was not worrying about her career, and when she heard the others, especially Lyn and Jeremy, ranting because their parents would not take them seriously, she could not think why they bothered themselves so much with the future. Her motto was, 'Sufficient unto the day', and she plodded on at school, neither working too hard nor slacking, shining only in gym and tennis. She passed several elementary dancing exams. in a few months, and then settled down to work for a stiff one. Nigel led a hard life during this summer term. He was taking G.C.E. in July, and all through the term he worked every minute of the day, and when he went to bed he dreamed maps of Europe and dates of Factory Acts.

One day his father remarked to him: 'I'm glad to see you've given up that ridiculous art business, my boy.'

Nigel was astounded. 'But, father, what makes you say that?'

'Well, you have given up hope of ever doing anything in that line, haven't you?'

'No, I have not!' Nigel almost shouted, 'and I never shall, however hard you try to make me be a stuffy old barrister!'

'Nigel!' pleaded his mother, 'that's not the way to speak to your father.'

'Sorry,' growled Nigel. 'I'm tired.'

When he had gone to bed Mrs Halford said, 'You must admit he's been working hard for his exam.'

'If he hopes that by putting up a good show in the exam. it will make me less set on his taking up law, he's greatly mistaken.'

'It would be different if he had some mad idea of an attic in Chelsea,' argued his wife, 'but he's got his wits about him. He can see that there is money to be made in commercial art, and that's what his flair is for, that and for stage scenery too.'

'But it's such a precarious living,' began Mr Halford, then stopped, surprised at the fixed gaze his wife had turned upon him. 'What's the matter?' he asked nervously.

'How funny!' she murmured. 'And when I married you, you told me that we should live precariously at first, till you got a rise, and I said that half the fun in life came from things being unsafe, and you agreed.'

'I was young and stupid then.' Mr Halford brushed away the argument.

'Isn't Nigel allowed to be young and stupid and enjoy himself?'

They were both getting heated, when Mrs Halford laughing said, 'What a good job Bulldog doesn't want to be a musician!'

Bulldog was spending all his spare time at the Blue Door Theatre, staring at the curtains in deep thought, but the inspiration for making them 'swish' would not come. Then he spent his evenings at the public library, poring over books on stage production and effects, but still could not find what he wanted. One day the librarian, who was sitting at his desk in the non-fiction room, received a shock. A boy, freckled and ginger, had been sitting on top of a stepladder, deep in thought, with his mouth open and eyes staring, when suddenly he shouted, 'Of course – I got it, I got it, I got it!' leaped off the steps, and disappeared. For the next few days all the hammers, nails, and saws had disappeared from the Corner House, and finally Bulldog confronted Nigel, who was learning irregular French verbs, and said dolefully, 'I've got a confession to make.'

'Oh?' replied Nigel uninterestedly.

'I've pulled down the curtains at the theatre.'

'Put them up again, then,' growled Nigel.

'I was only trying an idea that didn't work, but it's given me an idea for another, only I shall have to spend a lot of time and ingenuity on it.'

'Well, don't waste so much of it on me,' growled Nigel. 'Goodbye!'

Jeremy despite his vow to work, found himself slacking again. Dreaming and reading and composing were his life, only interrupted by the invention of excuses for undone homework. He passed another music exam. with distinction, and came bottom of his form every week.

'You really must speak to Jeremy,' Mrs Darwin urged her husband. 'He's come twentieth again.'

'That's not too bad,' replied her husband easily.

'There are twenty boys in the form,' she told him bitterly.

'Dear me! That *is* bad, then. Perhaps I ought to reprove him, but what shall I say?'

'Tell him that the harder he works this year, the easier it will be next year.'

'Perhaps he prefers to get all his swotting over next year.'

'I think he's hoping that if he works badly enough we shall let him take up music.'

Mr Darwin went on with his tea in silence.

'And that can't be allowed, can it?' urged his wife.

'What's that? Oh, no, no, of course not. When I've got a nice little berth for him in the office, it's sheer madness.'

Mrs Darwin sighed. 'And Lyn is such a nuisance. All this term she's been learning speeches from plays. She knows Juliet and St. Joan, and Portia, and I don't know what else! All she can do well in at school is Oral English. I don't know what she thinks she'll do when she leaves school.'

'Perhaps she'll be a librarian or an English teacher.' This was spoken without conviction.

'Perhaps not!' snapped Mrs Darwin. 'I can see trouble ahead, I'm afraid. And all the people that take an interest in her, the Bells and the bishop, they all encourage her in her acting nonsense.'

Up in her bedroom Lyn was being Portia in front of the mirror. She had evolved a new method of acting. After memorizing her words, which never took her long, she would imagine the scene as Felicity Warren would have played it, and then act Felicity acting the part. This was always more successful than acting

Lynette acting the part. Sometimes she would have fits of despair and fling the book away from her, realizing how bad she was, and how little chance she had of ever being able to improve.

Sandra lived quietly, sewing and cooking and practising her singing. She and Vicky sometimes went up into the fields; there Sandra sewed, while Vicky read aloud from books of plays. Sandra had undertaken the renovation of the theatre wardrobe, and was always to be found sewing on buttons and strings.

The summer drew on. Nigel sat for his exam and felt a free man again. Then one hot Sunday morning, as they sat in church with their respective families, Mr Bell announced, 'There is going to be a garden fête held in the vicarage grounds in aid of the South England Bible Campaign. Will all those interested attend a meeting in the parish hall at seven o'clock tomorrow.' After the service Mr Bell spoke to Nigel. 'Will you all come along tomorrow night? I think we shall need your assistance.'

On Monday evening the parish hall was crowded with benevolently minded citizens of Fenchester. The children felt lost, as refreshments and decorations were discussed in detail, but when Mr Bell, who was chairman, said, 'And now, regarding entertainment,' they pricked up their ears.

Mrs Potter-Smith stood up and gushed, 'Oh, dear Vicar, my Ladies Institute would love to do a little play for you. And in your too sweet garden a fairy fantasy would be just perfect.'

Lyn gripped Sandra's arm in agony, waiting for the vicar's reply.

'That's very kind of you, Mrs Potter-Smith, but I really think your Ladies' Institute will be invaluable in the refreshment line,' he told her diplomatically. 'You are so dependable and capable, and I'm sure that with you at their head the ladies will be quite able to cope with it.'

Mrs Potter-Smith bridled with delight.

'All those in favour of this arrangement please signify,' requested Mr Bell. Bulldog was rude enough to raise both his hands. 'That is settled. Now I propose we leave the entertainment in the hands of people who could do nothing else.'

One of the Primary Sunday School teachers stood up.

'I propose the Blue Door Theatre Company be asked to provide entertainment.'

'Seconded!' said several other voices.

'Very well.' Mr Bell turned to the children. 'Nigel, will that suit you all?'

'Yes, sir. It will be a pleasure.'

Mrs Potter-Smith stood up.

'I propose,' she said, 'that they do something with fairies in. People do love that sort of thing.'

Jeremy ground his teeth and looked imploringly at Nigel.

'Say something, Nigel!' hissed Lyn. 'Stand up and say something!'

To the surprise and horror of the Blue Doors, Nigel stood up and agreed complacently that they would do something with fairies in. Bulldog pinched him violently, and when he sat down said in a hurt voice,

'Nigel! Imagine me wearing tinsel and tulle and flitting round the vicarage garden!'

'It's O.K.,' Nigel calmed him. 'Trust your Uncle Nigel. I'll tell you afterwards.' When they got outside he said, 'Don't you think we could do one of the fairy scenes from *Midsummer Night's Dream*?'

No one was enthusiastic.

'I was Puck once,' Lyn told him, 'and I'm sick of the part, so don't make me take it.'

'Vicky could be Puck,' Sandra suggested. 'Then she could do an acrobatic dance.'

'Why shouldn't we do several little Shakespeare extracts?' suggested Lyn, 'because we've not got time to make anything up for ourselves.'

'Lyn wants to play Juliet,' Bulldog announced shrewdly.

She coloured up and acknowledged that she did.

'I don't see why she shouldn't be Juliet. We could have just the balcony scene. But what about Romeo?'

'Definitely not me!' put in Bulldog hurriedly.

'You'd make a better Falstaff,' Lyn told him cuttingly.

'Either Nigel or Jeremy must play it,' pointed out Vicky.

'I don't want to,' Jeremy told them. 'I'm tired of making love to Lyn.'

'Actually I prefer Nigel. He's got better legs than Jeremy.'

'As you told me at Stratford-on-Avon, this isn't going to be a musical comedy,' said Nigel.

'No, but you've got to wear doublet and hose.'

'Is there much to learn?' Nigel asked of Lyn, for he was not a quick learner.

'Not so much as Juliet has.'

'Who's going to be what in *A Midsummer Night's Dream*?' Vicky wanted to know.

'Sandra must be Titania, obviously.'

'Jeremy must be Oberon, then,' said Lyn.

'What about me? An odd fairy, I suppose?' asked Maddy.

'Right, first time. You can have your hair loose and be the fairy that has the conversation with Puck. You know, "Over hill, over dale".'

'Do I have to dance?' asked Maddy anxiously.

'We'll decide that later. And anyhow you're thinner since you were last extracted from between the boards of the stage, so you ought to be able to dance,' Jeremy told her.

'Whatever shall I be?' wailed Bulldog. 'They'll all laugh if I'm anything "fantastic", as Mrs Potter-Smith calls it.'

'You'll be fantastic whatever you are,' Lyn told him.

'I refuse to be a fairy or wear hose unless I can be funny. I couldn't be a funny fairy, I suppose?' he asked wistfully.

'No, you can't. It would spoil it,' said Lyn decidedly. 'I should think Sir Toby Belch would be more in your line.'

'Toby Belch! Of course,' cried Bulldog eagerly. 'I won't be anything else but Toby, and Maddy can be Maria.' His face clouded. 'What about Sir Andrew?'

Lyn giggled. 'Jeremy's legs would do well, but I don't

know whether he'd be funny enough.'

'I'd rather be Sir Andrew than Oberon,' said Jeremy.

'You'll have to be both.'

'Goodness! Two parts to learn! And in this hot weather. I'll be a nervous wreck.'

'Lazy hound!' Lyn reproved him. 'The play's the thing.'

So it was arranged, and when they started rehearsing at the theatre next evening they were all armed with immense copies of Shakespeare.

'Mine has an appendix,' announced Maddy proudly.

'Mine's got notes on acting,' Bulldog told her.

'Mine's lost the page with the balcony scene on it, confound it!' grumbled Lyn. 'I think it's a bad idea, lugging these great volumes around.'

The books proved a nuisance as they read through their parts. Maddy dropped hers on Bulldog's toe several times, the last of which was so obviously on purpose that a fight ensued. The next evening they sat round the dressing-room table and copied out their parts into exercise books.

'. . . maiden blush bepaint my cheek,' muttered Lyn as she wrote.

'. . . speak again, bright angel,' said Nigel, a bit louder.

'. . . laughing at their harm,' shouted Maddy.

'. . . he's a great quarreller,' screeched Bulldog, and Lyn and Nigel had to get quite tough in order to quell the pandemonium.

The next week they broke up and could indulge in extensive rehearsals. Lyn was in her seventh heaven, and as she had previously learnt her part, she had time in which to study it thoroughly. When they made descents on the public library she always went to the literature department, where there were many books on Shakespeare's heroines. Nigel and Bulldog were anxious about the balcony, which would be very difficult to erect in the vicarage garden. Luckily the other scenes were easily staged. For the fairy scene no properties were needed, and only a table and chair for the revel scene from *Twelfth Night*. They resorted to the hobbies section and read books on carpentry. Vicky and Jeremy did no studying of their parts to speak of, but practised the acrobatic dance for which Jeremy was playing the violin. For the first time in her life Maddy deigned to take advice from Lyn regarding her part. She hated being a fairy, but took Maria very seriously, and Lyn went over it with her till she had every inflection and gesture suited to the perky little servant girl.

Nigel was proving a poor Romeo. He could not remember his lines, and put Lyn in a muddle, and they would find themselves repeating speeches, and going round in a circle. As he was used to heavy-father parts he was too pompous and elderly, and Lyn would tell him in despair, 'Take twenty years off your age, for goodness' sake.'

Sandra had a glorious time getting the clothes ready. They were such picturesque characters that she allowed all her creative imagination to run riot, and spent extravagantly to buy netting for the fairies' dresses and cellophane for their wings. She had several fitting days, when she stuck pins into almost every part of their anatomy, and made them stand in the oddest positions, so that she could squint through half-closed eyes and see where the seams were wrong. She had very positive ideas about stage costumes.

'It doesn't matter how bad the material is or how bad the sewing; all they need is colour and line.'

'Do you take me for a pin-cushion?' roared Bulldog at Sandra as she stuck a pin into his shoulder.

'If you'd only stand still,' Sandra told him calmly, 'I might finish sooner.'

Maddy burst in excitedly, 'Look, I've been to see dear sweet old Mr Smallgood and Whittlecock, and see what I've got.' She thrust under their noses two old pewter tankards. 'They'll do beautifully for the knights to drink from.'

'Did he actually lend them to you?' asked Sandra with surprise.

'Well,' hedged Maddy, 'he didn't actually say—'

'Then you'll take them straight back,' Sandra ordered her sternly.

'Oh please not, Sandra! They're so lovely. And I left a note saying I'd taken them, but I'd return them.'

'You'll go in tomorrow and ask his permission.'

'Yes, Sandra,' replied Maddy meekly.

But when she did enter the antique dealer's he was so alarmed at seeing the Holy Terror again that he said quickly, 'Take what you want, but bring it back!' Then he disappeared into the blackness of his den behind the shop.

They decided to have the dress rehearsal the day before the fête, and the day before that the boys went to the vicarage garden to put up the balcony. They had already chosen the spot to be used as a stage. It was a grass patch in front of a shrubbery, with a slight bank downwards to a tennis court. They planned that the audience would sit on chairs on the tennis courts, and behind the shrubbery would be back stage. Mrs Bell had given them permission to use two bedrooms as dressing-rooms. The only drawback to this was that the stage was a long way from the house. They had spent some time gazing at a tree on one wing of the shrubbery, and wondering if it would do for a foundation for the balcony, when Jeremy said suddenly, 'I've got it!'

'What?'

'We'll borrow two trestle ladders from Blake's; that's where we got the glass for the theatre window, if you remember. We'll put them some way apart under the tree, with broad planks across the middle. Then you can paint the balustrade part in white on a piece of board and we'll fix that on the front.'

'Sounds O.K. But how will Lyn get up there?' asked Bulldog sceptically. 'Unless we build her in with it.'

'We could have a step-ladder behind,' suggested Nigel.

'But it would show.'

'Not if we draped the bottom with a white sheet.'

They set to work as soon as they had fetched the ladders from Blake's, and wrestled with the task for the remainder of the day. When the girls came to inspect it in the afternoon Nigel was still painting marble pillars with whitewash on a piece of black creosoted wood.

'The sides of the wretched thing keep on getting unequal,' he grumbled, rubbing his whitened hands down his dungarees.

'It looks better from a distance,' Lyn comforted him.

'So do you,' he told her.

She laughed. 'Wait till you see me in my Juliet dress. Sandra's made it beautifully. If that doesn't make you act Romeo, nothing will.'

Maddy had climbed up the ladder and was standing on the plank when Jeremy caught sight of her.

'Stand still, you little idiot,' he shouted urgently. 'It's only just lodging on one side, and I haven't roped either side yet.'

Maddy obediently stood still. 'Do I stand and wait for it to collapse?' she wanted to know.

'No; jump and I'll catch you. It's not too high.'

'I come, loved one, I come!' cried Maddy melodramatically as she dropped into Jeremy's arms.

By the evening the balcony was finished, and the final effect was good, although the actual structure was fragile. Two dark red curtains were suspended at the back of the balcony, through which Lyn was to enter, and the bottom was covered with a white sheet. The balustrade was very well painted, but Lyn had to be careful not to lean too heavily on it. Nigel and Bulldog surveyed their handiwork proudly.

Maddy giggled. 'It looks like a Punch and Judy show,' she said. 'Oh, I wish we could act a Punch and Judy show.'

'You could be the baby, and I'd be Punch, then I could drop you over the side,' Jeremy told her.

A lot of other parish workers were in the garden arranging their booths and sideshows, and Mrs Potter-Smith's shrill yap could be heard above the hammering and sawing as they cleared up the stage.

On their way home they stopped in front of the gate that led to Miller's Hill and the fields. The sun was setting behind the single tree on the hilltop, and the sky was black and yellow and gold.

'Thunder tonight,' remarked Jeremy.

'Good job we thought to cover the balustrade with the sheet,' remarked Nigel, 'and to take the curtains down.'

As they closed their front doors there came the first roll of thunder.

Lyn looked round the untidy bedroom of the vicarage. It was strewn with clothes and cosmetics, and Maddy and Vicky were sprawling on the bed, clad only in their undies. Lyn, still in her ordinary clothes, paced up and down impatiently.

'Do hurry, Sandra,' she urged. 'The boys are waiting, and they'll only start fooling around if you leave them.'

Jeremy's voice from outside asked, 'Aren't you females ready yet?'

'No,' shouted Maddy. 'I haven't got a single garment on.'

'Tut, tut! Turning the vicar's bedroom into a nudist camp! Do hurry, Sandra.'

'Oh, don't be such a worrit. I can't get the fairies' wings fixed on the dresses.'

'Can I come in and help?' Jeremy wanted to know.

'Not unless you can bear the sight of Maddy, *deshabillée*.'

'I'll wait,' sighed Jeremy resignedly.

At last the cellophane wings were fixed on the fairies' shoulders and attached by rubber bands to their wrists.

'You can come in, Jeremy.'

Sandra made up his face till he looked like the demon king in a pantomime.

'Gosh,' Jeremy peered into the mirror, 'what have you done with my real eyebrows?'

'Powered them out,' Sandra informed him. 'Now, are we all ready for the fairy scene?'

They went down to the stage and when they got there they stood still, dumbfounded. On the raised part stood a large trestle table bearing an urn, and Mrs Potter-Smith was draping the legs with pink crêpe paper.

'Hallo, kiddies! All dressed up?' she cooed. They did not reply, so she babbled on. 'Such a nice little place I've found for the refreshments, and we can have some tables on the tennis pitch' – they winced – 'and some behind the shrubbery, so my customers can sit either in the sun or the shade.'

'But, Mrs Potter-Smith,' expostulated Nigel, 'didn't the vicar tell you he's let us have this part of the garden?'

'No, my dear!' Her pale blue eyes popped out at them. 'The dear vicar said to me, "Mrs Potter-Smith, anywhere in this garden is yours, anywhere." That's what he said.' She smiled at them complacently.

'But, please, don't you see we have some of our scenery up and all ready?' Nigel drew aside the sheets that covered the balcony.

'Fair's fair, dear boy, fair's fair. You have your – er – buildings and I have my table.' She smiled sweetly at him, showing a large set of false teeth.

'Fair is fair!' shouted Nigel, forgetting his manners for once. 'All's fair in love and war, and this is not love!' He strode angrily off.

'Dear, dear! I think it must be the thunder that's made him get into such a paddy,' said Mrs Potter-Smith, still in a good temper, as she unwound reams of paper.

The Blue Doors stood helplessly watching her until Nigel returned with Mr Bell, both looking harassed.

'Vicar, dear,' crooned the high-priestess of refreshments, 'don't you think my table looks too dinky?'

'Very nice, Mrs Potter-Smith, very nice. But–'

'You're not going to make me leave this delightful little nook, surely?' she asked him in a coquettishly reproachful voice.

The vicar ran his hand through his grey hair; then his ever-ready tact came to the rescue.

'Well, to tell you the truth, I've just had a disturbing thought. You know that the old Countess of Brackenshire is going to open the fête?'

'No! But how lovely! The countess is a dear friend of mine,' claimed Mrs Potter-Smith eagerly. She had a weakness for the nobility.

'Then she will be sure to come and have some refreshments, will she not?'

'Why, yes, dear vicar, yes definitely.'

'I was wondering,' said Mr Bell gravely, 'if she would be able to manage the walk right down to this part of the grounds. She is nearly eighty, you know.'

Mrs Potter-Smith's large teeth bit her bottom lip, meditatively and regretfully.

'True. I see your point.' She gave in, beaming. 'Well, in that case, perhaps, I'll move nearer the gates.' She smiled at Nigel. 'You see, you have only to ask me nicely–'

'Shall I help you to carry your table?' Nigel asked politely, and his good breeding was restored in the eyes of Mrs Potter-Smith. Perspiring profusely, she trotted to another part of the grounds.

'Now perhaps we can start. Overture and beginners,' shouted Lyn at the back of the shrubbery.

Jeremy began to play and on to the grassy stage danced Maddy and Vicky as Puck and the Fairy.

'Stop, stop!' cried Lyn, in heartbroken tones. 'Maddy, less like an elephant with lumbago, please. Vicky, show her again.'

Vicky, a floating cobweb compared with Maddy, danced Maddy's steps for the few opening bars. The next time Maddy managed it, and they were able to get on with the scene.

'Don't stand like a statue,' ordered Lyn. 'Move about a bit, Maddy. More ethereal.'

Maddy's nerves were on edge, and she stuck out her tongue in a most unethereal manner. Just after Puck and the fairy had made their exit and Sandra and Jeremy had taken the stage, some loud hammering started near by. They stopped, exasperated.

'Go and see what it is,' ordered Lyn.

Bulldog came back a few seconds later grinning. 'Be

prepared to laugh. It's the coconut shies just going up. The man has hammered in one stake, and there are nineteen more.'

Lyn flopped on to the grass. 'Who'd be an amateur actress!'

The rest of the rehearsal of the fairy scene was accompanied by heavy blows, back-stage, that made Vicky fall over several times during her acrobatic dance. She finished up absolutely exhausted and pale in the face, leaned against a tree, and gasped, 'Gosh, I feel all dizzy.' Nigel carried her back to the girls' dressing-room and laid her on the bed.

'It's only the heat,' she told them, as they hovered anxiously round her. 'You get on with the rehearsal.'

When they came back after the revel scene, in which they all forgot their lines, she was much better.

'It's so muggy,' grumbled Lyn, 'I can't bother to have my face made up for Juliet.'

But when she was up in the balcony she regretted this decision, for several helpers, who had been erecting their stalls, came to watch. Miss Thropple, the tall spinster who sang 'Cherry Ripe' at the Ladies' Institute, was among them, and she chattered to the church-warden's wife all the time in her high-pitched, screechy voice. Lyn had just got to 'Hist! Oh, for a falconer's voice' when the first drops of rain fell. All day there had been thunder in the distance. The rain dashed down on to the grass and the trees bowed humbly.

Holding their clothes tightly around them, the actors ran for the vicarage. When they had reached the door Lyn turned to Nigel and panted, 'The balcony, cover it up!' and Nigel in his Romeo clothes had to brave the torrent, to sprint back to cover the whitewashed part, and to remove the curtains.

They dressed slowly and bad-temperedly. The dresses for Romeo and Juliet would have to be taken home and dried, and the balcony curtains were soaked. Nigel returned with them, using all the bad words in his vocabulary.

'That darned balcony has collapsed,' he told them furiously.

Lyn threw her head back and laughed. 'The end of a perfect dress rehearsal!'

11

GARDEN FÊTE

When the sun rose over Fenchester next morning it shone on a sad scene in the vicarage garden. All the gay draperies of the stalls were reduced to sodden masses of pulp, and the flags that were strung across the lawn hung damply and despondently. But when the Blue Doors arrived, about midday, they found the elements trying to make up for the destruction they had caused the previous night. The sun was burning fiercely and all the tables and chairs were drying, the sky was a continental blue, dotted with puffs of cloud.

'No bigger than a man's hand,' quoted Nigel biblically, 'and certainly there's enough blue sky to make a sailor a pair of trousers.'

Maddy did a hand-stand, expressive of delight. 'Gosh!' she cried, as she lumped down on her back, 'it's just the day for a garden fête.'

As they walked over the wet grass to the stage Lyn said anxiously, 'Do you think it will be O.K. tonight?'

It was the tenth time she had asked this question that morning, so no one bothered to reply.

'We didn't even finish *Romeo and Juliet* last night,' she complained, 'so we can't tell whether we should have gone on one of our circular tours or not.'

'We'll have to have prompters,' Jeremy decided. 'There's plenty of cover for them in the shrubbery.'

'I'll prompt for the fairy scene,' offered Lyn, 'and Vicky can for the revel scene, and anyone can for the balcony scene.'

When they arrived at the stage they found the balcony had not come to much harm. The sheet was soaked, but it had certainly protected the painting, and Nigel, after inspecting it thoroughly, pronounced that they would soon get it up again as good as new, and in a quarter of an hour the balcony, a little damp, but otherwise sound, was fit to be inhabited. The rest of the morning they spent in arranging all the costumes so that they could find them easily and in order.

'We don't want to waste a lot of time this afternoon,' said Sandra, 'laying out the make-up on the dressing-table.'

'I'm looking forward to it, aren't you?' asked Maddy excitedly.

'I'm not,' said Lyn, with a white face; 'I'm terrified. I'm sure we've bitten off more than we can chew. The audience will be bored and find it far too highbrow.'

'Nonsense,' said Bulldog, entering at this moment. 'I'm going to be anything but highbrow.'

'Oh, you,' Lyn was scornful, 'I'm talking about myself.'

'Perhaps, Lyn,' Sandra said, with a little crooked smile that meant more than her words, 'you'll be comforted if you remember that, even though people don't like the extract that you're in, they may like the others.'

Lyn took the rebuff sensibly, and for the next few

minutes tried to think less of her own part.

'I came to see if you could lend us some more cold cream, because the pot you gave us is half empty,' said Bulldog.

'Sorry. We've only got just enough for ourselves.'

'Bother you! I'll have to go down to Woolworth's and get some.' He came back a few minutes later and said, as he passed their door on the way to the boy's room, 'Whatever do you think I did? I went out in my filthy jeans and who should I meet but the bishop!'

'Bulldog! You awful boy!' reproached Vicky. 'What did he say?'

'He looked at me very hard, then said, "Hullo, Percy, I didn't recognize you at first." '

'He's so fastidious about clothes,' sighed Lyn. 'I'm sure he thinks that we girls ought to dress more neatly and conventionally.'

'What are you wearing this afternoon?' Sandra wanted to know, and there followed a discussion as to whether they should wear socks or tights.

'I'm wearing socks! I'm wearing socks!' said Maddy determinedly, and continued to repeat this statement until Vicky flung a cushion at her.

'Of course you're wearing socks!' Sandra quelled her. 'You're only a little girl.'

'I'm not wearing tights,' said Vicky the tomboy. 'I wouldn't if you paid me to.'

'I'm going to,' Sandra told them.

Lyn wrinkled her brow, then shook her head angrily 'Oh, why bother about socks and tights and footling things like that when there are big things at stake?'

'What do you mean?'

Lyn walked to the window and looked out over the green tree tops of the garden.

'I have presentiments and premonitions, and you know my prophecies always come true.'

She turned and faced the others, who were looking at her in puzzled surprise.

'Something important is going to happen tonight,' she cried. 'And I think it's going to happen to me.'

The other girls could never understand her when she was in this kind of mood.

'You're over-excited,' Sandra told her anxiously.

'I am,' she agreed; 'and I want to keep in this mood because it makes me act, but if Nigel is as dumb tonight,' she shrugged her shoulders, 'it's all up with me.'

Vicky, angry at the criticism of her brother, tried to say something, but Lyn went on:

'I'm sorry to say things about Nigel, Vicky, but really he doesn't seem to care whether he acts well or not as Romeo, and he must know how much I want to play Juliet decently.'

'He'll act tonight,' Vicky assured her. 'But you know that none of us, I or my brothers, can act well. Only Bulldog can clown a bit.'

'I'm sorry to get so het up,' apologized Lyn; 'but the mornings before shows are dreadful when there's not much to do. Let's go outside and see if we can help anyone else.'

They found Miss Thropple, who was presiding over a stall of mineral waters, staggering backwards and forwards with crates of bottles containing highly coloured liquids.

'Can we help?' asked Sandra, and under the influence of manual labour they began to forget their nerves.

Maddy sang tunelessly as she made journeys from the stall to the lorry that brought the drinks, and back again. She felt completely self-confident about Maria, and as for the fairy – well, she didn't mind how badly she failed in that, as long as she might make a hit in *Twelfth Night*! Short though her part was, Bulldog made a perfect partner for foolery, and he made all the people with whom he acted appear as funny as himself. He was happy this morning, knowing that it was in his power to amuse the audience.

Sandra's emotions were the least disturbed of the company's. The mirror told her that she looked pretty in her clothes for Titania, and she always managed the part well enough, but not outstandingly, and Jeremy, with whom she played the scene, was no better and no worse than herself. He, however, was feeling unhappy about his part as Sir Andrew. Bulldog could be depended on to make the scene a success, but Jeremy knew that in comparison his rendering of Sir Andrew would be feeble. He comforted himself with the thought that, to make up for it, he would play his violin extra well for Vicky's dance. Vicky, on her journey back to the lorry for another crate, practised steps from her dance with a light heart. None of the acrobatics were to be contortional, as the whole thing must be kept 'fantastic'. Vicky, in the middle of a series of *fouettées*, stopped to laugh a moment at the remembrance of Mrs Potter-Smith's use of the word.

Nigel trudged to and fro with a crate under each arm. He was unhappy. Tonight he would make a fool of himself, he felt certain, and it would let Lyn down and she would be furious. He did not know what was the matter with him, but his lines as Romeo just did not stir him. His previous parts had not been inspiring, certainly, but he had been able to feel that he *was* the character he was playing.

'Perhaps I've been working so hard I've forgotten how to act,' he thought sadly. 'I feel awfully grown-up.'

Suddenly he saw the Blue Door Theatre Company in a different perspective, not as his one burning interest in life, as, like the others, he had hitherto regarded it, but just as a small episode in his life. He saw himself, a grown-up, saying to someone else, 'When I was a kid we used to act little plays and things at parish functions. Quite fun!' The scene was so clear that he blushed and looked to see if the others had read his disloyal thoughts, for long ago they had decided that the company must go on for ever.

All the others, perspiring but looking happy on the whole, were carting crates and either talking or thinking of the coming performance. The birds were singing and the Ladies' Institute were chattering as they cut sandwiches. Nigel felt safe again, and once more believed in the Blue Door Theatre Company as the one thing to live for, as it embodied everything for which he cared. In a flash he saw himself painting backcloth after backcloth, and the others laughing and ragging near-by. He felt a sudden and overpowering affection for them.

This was how he meant to spend his life!

When they went into their houses for dinner Sandra said, 'What time shall we go this afternoon?'

'Not too early, or we shall have to listen to a lot of dreary speeches from that cow-like countess,' said Lyn.

'I know something we've got to do. We must sell all those programmes that the vicar typed for us,' Nigel reminded them.

'Oh, yes,' Sandra said. 'And if people say, "Don't bother about my change", as they so often do at sales of work and things, don't be polite and give it to them, because we need every penny we can get.'

That afternoon the Corner House was full of the sound of running water. Nigel got into a cold bath and wondered whether he would ever be as delightfully cool again. Vicky was pedicuring her feet, a thing she never failed to do when she went to dance, and which was more important than ever today, as she was to be barefoot. There were alarming thumps next door, and she went to investigate, and found Bulldog dancing in his dressing-gown.

'Whatever do you think you're doing?'

'I'm just practising some silly steps for the end of the revel scene, where Jeremy and I exit dancing.'

Vicky taught him some more, and he soon paralysed her with laughter as he bumped and twisted about the bedroom.

Maddy was just tying her hair in its usual untidy pony-tail when Sandra came in.

'Don't do that, Maddy; have it loose today. You've got to, for the fairy.'

'Yes, but I'm not going to all the time. I look such a clot.'

Sandra snatched the comb away from her and combed it out on to her shoulders, and forced it to wave at the back. She had magic in her fingers when she was hairdressing, and Maddy looked at herself with approval when it was done, ' 'Snice,' she decided.

'You look quite pretty,' Sandra told her. 'Your dress makes your eyes as blue as anything.'

Maddy was wearing a bright blue frock with white smocking at the neck and waist, black patent leather shoes and white socks.

'Yes,' Sandra nodded appreciatively, 'you'll do the family credit this afternoon.'

Sandra too was wearing a blue dress that she had made herself. Tights had been her final decision, and she wore blue sandals.

When they congregated at three o'clock Bulldog clapped his hand over his face in simulated dazzlement.

'My hat! what a bevy of beauties!' he cried; 'and they deign to walk down the street with me. Blow me down!'

'You look less like an errand boy than usual, I must say.' Lyn complimented him.

He bowed low, and a lock of ginger hair fell away from its neatly smoothed companions, into its usual position over his brow.

'Thank you, fair lady,' he said, as he brushed it back 'That word of encouragement has made me your servant for ever, and if you'd remove the smudge of powder from your left eyebrow I should be your slave.'

'Keep your fooling for tonight,' Lyn advised him.

They walked along chattering and laughing with the rather hectic excitement that overtook them before performances. The amplifier playing 'The Merry Widow Waltz' could be heard long before they reached the vicarage grounds, and when they walked through the big iron gates they found the fête in full swing. The grounds were crowded with elderly church people, eager to help a good cause, and young people, out to have a good time. The Blue Doors knew everyone and everyone knew them, so first of all they walked round talking to their acquaintances. John Flanders was there with his mother, a majestic horse-faced woman with long dangling earrings. He pounced on Lyn, with a delicate compliment on her appearance, and asked if she would mind if he introduced her to his mother.

'This is Lynette, Mother,' he said.

Lyn shook hands.

'So you're Lyn.' Mrs Flanders looked her up and down, and she felt sure she was standing with her toes turned in, and that she had not removed the smudge from her eyebrow. 'I've heard such a lot about your acting from John that I had to come and see your play today.'

John said, still gazing admiringly at her, 'I wonder if you'd come and have tea with us, Lyn, when it's tea-time?'

Lyn thought quickly. She knew very well that the Blue Doors had arranged to have their tea together, but how could she refuse?

'Yes, Lynette,' urged John's mother, 'we should be pleased if you would.'

Lyn crossed her fingers and told a lie. 'It's most kind of you, Mrs Flanders' – she smiled her society smile – 'but I never eat before I act.'

'How temperamental of you. I'm sure you must be destined for the stage, if you have these odd habits.'

Lyn decided that she disliked Mrs Flanders, and she did not like the way John was looking at her, so, crossing her fingers again, she said, 'If you will excuse me, I have to go and speak to my mother. She has a houp-la stall. I do hope you'll come and patronize it.'

' "Patronize" is the right word,' she added mentally. Mrs Flanders made a delicate *moue* of disgust, and her earrings jingled. 'The travelling-fair type of amusement has never appealed to me,' she said in a superior voice.

'Well, cheerio, John.'

'Goodbye, Lyn. I'll be wishing you luck all the time.'

For the sake of her conscience she made her way to the houp-la stall, where a roaring trade was going on.

'Mother, if a horse-faced lady and a boy in a Grammer School blazer come here, *that's*. Mrs Flanders and John, so be nice to them.'

She went to find the rest of the Blue Doors. They were watching Nigel, who was trying his hand at skittles.

'Hullo,' he said, when she came up. 'Where's the boy friend?'

'John? Oh, I left him with his mother.'

'Best place for him,' growled Bulldog. 'Come on, Nigel, knock one of those front ones, and you may get an embroidered penwiper.'

'Mrs Flanders asked me to have tea with them,' Lyn told Sandra.

She was impressed. 'What did you say?'

Lyn told her the excuse she had made, ending up loudly, in hopes that Nigel would hear. 'You see, I'd much rather be with the gang.' But Nigel had just knocked over two skittles with one ball. The proprietor of the skittle stand, one of the church bell-ringers, asked, 'What'll you have? Cigarettes or chocolates?' Nigel chose chocolates and shared them out equally with the seven. When they had eaten them Vicky asked, 'What now?'

'Let's try everything, then start selling the programmes.'

They visited every stall and threw rings at vases, balls at coconuts, and darts at boards with continual luck.

'What I like about charity fêtes is that you feel your money is going to a good cause – and you get more for it,' said Maddy ethically, as she hugged a coconut, a china vase, and a picture of 'The Monarch of the Glen'.

The grounds got more and more crowded with ladies in silk frocks and wide hats and children in their best clothes. Everyone to whom the Blue Doors spoke said that they intended to stay for the entertainment in the evening, and that they were looking forward to it. Mrs Potter-Smith, perspiring behind the refreshment stall, ladled out ice cream after ice cream, while Miss Thropple's mineral waters were drunk freely. As the afternoon wore on the sun got hotter, the amplifier blared louder, and the whole garden seemed to the children to be a kaleidoscope of colour. About half past four, when most of the people had retired to the little tables on the tennis court for tea, Sandra said, 'Now is the time to sell the programmes. If we attack people at tea they'll buy one to get rid of us.' The programmes were half sheets of foolscap, on which was typed:

THE BLUE DOOR THEATRE COMPANY
NIGEL, VICTORIA, AND PERCY HALFORD, SANDRA AND MADELAINE FAYNE, AND LYNETTE AND JEREMY DARWIN
Present to you extracts from Shakespeare.

I. A Fairy Scene from *A Midsummer Night's Dream*.
    Fairy .... Madelaine Fayne.
    Puck .... Victoria Halford.
    Oberon .... Jeremy Darwin.
    Titania .... Sandra Fayne.

II. A Revel Scene from *Twelfth Night*.
    Maria .... Madelaine Fayne.
    Sir Toby .... Percy Halford.
    Sir Andrew .... Jeremy Darwin.

III. The Balcony Scene from *Romeo and Juliet*.
    Juliet .... Lynette Darwin.
    Romeo .... Nigel Halford.
         Costumes: Sandra Fayne.
         Scenery: Nigel Halford.

They went round hawking the programmes. Maddy

was the most successful. Knowing the weaker sex, where money is concerned, she concentrated mainly on elderly gentlemen.

When they were all sold, they visited Miss Thropple and Mrs Potter-Smith and drank crimson raspberryade with lumps of ice cream floating among gassy bubbles.

'We go on at seven, and it's five now, so no one must eat anything else after this, understand?' ordered Sandra, as they sat down for tea at a little table. A Ladies' Institute member hobbled up with a tray, complaining of her swollen ankles.

'Cheer up!' grinned Bulldog. 'Think what it must be when a centipede has swollen ankles.'

He received a glare, and when his tea arrived it was slopped over into the saucer.

'Service with a smile . . .' quoted Bulldog. He was in a good mood. 'I say, don't you think these waitresses would look better in a uniform? Something snappy, like lift girls!'

Lyn with her mouth full of meringue and a smear of cream on her chin was laughing at an idiocy of Bulldog's when Maddy said. 'Lyn, don't look round, but the snootiest lady I ever saw is looking at you as if you were something the cat's brought in.'

Lyn looked, and found Mrs Flanders' agate eyes fixed on her.

'Gosh,' she spluttered into her cup, 'and I said I never ate tea before acting.'

'You wait till afterwards,' said Maddy. 'We'll have something worth eating then.'

At six o'clock all the old ladies of the parish began to

arrange themselves on the front row of chairs on the tennis court, and the Blue Doors went up to change. Immediately they closed their dressing-room doors they were attacked by the yellow demon, Stage Fright. Sandra alone was a calm rock of strength as her deft fingers dressed and made them up. They were all ready and on the landing by five to seven. The four who were in the fairy scene were enveloped in the black cloaks used for *Spanish Inn*, Bulldog in his *Twelfth Night* clothes, and Lyn and Nigel in their ordinary clothes. Lyn carried the big Shakespeare. They strained their ears and heard the vicar telling people to take their seats. Sandra looked at Nigel's watch and said, 'Come on.'

'We face the firing squad,' murmured Jeremy.

They made their way to the back of the shrubbery by a devious route to avoid peering eyes of the audience, and Maddy and Vicky shed their cloaks and solemnly wished each other good luck. Vicky stayed by the entrance near the balcony, and Maddy went to the other side. Jeremy, leaning against a tree trunk, struck up the overture, and Lyn and Nigel, shivering in sympathy with the two about to appear, sat together on a log, following the lines in the volume of Shakespeare. The audience said 'Sh!' to their neighbours when they heard the violin, and Maddy danced on. She wore a simple gold tunic and green cellophane wings. Her feet were bare, but for little wreaths of ivy leaves round her ankles, and her loose hair was twined with tiny roses.

'Doesn't Maddy look thin?' remarked her mother to Mr Fayne

With a little yodelling shout Vicky bounded on with

a jump she had learned at her ballet class. She wore a green bathing costume with tiny cellophane wings on the shoulder, and Sandra had made up her face with slanting eyebrows and scarlet lips. Her red hair had been brushed till it stood up on either side of her head, springy and bobbing.

Their acting was not extraordinarily good, but their appearance and vivacity helped them. They both spoke too fast and their voices did not carry, but their laughter when Puck described his tricks was most convincing. Then they ran off in alarm as the King and Queen of the Fairies entered.

Jeremy looked most fantastic. Sandra had cut out curly antlers from black cardboard, and he wore these on his head. His face was dead white but for crimson spots on each cheek, and his blue eyes were heavily mascara'd. He wore his Sir Andrew clothes under his black cloak, as there would be no time to change. Sandra looked a delightful vision. She wore drapery of light blue, and dark blue cellophane wings. Their scene was not brilliant, but the audience enjoyed the picturesque effect. Jeremy's last speech,

'Well, go thy way; thou shalt not from this grove
Till I torment thee for this injury'

was delivered with great gusto, and the Fairy King and Queen stalked off with their heads in the air.

As the audience applauded, even Mrs Potter-Smith had to acknowledge it was good. Behind the shrubbery Vicky stopped massaging her ankles, and, as Jeremy picked up his violin, she ran on to the stage. For the next five minutes she was a leaping ethereal sprite, her red curls tossing and flying as she made swift successions of hand-springs, back-bends, and fancy jumps. The sun was beginning to set with an orange glow through the shrubbery, and Jeremy played in a fashion that would have done credit to Oberon himself. She ended up with a high jump into the air, landing in the splits with her body bent backwards nearly parallel with her back leg.

As soon as Jeremy had played the last weird note he ran as fast as his legs could carry him back to the dressing-rooms, where he added his accessories for Sir Andrew. Sandra made him up when she had arrayed Maddy for Maria, and dispatched her in time for her entrance. Nigel and Lyn strolled back in silence to dress.

On the stage Maria and Sir Toby were back-chatting the slick Shakespearean lines. Bulldog wore a pair of outsize bloomers stuffed to an enormous size, a jerkin made of an old windcheater, and bright red stockings. His hair was brushed up on end, and Sandra had made up his face to a jovial and beery pink. Maddy had her hair in a bun, red cheeks and lips, and wore her sweetest smile. Her blue dress was plain and low cut, and she had a small white apron. Their acting was brisk, and had an almost French quality in its boisterous vivacity.

'For here comes Sir Andrew Aguecheek,' roared Bulldog cheerily, waving Mr Smallgood and Whittlecock's tankard.

Jeremy entered, dragging his heels, with his head hung. He wore very skimpy yellow trunks, long black stockings to emphasize his thinness, and a scarlet jacket that was far too big for him. His fair hair was parted in the middle, and, with the curls greased out, hung lankly on either side of his foolish face. He spoke in a weak, vacant voice that contrasted with the boisterous accents of the other knight. After Maria had been introduced to him she made her exit, to hearty applause. Sandra and Vicky banged her on the back.

'Gosh! you were wonderful,' Vicky told her, 'better than anyone has been yet.'

Maddy's eyes were shining. 'I felt like Lyn always looks as if she's feeling when she's acting.'

'Lyn couldn't have acted it better,' Sandra told her.

On the stage Sir Andrew and Sir Toby were frolicking, accompanied by frequent draughts from the beaker of ale, and a lot of laughter from the audience. Even Mrs Flanders laughed as they went off dancing.

'What a fool that boy is,' she remarked.

For a long time the audience broke into further chuckles as they clapped. The three players had to appear again to bow. Lyn and Nigel walked down the gravel path between the tall box hedges.

'You look beautiful,' Nigel told her seriously. 'John Flanders will never get over it. Just imagine it's him in my place.'

'Shut up!' cut in Lyn. 'I shan't be acting for anyone but Romeo.'

'But surely,' pursued Nigel, 'if you imagine I'm someone you like – '

'You're no one but Romeo,' she persisted. Then relenting, 'Well perhaps you're a *bit* Nigel, too.'

'Thank you. I can assure you that if I do happen to attain anything worth calling acting, it will be a tribute to you, not Juliet or Shakespeare.'

'I bet I can make you act better than you have ever acted before,' vowed Lyn. 'Remember, you've never acted opposite me in any of our other plays.'

She went up the step-ladder, assisted by Jeremy, who sat down on the bottom rung to prompt. Peering through a hole in the curtains she saw the audience gazing expectantly upwards. Nigel entered from the far side, and she saw that as he soliloquized, he looked much older. Her cue came, 'It is my lady, oh, it is my love!'

Slowly she pulled aside the curtain and stepped on to the balcony with her hands resting lightly on the top, looking up at the darkening sky with lips slightly parted. A murmur went round the audience. It was a masterpiece of costuming on Sandra's part. Her dress was mauve and slim-fitting, with a low square neck, and round it she wore a heavy gold chain. The sleeves were long and full, gathered in at the wrist, and slightly transparent. Nigel, who had only seen her under a cloak, was taken aback at her appearance and faltered most effectively.

Juliet's first utterance, a long sigh, floated through the shadowy garden. Nigel's next speech was quite impassioned, and when Lyn, speaking aloud to herself, cried, 'And for that name, which is no part of thee, take all myself,' the audience began to realize that they were about to witness a first-rate performance.

Lyn and Nigel went from strength to strength, Lyn

continually leading him on, and forcing him to act. He was so happy to find himself acting well that he forgot the argument in which he said the balcony scene should be acted soberly, and once or twice laughed gently, gazing up at Lyn with adoring eyes that, even if they were not so sincere, easily beat the eyes of John Flanders.

Lyn felt exalted and rash, exactly as she knew Juliet ought to feel, and forgot her effort to imitate Felicity Warren; consequently her performance was more natural and very much younger.

The bishop sighed contentedly. For the first time in his life he was seeing Romeo and Juliet at their correct ages, and he knew that by taking them to the Shakespeare Festival he had been instrumental in bringing this about.

Lyn made her exit on the famous words, 'Parting is such sweet sorrow that I shall say good night till it be morrow.'

Nigel murmured a blessing, looking up at the spot where they had ordained that the moon should be, and then walked determinedly off the stage. Behind the shrubbery Lyn and Nigel ran to meet each other. They could see the praise and delight in each other's eyes, but neither could speak. Nigel took her arm.

'Come on! We must take our bows.'

The whole company bowed to the audience, who clapped and the younger people cheered. The bishop had been sitting next to Mrs Darwin and talking earnestly to her between scenes. Now, as Lyn was called for again and again, he asked, 'And after this are you not convinced, Mrs Darwin, that your daughter is an actress?'

Mrs Darwin, watching her daughter, who, flushed and smiling, was bowing with complete self-confidence and charm, replied slowly, 'Perhaps I am, Bishop.'

12

AUTUMN LEAVES

The Blue Doors went back to school in the second week of September with not much inclination to work. Mr and Mrs Halford had sent Nigel, who had passed several G.C.E. subjects, back for another year to take accountancy and applied mathematics, and to these subjects he managed to add art. The idea of his being a barrister had now been abandoned, and his parents had settled for accountancy. The art master was a friend of his, and he was allowed to spend all his spare time in the art room, daubing vivid lettering on enormous pieces of paper to make posters, advertising everything under the sun.

After the excitement of the garden fête, everyone found it rather hard to settle down to work. Jeremy was supposed to be taking G.C.E. in the coming July, but in October it seemed so far away that he did not bother about it, and spent all his evenings at the piano. He was indulging in a fit of sentimental songs, and mournful strains could be heard issuing from the Darwins' house at all times of the day.

The girls also were slacking in a final period of enjoyment prior to a real 'swot' the next year. Sandra's form mistress told her that she, the eldest girl in the form, should be ashamed of herself for coming out bottom two weeks running. Sandra sighed, and comforted herself with the thought that, although she could not calculate equivalent weights in chemistry she could contrive *charlotte russe* fit to make a king's mouth water, and that the shorts she was working on in dressmaking had a better line than anyone else's in the form.

Lyn was working hard, but not at school subjects. The list of parts in which she was word perfect grew bigger every week. She had long ago learned the rest of Juliet, besides the balcony scene, and now, as well as her old favourites, St. Joan and Portia, she had Viola, Eliza from *Pygmalion*, Cleopatra, Ophelia, and Katharina from *The Taming of the Shrew*. These eight parts she rehearsed in turn each night before she went to sleep and at any other odd moment during the day, until they were as real to her as were any of the girls at school.

A touring repertory company would occasionally come to Fenchester, and the Blue Doors always went to the first night, when two seats were sold for the price of one. Lyn, however, went to each performance during the week, borrowing from her friends in order to do so, and then going without her pocket-money for the next few weeks so that she could pay her debts.

The weather became cooler and cooler, and the girls began to wear jumpers and blazers over their summer dresses, then thick skirts; by half-term it was blustery autumn weather. There was a half-holiday on the Friday with a long week-end to follow. In the afternoon they decided to go for a bicycle ride to Pendlebury Thicket, some woods about seven miles from Fenchester. They cycled merrily along through the sharp November air until they could see the brown cluster of trees in the distance.

'Doesn't it look super?' remarked Sandra, pedalling hard on her sedate bicycle. 'We must get some autumn leaves.'

'You're a hopeless person,' grumbled Maddy, rattling along behind. 'If we go to the seaside you collect seaweed, if we go to the woods you want autumn leaves. I believe if you went to the Zoo you'd want to take home a nice little bunch of Baby Pandas.'

They leaned the bicycles against a fallen tree trunk and entered the deep, dark woods. The soggy brown-tinted leaves made a soft carpet to their feet as they walked between the trees.

'I'm going up aloft,' announced Maddy, clambering on to the bottom branch of a tall fir. She made her way upwards until she was out of sight of the others, then they heard her voice crying, 'Do come up. It's marvellous. Just like being in a ship.'

'Shall we go up?' asked Nigel.

'I'm not very fond of heights,' confessed Sandra.

'It's easy as anything,' yelled down the pioneer. 'Like going upstairs to bed.'

Bulldog joined her at the top, where they sat and sang sea shanties at the top of their voices and rocked the tree perilously backwards and forwards, till Sandra called up to them to be careful. In reply she received a fir cone on her head.

'It shows how you originated, Maddy,' shouted

Jeremy to her. 'Substitute a coconut for a cone and the answer's a monkey.'

'Yo ho ho and a bottle of rum!' bawled Maddy and Bulldog. The others left them there and walked on to where a little stream rippled through a glade. Nigel was fired with a childish desire to dam the stream, and this he did with mud and twigs until the glade was sufficiently irrigated to please him.

'You're still a kid!' teased Lyn.

'Thank you, Methuselah.'

Vicky was looking for empty birds' nests, and Jeremy and Sandra wandered along humming tunes to themselves and shuffling their feet in the leaves.

'I'm bored!' said Jeremy suddenly.

'I'm very sorry if my company is as dull as all that,' Sandra told him, surprised. 'But I thought you wished to be left alone with your thoughts, like all true musicians.'

'Oh, it's not you I'm bored with,' Jeremy hastened to assure her. 'It's life in general.'

'Take some magnesia,' advised Sandra, who never suffered from either depression or exaltation.

'I'm sick of doing nothing,' complained Jeremy.

'Well, it's your own fault. You've got something to work for.'

'Yes, but I mean to fail. If I pass I go straight into father's office, and that's not going to be little Jeremy's fate if he can help it.'

'What good will it do you to fail?'

'A lot. I only need an extra year and I might possibly get my L.R.A.M., if I have time to practise, but if I'm sweating in an office all day – '

'I see your point,' agreed Sandra, 'and you're lucky to have music lessons at all. Look at me! Not a vestige of voice training have I had, and I don't look like ever getting it. Next year there's G.C.E. with Vicky and Lyn, and if I pass it, suppose I shall take full time Home Economics till I get my diploma. Hopeless, isn't it?'

'We ought to do something about it.' Jeremy slashed at a bush with a stick he had picked up. 'But what?'

'All we can do is to go on giving shows in the hope that we can persuade our parents to let us take up the careers we want.'

'Yes, I suppose so. Why don't we get going on another show, then?' Jeremy suggested. 'We could get it ready for Christmas. If only we could find someone who really knows about acting to see it, and say what they thought.'

'It beats me!' said Sandra. 'Mummy loves to hear singers on the radio, yet she won't hear of me taking it up. I tell her that if all mothers were as narrow-minded as she, there would be no good singing in the world. She thinks that just because I happen to be her daughter I am different from other people.'

'You know, I'm wondering . . .' began Jeremy.

'Wondering what?'

'I am wondering whether I shall be content just to be a music master or in an orchestra. I think I want to act as well.'

'Oh, same here,' agreed Sandra. 'I'd like to keep on acting.'

'I was reading about a stage school in London,' went on Jeremy, 'where pupils can take a course in acting and any subsidiary subject like dancing, elocution, music, and singing. That would suit you and me fine.'

'Was it expensive?'

'Pretty expensive.'

'And what should we do afterwards?'

'Why, it's obvious. We should come back to Fenchester and make the Blue Doors professional. You know, we've got the material for a really good repertory, a decent little theatre that we could improve in time, a large town with no other theatres, and a team of actors who are used to playing together. We've got Lyn, who, if she were trained, would make a first-class actress; we've got you, who can sing and make costumes, and when you'd been taught you would be able to act, I'm sure; and then there's Vicky, who can dance, and can be taught to act; and Nigel, who's a marvel at scenic art already.'

'And you,' added Sandra, 'who can do anything in the music line, and you're getting to be a good actor too. What about Maddy?'

'I don't know.' Jeremy frowned. 'She's rather a problem because of her age, but, you know, she's got a lot of stage sense already. Has she shown you the play she has written?'

'No. Have you seen it?'

'Yes; and although it's a bit crazy, it's definitely got something.'

'She's awfully keen on the stage. She said she'd be a wonder mite in a pantomime, if she had the chance.'

Jeremy was amused. 'I can't see Maddy as a Babe in the Wood for long. But you know, she acted Maria jolly well last summer.'

Sandra sighed. 'Oh, it would be so wonderful! Think of it – the Blue Door Theatre Company going on for ever!'

This conversation was only the first of many that occurred during the following weeks on the subject of the future. Then, one day, when for the hundredth time they had decided that they must study at a dramatic school, Vicky said sagely, 'We're absolutely nuts. We're living so much in the future that we're not bothering about the present. Look here, there are only four weeks to Christmas Day, and surely we're going to do a show for Christmas?' It was a Friday evening, and they were in the study of the Halford's house. Vicky's words put fresh life into them.

'Yes, Vicky's quite right. Let's shake off our grumbles and vain hopes and make the best of the moment. Now, any ideas for a Christmas show?' Nigel had fallen into his old role of chairman.

'Not a Nativity play!' begged Bulldog. 'Something more dramatic.'

'No, we don't want drama at Christmas time,' objected Nigel. 'We want something light and frothy.'

'Oh, a pantomime; do let's do a pantomime,' begged Maddy.

Nigel was sceptical. 'We haven't got enough people,' he objected.

'Oh, I don't mean an affair with a revolving stage and a beauty chorus and real ponies.'

'It would be rather fun,' said Jeremy. 'I've got positively tons of songs that would fit a pantomime.'

'What about *Cinderella*,' suggested Nigel.

'Oh yes, Sandra, you'd make a good Cinderella,' said Vicky.

Lyn was feeling hurt and lost. If they did *Cinderella*, whatever part could she play? She knew she had not enough voice to play the lead in a pantomime, but she did hope for a minor part. 'Perhaps I'll be one of the ugly sisters,' she thought angrily.

'Who'll be Prince Charming?' Maddy wanted to know. 'Nigel or Jeremy? I must say neither of them is a very good example of that title!'

'Who's got the best voice?'

'Nigel,' said Jeremy at the same moment as Nigel protested that it must be Jeremy.

'I will not be Prince Charming,' said Jeremy decidedly. 'I've had enough of hose and breeches for one term, thank you. Let me be one of the ugly sisters.'

'And I'll be the other.' Bulldog was eager for the part.

'O.K., I'll be the prince, then.' Nigel was secretly rather pleased to get the part.

'Vicky must be the fairy godmother,' Maddy insisted, 'so that she can dance. And what about me?'

'Page and guests at the ball, and Prince Charming's retinue,' laughed Nigel.

'Gosh!' said Maddy. 'What a whale of a part.'

Lyn spoke evenly but furiously. 'I suppose I may be allowed a walking-on part. I might even be capable of saying, "The carriage awaits without." '

There was a petrified silence.

Then Nigel exclaimed, 'Why, Lyn, I'd forgotten all about you. I'm sorry. Of course you must have a part!'

Lyn laughed sarcastically. 'Oh, don't bother. I quite enjoy scene shifting.'

There was another awkward pause, then Bulldog stepped into the breach by saying, 'We've forgotten Buttons!'

'We must have a Buttons, and Lyn would be super.'

Lyn thawed slightly at the compliment.

'Like to play Buttons?' Nigel asked her.

'Looks as if it's settled,' she replied sullenly.

'Will you attempt a song?' Jeremy wanted to know.

'If you can trust me with one.'

'O.K. I'll give you a duet with Maddy, perhaps.'

Jeremy scribbled down some notes in his pocket-book.

'It's rather an undertaking,' Sandra remarked.

'No worse than Shakespeare,' said Bulldog.

'You will give me a really funny song, won't you Jeremy?'

'I'll try, but you may have to make up your own words. I'm not so good at being funny to music. May I have Maddy to help me with the story part of it?'

Maddy was delighted to think that her beloved Jeremy needed her help.

As they went home Sandra whispered to Jeremy, 'Please write Lyn a good part, Jerry; she's rather upset.'

Lyn *was* upset, and furious at herself for being upset. 'I mustn't expect to get the chief part every time,' she told herself over and over again, but still she could not remove the little spark of jealousy of Sandra that persisted inside her.

For the next week Jeremy and Maddy were a fixture

after school in the dining-room of the Darwins' house, where they covered sheet after sheet of manuscript and exercise book paper. The script was finished by the following Saturday, and they went down to the theatre to read it over to the rest of the company. It met with the greatest approval. Even Lyn was delighted with her part, and they wanted to start rehearsing right away; but Lyn, as producer, ordered everyone to learn their words before they started to rehearse.

Over the garden fence one morning Mrs Fayne said wryly to Mrs Darwin, 'So they've started it again!'

'You mean acting?'

'Yes, a pantomime this time, if you please.'

'My goodness, they're ambitious,' Mrs Darwin said. 'But I don't think it will suit Lyn; she's all for tragedy and melodrama. What pantomime is it?'

'*Cinderella*, I believe.'

'It ought to be quite good. You know, I find myself looking forward to the children's shows,' confessed Mrs Darwin. 'Don't you?'

'Yes,' agreed Mrs Fayne, 'I do. I suppose it's because they're *our* children, but I prefer one of their little plays to the cinema.'

'You're not the only one. I was speaking to Miss Pritchard the other day – she's one of the Sunday School teachers, you know – and she said that she thinks they're quite as good as some of the professional companies that come here.'

'They're getting quite famous in a small way,' remarked Mrs Fayne.

'They are. I was introduced to a lady the other day

that I'd never seen before, and she said, 'Aren't you the
lady with the little daughter that acts?" She was at the
garden fête last summer.'

'I'm sure Lyn was thrilled to hear that, wasn't she?'

'I didn't tell her. I don't want her to get a swelled
head. She's got big enough ideas about going on the
stage already. I can see difficulty ahead.'

Mrs Darwin was getting heated. Mrs Fayne laughed.

'Oh, there's no need to worry. They're young yet, and
they'll soon forget all these foolish ideas.'

Her voice did not carry the conviction that it would
have done a year ago, and if the two mothers had seen
the rehearsal at the Blue Door Theatre that evening
their maternal hearts would have been still more
troubled. Even Lyn, usually hard to please,
acknowledged that if they went on rehearsing as well as
they had done that night, it ought to be a terrific show.

They went home after locking up the little theatre –
that little theatre that held the ghosts of so many songs
and so much laughter.

13

PANTOMIME

Miss Maclowrie, the headmistress of Fenchester Girls' School, was approaching the finish of her usual end-of-term address. 'And above all,' she said, 'think wisely, speak kindly, and act vigorously.' She was puzzled to see three Lower Fifth girls nudge each other at these words, and hide their faces to giggle, while little Madelaine Fayne turned round to them with an expansive grin. If the headmistress had been at the Blue Door Theatre the previous night she would have seen the joke, for the Blue Door Company had gone through the pantomime with scenery and properties, and all the time Lyn had been urging them, 'Put more pep into it; faster; get a move on; act vigorously.'

This morning was the twenty-first of December, and they had arranged for the show to be given on the day after Boxing Day. As the girls walked home with laden satchels slung over their shoulders Sandra announced kindly, but firmly, 'Fitting this afternoon, please, at the theatre.'

'At the theatre!' they groaned. 'It's so darned cold in that dressing-room.'

'Well, then, everyone must bring a lump of coal, and we'll make a fire.'

'Need I come, Sandra?' Maddy pleaded. 'Because you've tried all my clothes on.'

'Yes, you must come. I'm having Bulldog there to work the lights. I want to see the effect.'

Maddy stamped her foot angrily, and a cascade of books fell from her crammed satchel. She put down the case she was carrying in her left hand, the overall she had under her right arm, and repacked her satchel. When it was once more slung on her back she started off again, but this time a gym shoe fell out of her chemistry overall.

'Bother! Lyn, tie this shoe on the strap of my satchel.'

'There's not room,' Lyn told her; 'you've got your shoe-bag and your needlework bag attached already. You'll look like the White Knight.'

'I'll put it in my case, then.' Once more Maddy stopped in the middle of the High Street pavement and opened her case. She folded her gym, shoe into a ball and stuffed it into a corner, but then found to her exasperation that the lid would not close. She turned it broadside down on to the pavement and sat on it, bouncing up and down in an attempt to secure the lock. The other three stood watching her and writhing under the amused glances of passers-by. ''Sno use,' sighed Maddy, 'I'll have to repack it.'

Before Sandra could stop her she had emptied the case of its contents, school books covered with ink, paints and pencils, and all the peculiar junk she had accumulated in her desk during the term.

Just when she was in the middle of repacking, squatting hatless on the pavement with the ribbon coming off her pony tail, Vicky hissed in a deathly whisper, 'Look out, here comes Miss Maclowrie.' And sure enough, there was the tall thin figure of their headmistress threading her way along the crowded pavement.

'Gosh,' gasped Maddy, 'just look at all this! What am I going to do?'

Miss Maclowrie, though very fair in other matters of discipline, had strict ideas about behaviour in the street, and many a girl had been 'up on the carpet' for slighter misdeeds than emptying and repacking her case in the middle of High Street.

'Do something, do something,' said Sandra urgently. She had a horror of rows from mistresses.

Then help came from an unexpected quarter. While they were still staring at the pile of rubbish on the ground and waiting for Miss Maclowrie's cold grey eyes to light on it and to hear Miss Maclowrie's equally cold grey voice saying, 'And what is the meaning of this?' the bishop, like a great black bird, crossed the road to them.

'Hullo, girls,' he cried cheerfully, his thin face flushed with the cold, 'you look as if you'd broken up with a vengeance.'

'I'm at my wits end,' Maddy told him softly. 'All my worldly goods are on the ground, and Miss Maclowrie is just about to pass.'

The bishop, grasping the situation, said, 'Well, gather round this heap of stuff and she won't see it. She's quite a friend of mine.'

When Miss Maclowrie passed, all she saw was the Bishop of Fenchester talking to a bunch of her girls. He raised his corded hat to her in a courteous gesture. She nodded politely and passed on. The girls heaved a sigh of relief.

'Thank you, Bishop,' said Maddy gratefully. 'I'll do the same for you one day.'

'And how's the pantomime getting along?' he wanted to know.

'Not so badly,' Lyn told him. 'But we're suffering rather from having such a small cast.'

'How are you off for funds?' he asked.

'We haven't a penny, but we're going to take out of the proceeds whatever money we've spent on costumes.'

The bishop put his hand in his pocket and brought out a £5 note, which he gave to Sandra. 'There you are, wardrobe mistress, do what you can with that,' and he strode off before they could thank him.

'Oh, the darling man!' gasped Sandra. 'Now you can have some more tinsel on your fairy frock, Vicky.'

'I've got quite enough,' Vicky told her stoutly. 'You must have a better ball dress, that's what.'

'Nonsense. The one I've got is quite all right.'

'Oh no, it's not,' Lyn joined in. 'It's foul.'

If Sandra had a fault as a wardrobe mistress it was that she would not spend enough time, trouble, or money on her own costumes, however hard she worked on other people's.

'Look here,' pursued Lyn, 'one thinks of a marvellous ball dress the moment Cinderella is mentioned, and here you are trying to be Cinderella in a dress that your mother wore to dances in her twenties, with a few frills on the bottom. It's ridiculous. This afternoon you're coming into town and we'll buy some cheap but exciting stuff, and I'll jolly well *force* you to make yourself a dress.'

When Lyn's mind was made up on a subject it was impossible for Sandra to hold out, and by the time Maddy's case was packed safely Sandra had meekly acquiesced.

The fitting was postponed until the evening, and Vicky, Lyn, and Sandra sallied forth into the town, where nearly the whole population seemed to be doing their Christmas shopping. Maddy had decided to go down to the theatre with the boys and help with the electric lights.

'I'm afraid my presents aren't receiving much attention this year,' said Sandra, as they elbowed their way round Marks and Spencer's. 'I've been thinking of nothing but the pantomime. I don't even know what I'm going to give whom.'

'I'm going to do all mine on Christmas Eve,' said Lyn. 'Come with me? I adore Christmas Eve in the town. I wish it would snow.'

When they had some safety pins, a precaution for the dressing-room which Sandra never forgot, they went into a drapery store at the end of the town near the river, where everything was much cheaper. There they asked to see some materials suitable for a party frock, and spent a quarter of an hour inspecting bales of all kinds of light and silky materials, but could see nothing that would be suitable. Then Sandra caught sight of some material at the back of a shelf. She pointed at it.

'I'd like to see that, please.'

'But, miss, that's not dress material,' objected the draper, wooffling his moustache.

'I'd like to look at it,' repeated Sandra, and he brought it down.

She fingered it, looked at it from a distance, and then held it up to the light. It was very thin, but had a fine silvery sheen.

'I'll have as much of this as I can for a couple of pounds,' Sandra told him.

'But this stuff is only cheap, and there is no wear in it.'

Sandra insisted that she wanted a couple of pounds' worth of it. When they were outside again Lyn said doubtfully, 'Do you think it was wise to get such poor stuff?'

'Yes. Very wise. You see, if I'd got good stuff there would not have been enough, and then the skirt wouldn't have been full enough, and I might just as well have worn the old floral dress of Mummy's.'

The other two were not reassured until the next day. The fitting had once more been postponed so that Sandra could finish the frock. On the way to the theatre for the fitting she seemed very excited, but would say nothing about it.

When they got inside she turned to Bulldog. 'Would you put on the spotlight, please.'

Bulldog had rigged up at the back of the hall a rather amateurish spotlight, which was to be used mainly for the transformation scene, and at Sandra's request he fiddled about with it until the white glare was directed on to the stage. Sandra had gone into the dressing-room

and locked the door. The others danced on the bare
boards at the back of the hall until they heard the
dressing-room door unlocked. Then they looked up.

Sandra stood in the arc of light in a ravishing dress
of silvery-blue. The bodice was-tight-fitting and
unobtrusive, but the skirt – they could not believe
their eyes! Although prepared for a full skirt, they were
astounded at this cloud of shimmering silk that
seemed to fill the entire stage. Sandra, smiling
excitedly, made a low curtsey, and the skirt fell like a
lake around her.

'Do you like it?' she asked at length.

They found their voices, and told her how fabulous
she looked.

'And you really made it all yourself last night and this
afternoon?' Vicky asked incredulously.

'Yes; it was simple as anything, and you should see
how dreadful it looks in daylight! All anaemic and
uninteresting. It's the electric light that does it,'
explained Sandra.

'But how have you made it stand out like that?' Lyn
wanted to know.

Sandra lifted the skirt and revealed a white petticoat
around which were stitched hoops of wire.

'Elementary, my dear Watson,' she quoted.

'You're a wonder,' Jeremy told her. 'And now let's see
how our wigs are getting on.'

The Ugly Sisters had decided that their own hair was
not humorous enough, and so they evolved two wigs
from papier-mâché. Bulldog had used some of Mrs
Darwin's hair, and twisted it up into a bun on top of the

wig, so that when he wore it Maddy told him he looked like a cottage loaf. Jeremy had untwisted a length of rope, brushed and combed the flax until it was pliable, and then stuck it along the papier-mâché base on each side of a parting. They tried them on, and tested them to see that they were safe by standing on their heads; then Sandra began the make-up. By the time she had finished they looked two such remarkable creatures that the others were rolling about, helpless with laughter.

'Oh, Sandra,' moaned Maddy, 'if only you can make them look like that on the night!'

The rest of the fitting seemed tame after these first costumes, and Lyn looked angrily at herself in the glass. To her disgust she had got to dance, and Vicky said she had learned it jolly quickly, but she hated doing it. It made her feel uncomfortable and ridiculous, but she acted her part well, and always executed the dance in the snappy brisk way that she knew Buttons should. Frowning at her reflection, she still gazed into the glass, a full length one, filched from the Corner House.

Sandra, passing by, stopped and looked over her shoulder.

'You look nice,' she said. 'There's something wrong, though. It's your hair.'

For the past six months Lyn had been growing her hair, and it had now reached her shoulders. She had got rid of her fringe, and wore her hair parted at the side. Sandra took hold of it on each side and brought it up level with her ears, then pulled out a few ends and held them up in a fringe.

'That's what you want, a fringe and shorter hair like you used to have it, level with your chin. It'll make you look more masculine.'

'O.K.,' Lyn sighed. 'All these months I've been growing it, and now it's got to be cut off. What a bore.'

'The play's the thing,' Sandra reminded her, a *cliché* that was constantly on Lyn's lips.

The next morning Lyn sat sadly in the hairdresser's chair and watched the dark locks dropping on to the white robe, and then into a heap on the floor. When the fringe was cut and the assistant had finished telling her how sweet it looked, she sighed heavily, paid at the desk, and went out with a hood on her head to cover up the fact that she was a shorn lamb.

Jeremy greeted her with, 'That's much better than a lot of bush all hanging round like you had before; you looked as if you'd no neck at all.'

Mr Darwin, who had been against her growing it in the first place, did not notice it until she drew his attention to it. Then he said paternally, 'Now you look like my little girl again.'

The rest of the Blue Doors had spent the morning on their bicycles delivering programmes of the pantomime. These were printed on pink paper, and had a pattern of Christmas trees on the front. The expense had been more than usual, but on account of the bishop's donation they felt extravagant.

'The Blue Door Theatre Company,' it read (and here was a list of their names), 'present to you the pantomime of *Cinderella*. Come and bring your friends to the Blue Door Theatre, Pleasant Street, on December the 27th, at

7.30. There will be a collection in aid of St. Michael's Organ Fund.'

CHARACTERS

Cinderella	Sandra Fayne.
Prince Charming	Nigel Halford.
Buttons	Lynette Darwin.
VaselinaUgly Sisters	Percy Halford.
Iodina	Jeremy Darwin.
Fairy Godmother	Victoria Halford.
Page, Guest, Hairdresser, etc..	Madelaine Fayne.

Costumes: Sandra Fayne.
Lighting: Percy Halford.
Scenery: Nigel Halford.
Music: Jeremy Darwin.
Dialogue: Madelaine Fayne.
Dances: Victoria Halford.
Producer: Lynette Darwin.
Act I, Scene I: Hairdressing Salon.
Scene 2: Kitchen.
Act II, Scene 1: Ladies' room at Castle.
Scene 2: Ballroom.
Act III, Scene 1: Prince Charming's room.
Scene 2: Kitchen.

'Some programme,' remarked Lyn when she had read one through. 'I hope the show will be as good as it sounds. Rehearsal this afternoon, remember.'

They rehearsed solidly all that afternoon and evening, only stopping to dash home for a hasty tea, and all the morning of Christmas Eve they were at the theatre.

'Whatever is the use of having daughters,' grumbled their mothers, 'if they don't help with the mince pies?'

In the afternoon the Blue Doors went into the town to do all their Christmas shopping in one go. It was very awkward when they wanted to buy presents for each other, but they came back laden with exciting-looking brown-paper parcels and full of the Christmas spirit.

'Come into "ours" and have some ginger wine,' the Halfords invited. They joined in a broadcast carol service, and drank the burning brown liquid that glinted against the firelight. Maddy, sitting on the hearthrug, lifted her glass. 'Merry Christmas, and God bless us every one!'

'We need it!' they responded. The raised glasses clinked together.

The pantomime began with a fanfare of trumpets from a record-player behind the stage, and the curtains parted. They had rigged up another curtain that cut off the front quarter of the stage from the rest. In front of this Maddy was standing in page's uniform, made from an old red dressing-gown and the gold counterpane, previously used for the angel's robe and the fairy's dress. Her cheeks were puffed out at a tin trumpet, from which hung a banner embroidered with gold, a relic of Mrs Bell's box. Maddy lowered her bugle and spoke the prologue:

'A story to-night we have to unfold
Of a thrilling romance that happened of old.'

The rest of the doggerel was an apology for their small cast and stage. It ended up:

'We want to amuse you, dear people, and so
I'll blow my trumpet [she blew it]
AND ON WITH THE SHOW!'

The first scene took place in a hairdressing salon where Jeremy and Bulldog, as the Ugly Sisters Vaselina and Iodina, were undergoing a strenuous beauty treatment, aided by Maddy as the beautician. The audience were reduced to helpless laughter by their antics, particularly when they were doing the sliming exercise that Maddy taught the, and Iodina insisted on doing them all backwards because she wanted to put on weight.

When the curtain was pulled for the second scene the audience gave a gasp of appreciation. Nigel's kitchen scene was the best he had ever done. The backcloth was a panelled wall with plates standing on an immense dresser, and a curtained window. Up-stage was a table, and down-stage on the right a wooden settle, contrived of plywood and theatre chairs. They had arranged to have the fireplace off-stage, as Nigel did not feel capable of drawing a convincing fire and did not approve of a torch covered with red paper.

Full length on the settle lay Buttons asleep, snoring contentedly, a large apron over his red and green costume. Off-stage came the sound of Maddy's trumpet and a vigorous bang. Buttons still snored.

The banging and trumpeting went on, then Maddy walked in as Robin the page, and looked round the kitchen. Spotting Buttons, she went and stood over him angrily, hands on hips, then bent down and trumpeted in his ear. Buttons woke up slowly and inquired innocently, 'Did you ring?' then, seeing who it was, cried, 'Sorry, old man. I thought it was one of those old she-cats.'

They had a long conversation about the tyrannies of the Ugly Sisters, and Buttons confessed that the only thing that kept him in the house was Cinderella. Just as Robin was about to go, he remembered what he had come for: to bring a letter from his employer, the prince, for the sisters. He handed over a large, important-looking envelope spattered with sealing-wax. Buttons held it up to the light and read aloud:

'Prince Charming requests the pleasure of the company of Iodina and Vaselina at the Castle tonight for his coming-of-age ball. Dress will be worn.'

'I should think so, too,' broke in Robin. 'Two old hens like that!'

At this moment someone was heard singing off-stage.

'Sh!' Buttons warned Robin. 'It's Cinderella. Hide the invitation. She will be disappointed.'

Cinderella, sweet and innocent in artistic green rags, entered trailing a birch broom.

'Hullo. Why, it's my little friend Robin. How are you getting on at the Castle?'

Robin, with the invitation behind his back, answered, 'Nicely, thank you; good food and cheerful company. I must say the prince treats us well.'

'I think the prince is a wonderful man.' Cinderella's

eyes shone, and she clasped her hands. 'He's so good and handsome, and everyone loves him.'

'Especially the ladies,' put in Robin. 'He's to choose a wife by midnight tonight, and everyone in the realm will be going to the ball in hopes of being his choice.'

'I should love to go. Do you think I might get an invitation?' she asked them wistfully. They surveyed their feet and made no reply. She sank on to the settle. 'No, perhaps it's no use hoping for one.'

'Cinders,' faltered Robin, showing the envelope, 'this is an invitation for your sisters – but not for you.'

'Oh!'

There was a miserable silence, then Cinderella jumped up, forcing a smile.

'Don't let's mope. We can have just as much fun in a kitchen as all the grand folks in a ballroom.'

Nigel struck up a polka, and Cinderella danced with each of them in turn.

Suddenly the door burst open, and the Ugly Sisters sailed in. Cinderella picked up her broom and began to sweep. Iodina and Vaselina stormed at them until Robin held out the invitation. They snatched it and hurriedly opened it. Vaselina looked at it holding it upside down, and said, 'Fancy that.'

'Shall I read it out for you?' asked Robin cheekily. 'Prince Charming requests the pleasure of the company of Iodina, Vaselina, and Cinderella at the Castle tonight for his coming-of-age ball. Dress will be worn.'

'Cinderella can't go,' snapped Iodina.

'She's got nothing to wear,' added Vaselina.

'And it especially said dress is to be worn,' pursued

Iodina, in a satisfied voice. 'I shall wear my purple bombazine with the green fal-de-lals.'

'And I shall wear my new pink undies,' giggled Vaselina coyly. 'I'm sure I shall capture the prince. Come on, Cinders, I shall need you to padlock my corsets.'

They carried her off, leaving Robin and Buttons. Buttons confided in his friend that he meant to propose to Cinderella while the others were at the ball, then, sitting on the settle, with his arms clasping his knees, Buttons sang his solo. Then he relapsed into thought, and Robin crept sympathetically away. Then there was the sound of laughter, and Cinderella ran in and buried her face in Buttons' shoulder to stifle her chuckles.

'They're coming, Buttons. They look so funny.'

Vaselina entered in a terrific dress of purple, a big green bow in her built-up hair.

'Cinders, go back and help Iodina. She's got into her backless dress back to front.'

Cinderella went out, and Vaselina paraded in front of Buttons.

'Well, boy, how do I look?'

'Amazing, unique, and outstanding, especially at the back,' for indeed her bustle was a masterpiece.

Iodina came on in a long, shapeless, yellow dress, carrying an enormous raffia bag.

'Now, Iodina, have you got everything in your reticule?' Iodina stuck her head in it. 'Handkerchief,' she held up a violent red-spotted one, 'comb in case, and safety pins in case, and all our cosmetics. Lily lipstick for luscious lips, rose bloom rouge, and Dusky Night mascara.'

'That's right,' approved Vaselina, 'and remember not to sit down or you'll split your dress, and if the prince speaks to you, sparkle.'

'How?' queried Iodina.

'Like this.' Vaselina smirked, put a hand on her hip, and with the other under her chin cooed, 'Oh, Prince, you say the most lovely things.'

After more fooling Buttons announced that the coach was waiting, and Cinderella ran to the window and watched them drive off. She sat down on the settle, warming her hands by the fire, and Buttons came back and drew up a stool by her feet. They gazed into the fire till Buttons offered a penny for Cinderella's thoughts.

'I was thinking of – no one in particular.'

'But of someone!' pursued Buttons.

'Yes,' she confessed, 'someone of whom I'm always thinking.'

'What is he like?'

'Tall.'

Buttons' face fell.

'Handsome.'

Buttons looked sadder still.

'And kind,' went on Cinderella. 'He dresses in velvets and silks, and has many servants, but he's not selfish.'

'You are thinking of the prince!'

'I know it's silly.' She laughed. 'I do wish I were going to the ball tonight – just to see him. He would never speak to anyone like me, but just to be near him . . .' She broke off. 'Buttons, you said this morning you had something to tell me?'

Sadly Buttons got up. 'It doesn't matter – now.' He went off.

Cinderella mused aloud, 'He seems as miserable as I am. I wonder why?'

She sang her solo to Jeremy's careful accompaniment, and the lights gradually grew dim. Vicky entered, a typical pantomime fairy in an ankle-length ballet frock that she had worn in the dancing display. There were bands of tinsel round it, and in her hair shone a star, to match the one on the tip of her wand. As she danced, all the lights went off, and Bulldog followed her floating figure with the spotlight, over which was a piece of cardboard with circles of various coloured cellophane let into it; as it was revolved the fairy was lit with different colours. helped her on with the ball dress. Poised on tip-toe at the end Meanwhile Cinderella had slipped into the wings, where Lyn of the dance, the fairy, purple-lit, declaimed, 'Cinderella, your wish is granted. You shall go to the ball!' The spotlight swung on to Cinderella, standing ready in her billowy silk dress. The audience clapped and clapped, and for quite a minute Sandra had to be busy registering surprise at her transformation. The glass slippers, silver in reality, were produced, and she saw the carriage and horses from the window. The curtain fell on the fairy's injunction to be home by midnight.

During the interval all the friends and relations of the Blue Doors were telling each other how good they thought it was, and in the dressing-rooms the actors drank water and patted themselves and each other on the back.

'Aren't we getting *blasé?*' remarked Lyn. 'I've not felt a single twinge of stage fright.'

'I have,' Sandra said. 'Did you hear my voice shaking in "I wonder why"?'

'All the more poignant,' called Jeremy, from the other side of the curtain. 'I found the piano keys swimming with my tears.'

The first scene of the second act took place in front of the first curtain, while the kitchen scenery was changed to the ballroom scenery. The Ugly Sisters did some fooling in what was supposed to be the Ladies' Room, which greatly amused the audience, and then the curtains were drawn on to a corner of the ballroom. The backcloth showed marble pillars, and there were real ferns in pots at the bottom of them. The sisters went and sat on a seat and waited to be asked for a dance. The prince, resplendent in green and gold, came on, dancing with Maddy, who had changed into a Court Lady, wearing her new long party frock and her hair swept up on to the top of her head.

'How sophisticated she looks!' murmured her mother to Mr Fayne.

Down-stage the couple stopped, and the prince began to speak.

'Lady Rose, I have something important to ask you. As you know, tonight I have to make my choice of a wife. Will you' – at this moment Cinderella entered and sat beside her unrecognizing sisters – 'will you . . .' the prince faltered, gazing at the newcomer. 'Will you come to my wedding?'

Maddy heaved angrily, stamped her foot, and ran off.

The prince went up to the seat where the three sat. The sisters nudged each other.

'Oh dear Prince,' began Vaselina, but the prince said cuttingly:

'I don't think I have ever had the misfortune to be introduced to you.'

'Oh, Prince,' cooed Iodina, 'what lovely things you say!'

Her sister pushed her off the end of the bench.

'May I have the pleasure . . .'

Vicky, who was working the record-player off-stage, put the needle on to the silently whirling record of a Strauss waltz, and the prince and Cinderella danced round the stage. The Ugly Sisters sniffed disapprovingly, as the dancers' faces got closer and closer together, and finally they walked off, heads in the air. The prince embraced Cinderella and kissed her.

'I don't know your name,' he confessed, 'but will you marry me? It is love at first sight.'

The prince turned, and, cupping his hands, shouted off-stage, 'Guests, friends, courtiers. I have a proclamation to make. I have chosen a wife.'

The clock struck twelve and Cinderella slipped away, leaving a shoe on the floor. The prince, not noticing her exit, continued to speak. 'Here, as the clock strikes twelve, I present to you the lady . . .' He turned round, and the curtains were drawn on his surprise and consternation.

The next scene was in front of the middle curtain, and represented the prince's room next morning, where he was ordering Maddy, as Robin, to take the shoe to every house in the realm to find its owner. The back curtains parted, showing the kitchen once more; where Buttons was dancing with a breakfast-tray in his hands.

Vaselina, in a bathrobe *negligée*, entered to tell Buttons to take Iodina her breakfast, as she was suffering from a relapsed liver on account of the ball last night. She called out to Cinderella, but, getting no reply, stamped out to find her, and came back dragging her by the shoulder. Cinderella wore a becoming dressing-gown of quilted blue silk. Vaselina lectured her for not being down in time, then sent her off to dress. Just as Vaselina was singing a rather vulgar but very amusing song about the complaints of 'the morning after the night before', there was heard the page's trumpet off-stage, and the prince and his retinue walked on. The retinue was Robin, who carried the shoe on one of Mrs Fayne's best drawing-room cushions. Vaselina tried to fit the shoe in vain, and Iodina, entering in a flannel nightgown with frills at neck and wrist, also made an effort, but it was no good. At this moment Cinderella entered in her rags with a green handkerchief over her head, and begged to be allowed to try it. The shoe fitted. She took off her handkerchief and the prince recognized her. The final curtain fell on the entire company singing 'Happy Ever After', another chorus of Jeremy's composition. Vicky stepped in front of the curtains and spoke the epilogue, then the bishop handed up a bunch of flowers for Sandra and boxes of chocolates for the others.

In the dressing-room Maddy stretched herself out and sighed happily as she munched a chocolate with truffle in the middle, 'Who wouldn't be a babe in a pantomime!'

14

THE BISHOP TO THE RESCUE

With the coming of spring the thoughts of the Blue
Doors were turned again to the stage, and the ides of
March found them once more in consultation over the
dressing-room table.

'It may be the last concert we shall give,' sighed
Sandra, 'so it *must* be a good one.'

'The last?' echoed Maddy, horrified. 'Why?'

'Nigel leaves at the end of next term, presumably;
Jeremy takes G.C.E., and he'll leave school and go into
the—'

'Shut up,' cut in Jeremy. 'Don't remind me about my
fate. Anyhow, I shan't pass.'

'Then you'll take it next year, when Lyn and the
twins and I do. We shan't be able to have concerts
without Nigel, and I fully intend to swot next year, no
matter what anyone else does.' Sandra delivered her
ultimatum in decided tones.

'The future's pretty blank and undecided,' remarked
Nigel.

'I intend telling Mummy and Daddy that the
only thing I'm going to work at is the stage,' Lyn
informed them. 'But I'll wait until the Easter concert
is over, because there'll be a pretty big row, I expect,

and they might stop me appearing in it.'

'They're going to have a pretty bad time of it,' groaned Jeremy, 'because I take my last exam. before L.R.A.M. in July, a week after G.C.E., and I can't work for both, so you know which I'll choose.'

Bulldog, as usual was complacent.

'Thank goodness I'm not aching to work at anything,' he remarked.

'But, Bulldog, what are you going to do?' asked Lyn seriously. 'You must decide sooner or later.'

'I'd like to be something to do with electricity,' he told them vaguely. 'Or an actor,' he added.

'The old, old story again!' sighed Nigel. 'We *must* all go to a dramatic school! Who can we get to help us persuade our parents?'

'The bishop,' said Maddy promptly. 'He's on our side, very definitely.'

'But would it be proper to ask him?' queried Sandra.

'Proper!' flared up Lyn angrily. 'Seven careers at stake, and you wonder if it's proper!' Sandra bit her lip. 'Sandra, you have a soul of the Mrs Potter-Smith variety.' Lyn had a way of saying things that hurt.

On the day of the dress rehearsal, exactly two years after he had revealed his ambition during the morning at Browcliffe, Bulldog realized it. He invented something. He invented the elusive swish of the curtain. It was merely a matter of curtain rings and cord. He sewed the rings diagonally across each stage curtain, threaded cord through them in a complicated fashion, fixed one end, leaving free the end near the dressing-room. He pulled the cord, the curtains slid apart and up, hanging in heavy festoons in each of the top corners of the stage. The 'swish' was sweetest music in his ears. The rest of the company were in the dressing-rooms, and he did not tell them of his invention. When they came out he suddenly raised the curtain.

'Shut up, we're not ready,' snapped Lyn, then stopped, open-mouthed, staring up at the bunches of curtain.

Bulldog let go of the cord, and they gasped with delight at the definite, satisfactory rustle as the folds of the curtain swung into place.

'Bulldog's beaten us all!' cried Jeremy. 'He's realized his ambition!'

'What is it now? You must have another,' urged Lyn.

'To be an actor.'

They smiled their approval on him.

All through the Easter concert the curtains swished dutifully, to round after round of applause, from a wildly enthusiastic audience. At the end Nigel stepped forward.

'Ladies and gentlemen, we cannot thank you enough for the splendid reception we have had tonight. It has made happy what is really a very said occasion for us. Tonight, owing to circumstances and people,' his eyes swept the parents in the front row, 'sees the last performance of the Blue Door Theatre Company in this theatre as amateurs. But we hope and pray that one day you may see us back on this stage as professionals.'

They bowed and smiled with heavy hearts as the last curtain fell at their last concert.

Lyn tried to speak, then burst into miserable tears.

★   ★   ★

Early one Wednesday evening in May, a month after the Easter show, the seven sat in a row along a pew in St. Michael's, listening to the swell of the new organ. *Their* new organ, for they had helped to buy it. Tonight was merely a recital by the organist; it was not to be dedicated until the following Sunday. The music only formed a background for their thoughts.

'This is the first peaceful moment I have had for weeks,' thought Nigel, staring at the stained-glass window that was mottled with sunset rays.

Ever since Easter the Corner House had been a den of raging lions, rather than the happy home that it had been up till now. Three weeks ago Nigel had interviewed his father and begged to be allowed to have a year at a dramatic school when he left school at the end of the term. If at the end of two or three years he did not show promise, or if at the end of two or three years he could not get a job, then he would give it up and be an accountant. Mr Halford refused point-blank, and would not argue. Nigel, swallowed up in helpless fury, set his teeth undaunted.

Meanwhile Vicky had tackled her mother on the subject of the stage as a career, and found her an enthusiastic ally. They decided that as soon as she had passed G.C.E. she should go to a dramatic school to study dancing and drama. Against the sound of the organ Vicky remembered the ecstasy in which she had lived until her mother had discussed it with her father; the result was a domestic upheaval. Meal-times were silent and gloomy, and at any minute of the day when

Mr Halford was at home quarrels sprang up like toadstools. Bulldog thought fit to put his oar in. At dinner he said one day, 'Father, while your thoughts are on the subject, please include me in the dramatic-school idea.' Mr Halford looked like a drowning man from whom a straw has been snatched.

Matters in the Darwin household were worse, for both parents objected to the idea. Jeremy, with his long legs tucked uncomfortably under the pew, remembered the long rambling arguments with his father and the angry interludes with his mother. Gosh, how his head ached! At tea that evening Lyn and her mother had been going on at each other until he thought his head would burst.

Mr and Mrs Fayne were treating the matter most sensibly. They discussed it in their usual placid manner, and did not treat it as if it were some outlandish plan not worth considering. Certainly, it did not affect them so immediately, for their daughters were not ready to leave school.

Maddy was twiddling her thumbs, and Lyn nudged her short-temperedly.

Sandra, noticing it, thought, 'We shall all have nervous breakdowns if we go on like this, not acting anything and believing that we never shall again.'

Mr Bell, from his seat in the chancel, pondered the melancholy appearance of the Blue Doors. They all looked pale and miserable, and Lyn had definitely been crying. He hoped it was not a quarrel. This ought to be a great night for them, the first appearance of the organ, which they had helped to buy. He had expected them to bear their usual alert intelligent expressions, and to whisper amongst themselves, and possibly to giggle, but here they were, looking as if it were a funeral they were attending. At the end of the recital he pronounced the benediction, and the Blue Doors walked out into the evening sunshine, answering mechanically to the remarks made to them by the other members of the congregation.

'Where shall we go?'

'Not home,' said Lyn emphatically. 'I'm not going until bed-time.'

Sandra looked anxiously at her, feeling glad that the tension in her own home was not so bad that she had to keep out of it.

'Let's walk down to the library,' suggested Nigel, 'and have a browse in the reading-room.'

The High Street was cool and empty. Usually when they walked down to the library in the evening they walked right across the path and swung along in good spirits. Tonight there was no elasticity in their tread, and their utterances were only sighs. After the hubbub that they had been living in, they felt they needed quiet for a little while. Arguments, reproaches, and pleadings were still swimming in Lyn's head.

In the reading-room she made straight for the magazine, *Amateur Drama*, before the others could reach it. When Maddy tried to look at it over her shoulder she elbowed her away, and settled down to read it all through, starting with the advertisements. On the first page was a notice in large type that caught her eye: 'One-Act Play Contest'. She read it idly, and saw that

the adjudicator of some board of acting was touring in
the south of England to judge amateur companies in
one-act plays. The contests would be held at
Bournemouth, Portsmouth, and Brighton in May; in
June at Bath, Reading, and Fenchester.

Lyn made a loud exclamatory noise, to the disgust of
several elderly gentlemen who were nearly asleep in
their chairs. She pushed the magazine across the table to
Nigel, who was reading the *Art Gallery* on the other
side, and stabbed at the notice with an excited finger.
He read it, then looked up, and they saw the light of
battle in his hazel eyes. He beckoned the others and
they gathered round and read it through. Jeremy took
out his notebook and scribbled down the rules for
entering, and the address to which applications were to
be sent. Still obeying the golden rule of silence that was
enforced, they left the reading-room.

'We'll go in for that, if we die in the attempt,' said
Nigel forcefully.

'Our parents won't let us,' Sandra demurred, 'not after
the ructions of the past week.'

'But they can't be so cruel as to stop us from taking
an opportunity like that,' wailed Lyn, almost in tears
again. 'They can't!'

'They will,' said Bulldog. 'I would, wouldn't you?
Think of it, if your children had been behaving as we
have, would you let them?'

They agreed dolefully that they supposed they would
not.

'But it won't do *them* any harm if we go in for this.'
Lyn shook herself angrily.

'It will do Jeremy some harm,' said Sandra. 'It will distract him from both his exams.'

'It won't, Sandra. Only from one. I'm not taking G.C.E.,' he said suddenly, aware that he was causing a sensation.

'Not taking it?'

'No. The Head told me this morning that my form master told him that I should never pass in anything but music, so I've got to have another whole year at it. That's just as I planned,' he said in a satisfied tone. 'I can get my L.R.A.M. by next Easter, heaven willing, weather permitting.'

'But why didn't you tell us?' Maddy wanted to know. 'Then we could have rejoiced with him that rejoices.'

'I thought that as they that weep were in the majority, I'd weep with them for a bit, and also I don't want it known at home till things have settled down a bit. It would give them the last straw that breaks the camel's back.'

'That it would! But it's a good thing really, because there's no real reason why we shouldn't go in for this contest.'

But when they told their parents about it there were *many* reasons produced.

'Certainly not, after the way you've been behaving,' was Mr Halford's ultimatum.

'Another play just before your exam.? Certainly not, Jeremy! Don't be so silly!' rebuked Mrs Darwin; and when he took a deep breath and informed her that there was no exam. for him this year she was so furious that she said, 'All the more reason why you should do a bit of work now, instead of wasting your time acting.'

Mr and Mrs Fayne might easily have been persuaded by the use of kind words and gentle tones, but Sandra and Maddy did not try. Instead, they all held an indignation meeting that evening in the garden, and talked and talked until everything there was to be said had been said ten times over.

'I can't even cry now,' grumbled Lyn. 'I just go all hot and get in a temper. We must do something about it.'

'Now is the time,' said Nigel slowly, 'when we need the help of the bishop.'

Maddy jumped up. 'Let's make a crusade down to Bishop's Court and beg him to help! Come on. Let's go while the fit is on us.'

The girls insisted on doing their hair and putting on their best coats before making their way to the bishop's house. They climbed the grey stone steps up to the imposing front door and read out loud: 'Do not ring unless an answer is required.'

Lyn pulled the old-fashioned bell rope, and it pealed and pealed and had not stopped ringing when the door was opened. An elderly housekeeper stood on the mat – a most superior person, who surveyed them in acid surprise.

'She looks as if we're the dog's breakfast,' whispered Maddy from the bottom step.

'Good evening. Is the bishop in?'

'He is.'

'Er – may we speak to him?' Nigel was rather cowed by her haughty manner.

'He is writing a sermon.' She said this as if it closed

the question, and made as if to shut the door.

'But, please, we must see him. It's very important.'

'He is writing a sermon and does not wish to be disturbed.'

'Will you take him a note, then?'

'I could do that.'

'Make it nice and dramatic,' urged Maddy, as Nigel wrote on a piece of paper, leaning it against the wall, 'then he'll see us.'

He wrote: 'We are in trouble. Please, Bishop, may we see you and have your advice? The Blue Doors.' He handed it to the housekeeper, and she stalked away with it.

A few minutes later she returned to say sourly, 'The bishop says he will see Nigel, and the rest of you will come in and wait.'

They followed her along the dim, lofty hall into a large drawing-room, full of massive furniture and dark curtains. She ushered Nigel into a study lined with bookshelves, across the corridor, then returned to the drawing-room, standing in the shadows and fixing her eye stonily on the six who sat nervously on the edge of the heavy furniture.

'Does she think we're going to chew the antimacassars?' whispered Maddy.

'What a funny room to find in the bishop's house,' thought Sandra. 'I always thought he had good taste.'

The study that Nigel entered was far more the bishop's style. There was a blazing, cheerful fire, although this was summer; water-colours hung on the walls between shelves of books that reached from wainscot to ceiling. The bishop sat at a desk littered with papers.

'Hullo, Nigel.' A friendly smile lit up his cadaverous face. 'Sit down. Now can you help me with my sermon? I want a little story to illustrate the maxim that a thing worth doing is worth doing properly.' He tapped the desk with his pen.

'How about the parable of the man who came upon treasure when ploughing the field, sir?'

'Of course! Excellent.' The bishop wrote it down and talked on about his sermon until he had made sure that Nigel had lost the strained expression that he wore on entering. At length he said, 'Well, Nigel, what is it you want to tell me?'

Nigel took a deep breath and began. 'We've come for your advice and help. Bishop, what profession do you consider us most suited for?'

The bishop smiled. 'I think I know what you're worrying yourselves about. You all want to go on the stage, and your parents object.'

'That's right, sir. How did you guess?'

'I have eyes and also ears.'

'Well, what is your opinion on the subject?'

'Let me answer your question with another. If you go on the stage what will your aim be?'

'To make the Blue Doors a successful professional company. We've planned it all, sir.' Nigel's eyes shone as he described it. 'We should each have three years at a dramatic school, and I should have one year at scenic art, then we'd come back to Fenchester–'

'You're sure you'd come back?'

'Why yes, sir! This is just the kind of town that needs a theatre.'

'But yours isn't big enough.'

'We'd use it until we raised enough money to build a better one.'

'And if it didn't pay?'

'Then we should have to drop it and take up what we call our auxiliary careers. Mine is accountancy, Sandra's cooking, Bulldog's electricity – we've all got one. Does it sound such a feather-headed plan as our parents think?'

The bishop shook his head and spoke musingly.

'It sounds quite feasible, and as a lover of Fenchester, I'm sure you could help the town considerably. What your parents fear is that once you got to London you would stay there, mix with a lot of irresponsible young people, and turn into Bohemians of an unpleasant type. I quite see that point.'

'And also,' joined in Nigel, 'they don't like the sound of it. They bother about what people will say.'

'I suppose, as a bishop I should discourage you from this idea, but let me give you this piece of advice – don't bother about what other people say, if you think that what you're doing is right.'

'We don't consider we'd be doing wrong in going on the stage, but our parents do, excepting Mrs Halford, who was a dancer herself.'

The bishop rose.

'Well, Nigel, I'll do what I can for you. I'll call round and see your parents later this evening. Now I should like to see the others.'

He went across to the drawing-room where they sat waiting, and dismissed the housekeeper. When she was out of hearing Maddy said in a relieved tone:

'Gosh, I'm glad she's gone. She's been fixing me with an evil eye as if she were about to turn me into a rat.'

'That is my chief retainer, Mrs Griffin by name.'

They agreed that the name suited her, and he told them that beneath her stony exterior lay a heart of gold.

'But come into the study,' he invited them. 'I never stay long in this gloomy room.'

In the study he heard all their grievances, and they discussed the problem from all angles. He ended up the hearing by saying:

'I would not advise the stage as a career for any other young people that I know, but I believe that you seven, if you work hard and stick together, could make a real success of your enterprise, which will have my blessing.'

'And you'll try and persuade our parents to let us try the competition?' asked Lyn in a little voice, shaky with hope.

He nodded, smiling, while they tried to find words to thank him. Nigel wrung him by the hand.

'Thank you, sir, you're a sport, and even if you don't succeed it will be something we shall never forget!'

The atmosphere was emotional, until the bishop said, 'Now you must come and have some supper with me.'

He rang the bell and the Griffin appeared.

'My guests are staying to supper,' he announced. 'We will have ginger beer to drink. And now,' he said, 'how about a little music?'

He led the way into the dark dining-room, where

stood an immense Bechstein grand piano, with a glimmering ebony top. The bishop put his long fingers to the keys, and they sang with him, for he had a beautiful bass voice and played with great skill.

'May I try the piano?' asked Jeremy shyly.

'Certainly.'

'Oh, it's marvellous.' His fingers caressed the milk-white keys. 'So different from ours at home, that we spoilt when we were kids. It's got several notes that won't play, and the ones that play sound like a barrel organ.'

'You may come and play on this any time you like,' the bishop told him, 'so long as you don't play jazz. But it'll be nice to have you playing on her, for she doesn't have enough use to keep her in trim, as I have so little time.'

They noticed that he spoke of his piano in the feminine, as a sailor does his ship.

'Why are you so kind to us?' Maddy wanted to know.

'Perhaps because I have no children of my own to spoil.'

'I'm glad you haven't any children,' said Maddy candidly. 'I should be very, very jealous of them.'

Then Griffin came to announce that supper was served. It was an epicurean meal of mushroom soup, *poulet sauté*, and fresh fruit salad.

'I've had a full sufficiency,' groaned Maddy at length, 'and if I have any more I shall bust.'

Even Sandra was too merry with ginger beer and laughter to reprove her. After supper they wandered round the garden until the sermon was finished, when the bishop would walk home with them. The garden was large and well kept, with such perfectly trimmed lawns that it seemed as if they ought to wipe their feet before crossing them.

'I feel more hopeful than I have for weeks,' remarked Sandra, as they strolled along the twilit paths.

'Same here. I really think he'll do it. Even if he only persuades them to let us try the contest it will be something.'

'Then some big producer will watch the competition and offer us a contract,' laughed Sandra.

'A lot of good that would do,' said Lyn bitterly. 'They'd prosecute him for attempted kidnapping.'

'If by "they" you mean our parents, you'd better not let the bishop hear you say that. Remember how he hates your cynical remarks.'

'I wonder why he thinks we ought to be angels?' pondered Lyn.

'Because he's an angel himself,' replied Maddy.

'We *do* know some different types of people, don't we?' remarked Vicky. 'Nice ones like the bishop and the Bells, and nasty ones like Mrs P.-S. and Mrs Flanders.'

'Then there are people who look nasty at first and are really nice, like Miss Maclowrie and the Griffin,' added Lyn.

'Are we nicer than we look, or do we look nicer than we are?' queried Maddy.

'Look nicer than we are,' said Lyn. 'At least I hope I look better than my soul does at times.'

'Where is your soul, and what does it look like?' Maddy wanted to know.

'I think it's my heart. I always imagine it like a heart on a Valentine, although I know it's really an ugly affair with auricles and ventricles and what not.'

'I keep my soul in my waist line,' observed Maddy, 'and it's round and flat, rather like a pancake.'

'So when you're eating you heart out for anything you're really having pancakes for dinner,' remarked Bulldog facetiously; he was feeling rather out of his depth in this introspective conversation.

'It's a wonderful night,' observed Sandra, after a while. ' "On such a night as this" all sorts of things could happen.'

'A miracle may happen before the night is out,' said Jeremy. 'Won't it be good to look back on tonight when we're old and have nothing but dreams to live on.'

'We have complete faith in the bishop, haven't we?' said Lyn. 'It'll be awful if he can't manage it.'

But there was no conviction in her doubt. The talk and the music and the peace of the garden had calmed their troubled nerves, and it seemed that nothing could go wrong any more.

It was a little past nine when the bishop came out, with his black hat on, and said he was ready to walk home with them. A pale moon was beginning to show as they made their way along the quiet streets, all angling to walk next to their benefactor. By the gate of the Corner House he said, with the air of a conspirator, 'Now I am going to call on Mr and Mrs Halford. Sandra and Jeremy, will you tell your parents that they're wanted urgently at the Corner House, and then you can all go to bed and sleep the sleep of the justified. I'll do my best. Good night, children.'

'Good night,' chorused the Faynes and Darwins.

'Dear, sweet Bishop,' added Maddy, standing on tiptoe to kiss his cheek.

Nigel and the twins took him into the house, and when the door banged behind them Lyn said dramatically, 'There go our futures, our careers, and our happiness,' and added, as they turned in at their gates, 'I'm going straight to bed, and I'll say my prayers till I drop.'

15

THROUGH THE KEYHOLE

Sleep was impossible. Jeremy stood shivering in his pyjamas at the open window. Staring out into the darkness, over many back gardens, he could faintly discern the sentinel tree on the top of Miller's Hill. He could hear the slow pad of Lyn's feet in the next room, and knew she was walking restlessly up and down, biting her finger nails and trying to calm herself by reciting Shakespeare. He wished he could smoke, it might calm his nerves, but it always made him feel dizzy. He drummed his fingers on the window ledge and wondered for the twentieth time what was happening at the Corner House.

The heavy silence was suddenly shattered by peal after peal at the door bell. He slung on his dressing-gown, groped for his slippers, and was down to answer the door a fraction of a second before Lyn. A peculiar sight met his eyes. The young Halfords and Faynes, in their night clothes and dressing-gowns, were huddled on the doorstep talking in excited whispers.

'Hullo, have you heard the verdict?' Jeremy asked excitedly.

'No; but will you come round and listen in with us? We can hear perfectly in the hall.'

'O.K. What's it like out? Do we need anything more than we've got on?'

'No. Hurry up. It's dark, so nobody can see us.'

They crept silently in slippered feet along to the Corner House, with no awkward encounters. Two ladies passed on the other side of the road, talking in high-pitched voices, but did not notice the seven figures that slunk in the shadow of the fence. Cautiously they entered by the front door of the Corner House and grouped themselves round the closed door. The voices inside could easily be heard. Nigel mouthed, pointing to the keyhole, 'Take turns in looking,' and pushed Maddy forward. She glued her eyes to the hole.

'They're drinking sherry,' she reported, 'and the men are smoking.'

'. . . and so,' the bishop was saying, 'I promised them to do my best.'

There was silence, then Mrs Darwin said in the tight voice that Lyn often used when annoyed, 'It is very kind, I'm sure, Bishop, but hardly necessary.'

'It is more necessary than kind,' disagreed the bishop firmly. 'It is not a nice thing to have to say, but if you disappoint your children now they will never forget it for the rest of their lives.' He tapped his fingers emphatically on the table.

'I think you exaggerate slightly, sir,' said Mr Halford politely, flicking the ash of his cigarette into the fire. 'This fit will soon pass.'

'*Will* it? If I thought *that* I should not be pleading for them tonight. I feel certain that, if they are frustrated in this matter, they will take up without enthusiasm the careers that you force them into, and when, through lack of it, they fail, their excuse will be, "How different things might have turned out if only we had been allowed to go on the stage." '

'Hear, hear,' came the firm voice of Mrs Halford from her invalid chair. 'I quite agree that the stage is their vocation, and I will do everything in my power to make it possible.'

She looked happily round the room at the disapproving faces of the other parents.

The bishop said, 'Now, Mrs Halford has been a dancer, and has it spoiled her?'

'But, Bishop,' said Mrs Fayne in a puzzled voice, 'I can't understand your advising us like this. We've all read about the ways of theatre people in London.'

'I consider, Mrs Fayne, that there is no more evil in the theatre than in any other walk of life.'

'But what we don't want to happen,' put in Mr Fayne, 'is for our girls to come home with false and superficial values.'

'Impossible!' cried the bishop. 'Sandra is too fastidious and Maddy has too much sense of humour, and Lyn and Vicky would do nothing to harm their careers. In a dramatic school today there is some danger of these things happening, but no more than at any university, and I know that all your daughters are dependable and straight.'

Mr Halford murmured something about the stage not being a man's job.

'If by "a man's job" you mean strenuous, then I must

disagree. And it calls for as much brain work as any other profession.'

'But what will people say?' burst out Mrs Darwin, 'when they hear that both of my children are on the stage?'

'They would possibly think, "Those children will not come home the delightful people that they left." ' The Blue Doors nudged each other. 'But when they *do*, and people see them and are entertained by them at the theatre–'

Mrs Darwin laughed cynically. 'So you think they'd come home?'

'I am sure of it. That is their aim, to make the Blue Doors a permanent repertory for Fenchester.' He leaned forward eagerly in his chair. 'Now let me outline the plan of action that Nigel put forward in his most sensible and business-like way.'

Maddy pulled a corner of Nigel's red-and-black dressing-gown and whispered laughing, 'That's you!'

'Nigel leaves school in two months' time. He goes to a good dramatic school for three years' training. All the others, except Maddy, take G.C.E. in a year's time, then for six months pursue their "auxiliary careers". They will then all be around seventeen, and could go to a dramatic school for three years. As Nigel will be a year and a half ahead of them, he will have an extra year at stage design and then learn a little about the business side of it. To complete their training they would like a few months' working in some small repertory company as apprentices, and then by the time they are twenty they will be ready to open the Blue Doors professionally.'

'And Maddy?'

'By that time she will have taken G.C.E., and they can take her as an apprentice and train her themselves.'

The parents were human and could not but feel a slight stir of the pulses at this scheme. Mr Halford found himself so weakening that he said loudly and firmly, 'It is a ridiculous scheme. Supposing they have no talent? Suppose they're a flop? Suppose—'

The bishop raised a hand for silence. 'That is a point I omitted. They would all, at the end of their first year, consult the principal of their school as to whether they showed promise; if they are advised to give it up, they will forsake the stage for their auxiliary careers.'

'A waste of time and money,' said Mr Fayne cautiously. 'If we could make sure the idea would be a success . . .'

'We don't even know whether they're really good, or whether we only think so because they're ours,' his wife backed him up.

'But you could know. This one-act play competition for which they are so keen to enter is judged by an elderly lady who was once an actress, and is now on the board of the British Actors' Guild. If they were to win it . . .' He stopped, looking hopefully around.

'Win it?'

'But that's impossible!'

'Why should they?'

'If they could not win it, it would show that they are only average amateurs, not really fit to be trained, when there are so many young people crowding the stage. But if they won it – it would help them to get places in some good school, perhaps, and also assure us that they are good actors.'

There was a dubious silence, and the bishop and Mrs Halford exchanged quizzical looks.

'Go on,' she urged, forming the words with silent lips. 'Say some more.'

He thought for a second, then began again. 'As a lover of Fenchester, I feel the need for a good theatre. Although they do not know it at the moment, people would relish good drama, were it made possible. And *we* know, don't we, that the children have a knack of knowing what will entertain? If they can entertain us now, untrained and merely babies, how much more of a success will they be in four or five years' time, fresh from their teachers and at ages of discretion?'

'But supposing in those four years another company comes along and plants itself in Fenchester, what then?' asked Mr Halford.

The bishop smiled.

'They would have to get permission from the town council, and I, as bishop, would advise the council to refuse permission and wait for the Blue Doors. The town council,' he stressed the words, '*they* take my advice.'

'We'll think it over.' Mr Fayne made as if to rise, but the bishop shook his head.

'No, please! I beg you to decide once for all tonight. Your children are in such a state of nerves that it would be cruelty to keep them at that pitch. Won't you discuss it among yourselves for a while, remembering that their careers will always have my interest and blessing?'

He retired to the window seat, picked up a newspaper and pretended to read it. Outside the door the children sank on to the stairs, worn out with eavesdropping. They looked at each other, eyes large with mingled hope and despair. Lyn drew her house-coat more tightly round her and whispered with chattering teeth, 'May I never go through another night like this!' Nigel went into the dining-room and came back holding a cigarette between trembling fingers.

Bulldog rubbed his flushed cheek along the banister to cool it. 'I wish this were the Middle Ages, then if they wouldn't take the bishop's advice he could excommunicate them,' he said forcefully.

On the other side of the door earnest confabulation was going on.

'Please, please, darling Murray,' wheedled Mrs Halford, 'do say yes!' She gripped his hand in her own. 'The bishop has been talking sense, hasn't he? And if Vicky ends her career by marrying someone as good as you . . .' The flutter of eye-lashes was Mr Halford's undoing.

'Oh, have it your own way, woman – that is, if they can win the contest.'

She squeezed his hands excitedly. 'It'll be worth everything to see the look on their faces when we tell them.'

'Come on, Madge,' said Mr Darwin. 'We can't defy the bishop, can we?'

His wife's dark eyes were troubled.

'I don't know what to say! Still, it'll be fairly safe to

say they can if they win the competition.'

'Yes, my dear. Of course, only if they manage to do that. They'll deserve to.'

'It'll be nice if after four years, they're back in Fenchester for good, won't it?' observed Mrs Fayne. 'If they took any other job they'd probably only come home for holidays.'

'There's that about it. Well, I suppose we give in if the others do.'

They went across to hear the other two verdicts. Bulldog was at the keyhole and watched these movements, saw the nods and sighs, and then sheepish smiles. The others understood what was happening by the panorama of expressions that crossed his features. Then came the bishop's low, modulated voice.

'Well? You have decided?'

The girls clung together in an agony of suspense, and it seemed decades and centuries before Mr Halford pronounced the verdict in painfully slow tones.

'We've decided, Bishop, that we will let them enter the contest. If they win they may go to a dramatic school, on condition that they have also some training for another profession, and that they return to Fenchester five years from now.'

'A most sensible decision, and I —' began the bishop, but the sentence was never finished, for the seven adults were engulfed in the rush of seven thrilled figures in night attire, who kissed and hugged them and shook hands with them as if demented.

'You wicked children,' scolded Mrs Fayne, her voice muffled by Maddy's embracing arms. 'You'll catch cold.'

Mrs Halford switched on the electric fire and gave them sherry diluted with water, to warm them up after their draughty vigil in the hall. The parents reminded them every other minute: 'You haven't won the competition yet, remember,' but the Blue Doors were so overjoyed that they could think no damping thoughts. It was past eleven before they could be persuaded to break up the meeting.

Their cheerful good nights were kept up from the door-step until Mr Halford shut it by force.

When the children were finally sent up to bed he and his wife had another chat with the bishop.

'Aren't they sweet when they're happy?' said Mrs Halford.

When they're happy they're very, very happy, and when they're not they're wretched,' misquoted the bishop.

'It's the artistic temperament,' she sighed contentedly.

The next few weeks were ones of intense mental concentration. The Blue Doors sent up for details of the contest, and received full instructions. The name of the lady organizing it was Roma Seymore; in each town she was offering a trophy to the winners. In Fenchester the competition would start on the Wednesday night of the last week in June, for as long as it took for every company entered to perform. The Palace Cinema was to be used; this at one time had been a theatre and was fully equipped for plays. One rehearsal only was allowed in the Palace, and companies could arrange with the manager about their time, which must be in the week before the contest, and some time when the cinema was not being used for films.'

'That means,' said Nigel, 'that we must get it on the Saturday morning, because we shall still be at school, and they'll be showing films in the evenings.'

'Let's go down and bag Saturday morning at once,' said Maddy, who loved to be going places and doing things.

They went, and interviewed the manager, a jolly little man in sandy tweeds with a bald head and waxed moustache.

'Sorry, my dears, it's already booked,' he told them. 'A lady came in here this morning and said she was bringing her company on the Saturday morning, and would I see that the dressing-rooms were clean enough for them to go in. I nearly told her to see if her ladies were clean enough to go into my dressing-rooms. She stank enough of scent and I don't know what.'

'I say,' said Nigel, 'it sounds like Mrs P.-S. Potter-Smith was the name?'

'Couldn't say. But she was head of some parish ladies' institute.'

'That's her,' crowed Bulldog. 'Oh, let us be joyful!'

'I wonder if she would change places with us,' mused Nigel, 'because her ladies can rehearse any time. Still, if she won't . . .'

'Sunday is still free, all day,' the little manager suggested, but Nigel shook his head.

'Sorry, no good.'

'It's bad luck to rehearse on Sundays,' murmured Lyn.

'And the bishop wouldn't like it,' said Sandra.

'Put us down for Friday morning, then,' Nigel said, 'and we'll try to change places with Mrs Potter-Smith.'

As they walked away from his office down the soft-carpeted corridors he added, 'If she won't change we'll have to cut school that morning.'

'We could all catch cold,' suggested Maddy unoriginally.

'Too fishy!' they decided.

'We could eat something, all of us. Something peculiar like – oysters, then get awful pains. That would explain us all being away.'

'Oh, Mrs P.-S. will change. We'll wring her fat neck if she doesn't,' vowed Jeremy.

The same evening they went up to her house. It was a small detached villa with a crazy pavement and a sundial, and several stone figures crowded into the pocket-handkerchief lawn. The door was painted a sickly pink, and, to crown all, it was called 'Chez Moi'.

'Cheese Moy,' read Maddy. 'What a silly name! It ought really to be called "The Potter-Smithy".'

They knocked at the pink front door with a minute door-knocker in the shape of a pixie, with 'A Present from Cornwall' engraved on it. Mrs Potter-Smith had a craze for anything 'dinky', as she called it.

'Has she got a husband?' whispered Maddy, as they waited for an answer.

'No. She's a widow.'

'What a happy deliverance for some poor man!' said Bulldog piously.

A little maid, also in pink, showed them into a room crowded with 'dinky' ornaments and little stools and tables, and soon Mrs Potter-Smith fussed in, in great good humour. When they revealed the reason for their visit she shook her head sadly, disturbing the repose of her double chins, saying:

'Now, isn't that a pity! Saturday morning is the only time I can manage. You see, my nephew from Bristol is coming in to watch the rehearsal, and he will only be in Fenchester on the Saturday.'

'But couldn't your nephew come in to the actual performance?' pleaded Nigel.

'I'm afraid not. He'll be here on business on Saturday, so he won't want to come in again.'

She shut her loose mouth tightly for once, to show that the matter was at an end, and made a move towards the door. They went out despondently, Nigel alone being polite enough to say 'Good night.'

'Come on,' he sighed, picking his way down the narrow crazy pavement. 'We'll go down to the Palace again and take Sunday afternoon. If it's still there.'

'Oh, Nigel,' pleaded Sandra, 'don't let's.'

'Well, look here: is it more wicked to rehearse on Sunday afternoon if we go to church in the morning and evening, than to cut school on Friday morning?'

They could not decide this, and found themselves at the cinema before it was settled.

'Well,' asked the manager kindly, 'did you succeed in changing?'

'No. The beastly old woman wants Saturday just so some beastly nephew can come and watch her still more beastly play.'

'Hard luck! And all day Sunday is booked.' He

showed them his pad. 'Since you've been out I've had phone calls from Fenchester Amateurs, the Police Force Dramatic Club, and the St. Anne's Amateurs.'

'Gosh, what a lot of people are entering. It'll fill up the programme for nights and nights.'

'Yes, it will. But these things always get large audiences, you know.'

'Do they? My goodness!'

'Well, will you keep to Friday, or–'

Suddenly Jeremy asked, 'When do you open in the mornings?'

'Nine o'clock sharp.'

'Oh!' Jeremy's face fell. 'I only wondered if we could come before breakfast one morning.'

The manager looked at them kindly. 'Well, it might be managed. I could arrange for one of my men to be about to open up for you at six o'clock. Would that suit you?'

'Thank you, sir. That's splendid.' They beamed gratefully at him. 'Friday morning before school, then?'

'Certainly. It's a pleasure.'

As they made their way home, Sandra said, 'Aren't people nice to us? Generally speaking, not counting Mrs P.-S.'

'We must be conducive to niceness,' observed Jeremy complacently.

Lyn said, laughing, 'Has it struck you that we've decided to win the contest and arranged for the dress rehearsal, and we've not decided what to act?'

'Gosh, no! And there's only a month. How awful! Anyone got any ideas?' There was silence. 'Don't all speak at once.'

'I bags we write it ourselves, then they'll excuse anything wrong with it, because we're young,' said Jeremy artfully.

'Let's have it modern,' said Vicky.

'And morbid,' said Lyn.

'And – what's the word they use to describe highbrow novels – forceful, that's it,' said Jeremy.

In a week the forceful play was written. They called it *Saddler's Circus*. It was like many one-act plays, not so much a narrative as a character study. The nucleus character was Samuel Saddler, manager and ringmaster of a small circus, a brutal man who dominated and oppressed every member of his troupe. This part was to be played by Nigel, whose dark face could easily be made to look villainous. Sandra was playing the part of his French wife, Annette, whom he had met in Germany where she was studying music, married and brought her back to England to lead a sordid, miserable life, tenting. Through her persuasion Jennifer, a village girl, was induced not to join the circus; she had intended to do so, being in love with Peter, one of the tent-hands. Vicky was Jennifer, as there was a scene where she did acrobatics to show Saddler that she would be some use in the circus. Jeremy was Peter, and played his violin for the acrobatics.

The play took place outside Saddler's caravan, before and during the last evening show in a southern England village, and the theme was the way Annette dissuaded Jennifer from joining the circus. Bulldog was Jock, a clown, whose desire it was to leave the circus and with his savings to buy a little cottage and grow marigolds and hollyhocks. But Saddler, knowing that he was a fine clown, had tricked him into signing a contract that bound him to work till he was unable, and he was forced to keep on under his hard taskmaster.

Another incident that made Jennifer change her mind was the accident that occurred to Bobby, the little brother of Pearl, the bareback rider. These roles were played by Maddy and Lyn respectively. Bobby was learning trapeze, and the night that Jennifer was with Annette at the caravan the trapeze artist was ill, and Saddler made Bobby go on and use the high trapeze, in which he was very inexperienced. He slipped and hurt his back, and the doctor said he would have to lie on his back for the rest of his life, so Saddler sent him to a Home without consulting Pearl. There was a very striking climax. Jennifer having left Peter, the circus members decided to revolt; but as soon as Saddler appears they were once more cowed into submission by his brutality.

They worked with a feverish intensity, rising to rehearse before breakfast on week-days, and spending every evening and all day Saturday at the theatre. Nigel did a backcloth of a caravan, with a matchboard door that opened, and made real wooden steps to sit on. Flopping into bed thankfully after a fifteen-hour day of hard work, they had only time to murmur a sincere prayer before falling into heavy slumber. They knew the play perfectly in two weeks, as it was very short, and took a mere half-hour to perform. It began to get mechanical after a while, but Lyn said that this was good, for it would mean that they could not go wrong in the dialogue, and once before an audience, it would become fresh and spontaneous again. Sandra was sadly disappointed that there were no splendid costumes to prepare, but found for the first time that a part well studied was easier to play.

They took to being the characters in everyday life, bewildering their school friends. Sandra, sprung on to answer in class, would reply with a flutter of hands and a French accent, while Vicky acquired a permanent Somerset drawl. Nigel, when riled, often found himself trying to twist the black moustache he wore in the play, and his language became shocking. Bulldog grumbled that he only felt at home in his white clown suit, borrowed from a member of Vicky's dancing class. Maddy and Lyn studied Cockney from the butcher boy, who was a Londoner, and used some of his choicest expressions to shock their parents. In order to get used to the feel of their clothes they wore them whenever possible about the house.

Nigel assumed splendid attire: a scarlet tailcoat – also borrowed from Vicky's dancing-class friend, tall riding boots, buff breeches that his father had had in India, and Mr Fayne's top hat. An immense whip was borrowed from a leather shop in the town, and a sweeping black moustache completed the effect. Sandra wore a black dress and a white shawl, Lyn a ballet frock of Vicky's, Vicky a blouse and button-through skirt, as she wore tights underneath, Jeremy an old pair of flannels and a grey polo neck jumper, Bulldog the clown suit, Maddy dungarees and a cap to hide her hair. There were no lighting effects, and the only stage properties were the steps and a few soap boxes.

'It's simplicity itself to act,' declared Lyn, 'so I think we ought to try to get real tears where needed, don't you?'

Maddy, of course, could do this with ease, Lyn found it a more difficult job, and Vicky simply could not until the dress rehearsal. This was held before breakfast on Friday, a week before they had to appear, and as the theatre was chilly and unfriendly at this early hour, it helped to make the play still more depressing.

'If it doesn't move the audience it ought to,' pronounced Lyn, when it was over. Then she put the question that had been on their lips for weeks, 'Do you think we'll win?'

'I don't know.'

Nigel slashed with his whip, stepped to the end of the stage, and glaring fiercely out over the empty seats, said firmly, 'But we'll make a good try.'

The deserted theatre echoed the words exultantly.

16

THE SEYMORE TROPHY

Their hands ached with clapping, but still they went on, stamping their feet to supplement the appreciative noise. The members of the Fenchester Teachers' Dramatic Society bowed again and again to the applause, and little bursts of laughter broke out as the more humorous characters took their bows. They had acted a very witty comedy about a village council meeting, and had had the audience eating out of their hands two minutes after the rise of the curtain. They were all elderly, but had the sharp humour peculiar to school teachers. When the curtain fell: 'Gosh,' sighed Lyn, 'we shall never beat them. They deserve to win!'

'That Mr Pringle ought to be on the stage,' remarked Nigel. 'He's better than any actor in touring companies that have been here.'

'Look at Roma Seymore,' said Vicky. 'She's laughing like anything.'

Mrs Seymore was a tall, stately lady with an abundance of jet black hair. Age had not been able to spoil the beauty of her calm white face, and she had luminous, sympathetic eyes. She sat at the table in the gangway of the gallery, and with her was the president of the B.A.G., an elderly gentleman with white hair, and the local secretary, who was a member of the Fenchester Amateurs.

This was the second night of the three, and five of the eight performances had been given. The previous night the contest was opened by the Fenchester Amateurs, who did a scene from *The School for Scandal*. It was well performed, and the Blue Doors felt sure they could not beat it. The St. Anne's Amateurs were next, a small parish club with more enthusiasm than ability. They did a rather sickly play called *Sir John's Bride*. The Fenchester Boys' Brigade completed that night's programme with a thriller that was amusing rather than thrilling, especially in parts that were meant to be serious. Tonight had been very successful, so far. The Police Force Club gave a tough performance in a play taking place in a transport café on the Great North Road, in which there was some excellent fighting, but the teachers were definitely the winners so far.

The Blue Doors had arrived early on both nights to obtain seats near the adjudicator, so that they might study the effect of the various plays on her, as she chatted during the interval with the president and the secretary. The Blue Doors began to feel as if they knew her personally.

Nigel looked on the programme.

'It's Mrs P.-S. and her ladies now,' he observed.

'It's called *The Statue*, said Vicky. 'I expect we'll see Mrs Potter-Smith as Venus.'

'Sh!' said Sandra, as she had been saying every time people made personal remarks. 'There may be friends of hers behind us.'

The curtain rose. Mrs Potter-Smith in her favourite Greek tunic stood in a wobbly pose on a white pedestal, holding a garland of flowers. A group of Bacchanalian 'ladies' ran in, and the Blue Doors wriggled ecstatically in their seats. A slow smile spread over the mobile features of Roma Seymore. It was a ridiculous play, the theme being the return to life of a statue of some Greek goddess, and her romance with a present-day young man. The modern young man was played by Mr Bell's junior curate, who looked like a most mournful relic from the Victorian era, and spoke in a muffled undertone. The Greek goddess thumped about the stage, striking dramatic poses and declaiming in her weak, sugary voice. Agony replaced the amusement of the adjudicator, and she scribbled in her notebook. Some impolite people, noticeably those who had performed their plays, actually laughed aloud, but the Blue Doors stuffed handkerchiefs in their mouths, and were relieved to think that, after this, they could certainly not be bottom.

When the statue had at last returned to her pedestal and the curtain fell Sandra said, 'Come on, now, home and bed, and we must sleep late in the morning, even if it means being late for school. We don't want headaches tomorrow night.'

They hurried home discussing the plays hypercritically. At their gates Lyn said, 'Do you think we'll win?'

No one answered, for the Fenchester Teachers had made a big impression on them.

'We can only try,' Nigel said at last, and they went

to sleep with valiant hope in their hearts.

'Can you answer that question, Madelaine?' asked Miss Green suddenly.

Maddy jerked herself away from her dreams.

'No, Miss Green.'

'Can you if you think carefully?'

'No,' said Maddy.

'Did you hear the question?'

'No,' said Maddy.

'Have you *any* interest whatsoever in what I've been saying?'

'No,' said Maddy truthfully, and received her third order mark that day. The first was for over-sleeping and being late for school, and the second was for breaking a pipette in chemistry.

The other girls, now in Middle Five A, had hardly fared better. Vicky had an order mark for turning round to talk to Lyn, Sandra burnt a pudding in cookery, and Lyn felt sick with nerves and had to go and lie down. In the afternoon at the Grammer School Bulldog played so horribly in a cricket practice that he was put out of the second team.

They met at the bottom of the Grammar School hill and strolled slowly home.

'Shall we go up on the fields and have a rest as usual?' asked Sandra.

'I've got to go and have a bath and do my feet,' objected Vicky.

'You'll have time afterwards,' Jeremy told her. 'The show doesn't start until half past seven, and we're the second and last to perform. That means we shan't be able to see the Hanston Dramatic Class show.'

'I was thinking,' said Sandra, 'that if we don't win we could join Miss Hanston's class.'

'About all we'll be fit for.' Nigel moodily picked leaves off a hedge as he passed, leaving a trail of green behind him.

'I think I shall be a school mistress if we don't win, then I shall join the Fenchester Teachers,' said Lyn.

'What will you teach? Maths.?'

'Don't be sarcastic. English, of course.'

They lay under the tree on Miller's Hill, pretending not to be frightened.

'Won't it be annoying if we only lose by one or two marks?' said Nigel.

'It'll be more annoying if we lose by *more* than two or three.'

'Yes; but it won't be a "so near and yet so far" feeling.'

'It'll be an anticlimax,' said Lyn, her hands under her head, gazing up into the dizzily blue sky. Lyn hated anticlimax.

They went home to tea, to find their parents in as nervous a condition as themselves. Mr Halford surprised his children by saying, 'Well, I hope you're going to do me credit by winning tonight.'

'We hope so, Dad!'

The parents were coming to watch that night, but did not start out with the children, who had to go to the Blue Door Theatre to fetch their costumes. They went into their little haven and surveyed it lovingly.

'I do wish we were acting here tonight. We'd feel so

much more at home,' sighed Sandra regretfully.

'But it'll be nice to act on a really large stage, won't it?' said Lyn.

'Yes, but we'll have to speak up. Inaudibility is one of the greatest sins,' remarked Nigel.

'Where shall we put the trophy if we win it?' asked Maddy.

'We could put up a bracket over the door.'

'What's the trophy like? Does anybody know?'

'A cup, I should think,' Vicky speculated.

They looked up at the door, trying to imagine a cup reposing above it, then Nigel said, 'Come on, there's an hour and a half before we go on at nine.' He picked up the immense roll of paper, thickened at one end with cardboard, that was the caravan backcloth. Bulldog took up the wooden steps, and the girls the attaché cases; they made their way to the Palace Cinema. Tonight there was no need to show their little badges with 'Performer' to gain admission, for the girl in the box office, seeing their luggage, smiled and wished them good luck.

'I advise you to go round to the stage door,' she said. 'It'll be easier than by the manager's office.'

'Of course, how stupid of us!'

As they retraced their footsteps from the foyer many people turned to stare at these extraordinarily young performers. They were shown into two tiny bare dressing-rooms by the manager, who expressed his earnest hope that they might win.

Sandra set out their cosmetics and brushes and combs on the dressing-table, their flannels and soap at the wash basin, and pronounced that it looked more homely. Lyn was thrilled to find a notice on the wall saying that Mrs Siddons had once used the dressing-room while on tour.

'Gosh! This part of the theatre must be pretty old,' she said. 'I wonder if *she* had stage fright?'

Jeremy knocked at the door to ask Sandra to come and make them up.

'It's funny not to be able to hear you on the other side of the curtain,' he said with a grin. 'Quite a rest cure.'

The boys' dressing-room was already in a litter, and she gave them a good scolding as she bustled about, tidying up.

'This isn't the way to win trophies,' she said. 'The place looks as though a pig has been let loose. Bulldog, fold up your shirt, and have you got enough on under your clown suit? It'll be draughty on the stage.'

'Don't fuss,' rebuked the clown, doing a somersault. 'I pity your children, Sandra.'

'If I didn't fuss, no one else would. Come here and be made beautiful.'

She slammed on the conventional clown's make-up, red nose and cheeks on dead white face.

'You don't need much make-up, Jerry,' she told him. 'Or rather, you wouldn't if we were at the Blue Door, but here, with footlights, you'll have to. I've bought some real grease paint.'

She made him up with a pale face and heavy blue lines under his eyes, brushing his fair hair till it shone.

'Yes, you look just right; attractive but weak.'

'That's me all over,' he said complacently.

Nigel was still looking peaceful and law abiding in his ringmaster's clothes, but without any make-up. Sandra gave his eyes emphasis, and made the contour lines of his face less pleasant, and the moustaches completed the evil effect. He twirled them joyously.

'Sing ho, for the life of a cad.'

'And now I must dash and see to the girls. How much longer, Nigel?'

'Three-quarters of an hour.'

The familiar sights met her eyes in the girls' dressing-room – Lyn pacing the floor like a caged lioness; Vicky limbering up, holding on to a chair; and Maddy screwed up into a tight little ball, sitting on a chair with her face on her knees.

'Come on,' Sandra said calmly, 'who's going to be made up first? You, Vicky, because you're easiest.'

She gave her a normal, beautifying make-up and told her to hurry and dress, so there would be no need to dash at the last minute. Lyn was made up with scarlet lips, white face, with a trace of colour high on the cheekbones; but try as she might Sandra could get no resemblance between her and Maddy as brother and sister. She gave Maddy a sunburnt face, and was just about to settle down to her own make-up when Vicky said, 'Good Lord, you're not going to leave the child like that?'

'Why not?'

'Look at her lily-white arms and feet.' And Sandra had to use nearly all the stick of sunburn tint on her sister's fair limbs.

Her own make-up was not easy, as she was supposed to be getting on for forty, and by the time she had reduced her face to a harassed and lined but faintly beautiful condition, there were only another ten minutes before the end of the play the Hanston Dramatic Class was performing.

Lyn, in her ballet dress, hurried distractedly up and down the room, despite her shaking knees. She knew that if she could only act well there would be a better chance of their winning, but if she was still feeling as she did now, it would be impossible. But it was essential that they should win. They must, they must, they must! She murmured the words aloud.

'What did you say, Lyn?' asked Sandra.

'Nothing. Sandra, do you feel all right?'

'I don't feel as bad as I did before our first concert. Remember?'

'Don't I!'

The next few minutes were filled by reminiscing, but when they stopped, the clock still showed five minutes to go.

'Come on. Let's get into the wings.'

They put on their cloaks, either party or *Spanish Inn* ones, and went along to the boys' dressing-room. Nigel and Bulldog were smoking. Sandra eyed them with disapproval.

'Don't be sick, Bulldog, for goodness' sake.'

'I hope you haven't had any cigarettes, Jerry,' said Lyn. 'You know that they always upset you.'

'Oh, you women!' grumbled Nigel. 'You even grudge us our simple pleasures. What's that stink?'

'Maddy eating peppermints for her nerves.'

'Thank goodness I don't have to kiss her.'

Suddenly all their banter seemed meaningless and futile, and they were silent. Lyn looked at everyone as if seeing them for the first time.

'We'll win,' she said simply, 'if we're meant to.'

They nodded agreement.

'Come on,' said Jeremy, without making any movement towards the door.

They seemed rooted to the spot. Then a knock at the door, and the manager stood on the threshold, holding out a note.

'The other play is just ending. Good luck again.'

Nigel opened the note.

'Act well, Blue Doors,' it read. 'We shall clap our hardest', and was signed by the Bells, the bishop, and their parents.

Maddy laughed softly. 'How kind of them!'

'Come on,' said Sandra. 'Don't forget the backcloth and tacks.'

The corridor to the wings was bare and draughty and echoed with the applause given for the play that had just ended. The boys hurried on to the stage with a step-ladder and hung the backcloth, while the Hanston Dramatic Class came off, laughing and talking. Miss Hanston, their producer, looked hard at the girls as they stood, arms linked, in the wings.

'Who is your producer?' she asked them, in a kind but partonizing tone.

'I am,' said Lyn sweetly, looking about six in her ballet

frock, and Miss Hanston asked in surprise, 'Are you from some school, then?'

'No, not really.'

'You're not professionals, I hope,' she said with distaste, glancing at Vicky's legs, which were typically of the ballet.

'Oh no, we're still amateur.'

'Come on, Sandra and Maddy,' called Nigel.

They sighed and took up their places, Sandra sitting on the steps, Maddy cross-legged at her feet, whittling a stick. As Jeremy passed, on his way back to the wings, she caught his hand.

'Oh, Jerry! . . .'

'You'll be all right, Maddy. You look splendid; a real little tough.'

'I can't remember a word,' murmured Sandra, bringing out her knitting. Since they started rehearsing she had done nearly a whole scarf.

'Ready, Maddy?'

Maddy settled herself more comfortably.

'O.K.'

Sandra nodded across to the man who was working the curtain. It rose, displaying the vast expanse of 'wondering upturned eyes of mortals'. Maddy and Sandra had a shock when a burst of clapping broke out. The audience were showing their approval of the painted caravan. It was by far the best piece of scenery in the contest. Maddy threw down her stick and yawned loudly, stretching like a puppy.

'You are tired, my Bobby?'

'Gosh yes, Aunt Annette.'

And the play was swinging on its way in the words and actions that they knew so well and which had become a part of their lives. Bobby, leaning against Annette's knee, begged her to sing to him. She sang to the tune of Brahms' 'Lullaby' an old. French rhyme; while she did so Vicky, as Jennifer, entered, asking Annette if she could see Saddler, and find out if she was good enough to join the circus.

He growled that he did not want any more women on his hands, but said he would see her. She slipped off her skirt and handed it to her sweetheart Peter with her handbag, and politely asked if she might use the steps. Annette and Bobby moved off, and she began to twist and turn into her complicated contortions

Roma Seymore whispered to the president, 'I fear this is going to turn into a variety show. She's very good, though.'

'And young,' he remarked. 'I wonder if they're all juveniles?'

After a final whirl of cartwheels, Vicky as Jennifer mounted the second step, and facing the caravan, bent back till her hand grasped the first step, then walked down till she reached the ground. She heard the gasp from the audience, and so mounted a second time on to the third step. As she bent back, she saw first the tangle of ropes and pulleys on the floor, then the players upside down, then, finally, the bottom step and the ground.

She strained the muscles of her abdomen; she stayed arched, with hands not touching the floor, and suddenly she remembered her old ambition, the acrobatic feat she had tried so many times and failed to perform.

She would do it now or never. She relaxed her stomach muscles for a second, kicking with her legs. For a brief second she was in the air, then her hands, giving at the wrists to break the shock, came into contact with the boards of the stage, and her feet followed a second later. She stood up amazed and triumphant. The others only just remembered in time that to circus folk this would not seem marvellous. It seemed so to the audience. They clapped vigorously, and Vicky was about to bow to them when she saw Lyn in the wings shaking her head.

Saddler gave his permission for her to join the circus, and strode off to officiate in the ring, roaring at Peter to go and help in the stables. Left with Annette, Jennifer heard all about her sad life.

'What do you think of them?' asked the President.

'They're good, very good. Look, she's really crying,' and Sandra was, easily, but controlledly, as she told of how she had left the life on the Continent that she adored.

The rest of the play, telling how each member of the circus did his best to dissuade Jennifer from joining them, went better than it had ever done before, and the silent audience were clearly enthralled. To the cast, the time sped by, and it seemed incredible that they should have reached the closing lines.

'Why, why, why . . .' cried Annette, advancing towards the footlights, 'does he treat us like this?'

'Why do we put up with it?' asked Peter brokenly.

'We belong to Saddler's Circus . . .' said Pearl dully.

'A riot of fun and splendour,' added Jock, and they

laughed, softly at first, then rising to a crescendo of mirthless hilarity. They split their sides, but it was not infectious laughter, and the audience gripped the sides of their seats.

'What actors!' murmured Roma Seymore as the curtain fell.

Nigel ran down the steps to the others, and they danced madly round, hugging each other, till the curtain man told them he was going to raise the curtain for their bows. Amid thunderous applause they acknowledged the appreciation of the audience. Their parents were waving and smiling from the front row of the balcony.

'Roma is clapping,' whispered Maddy, doffing her cap so that her pony-tail escaped.

'My goodness,' gasped Roma, 'I thought it was a little boy!'

'And so did I!' The president leaned forward. 'By jove, that was good make-up and characterization.'

The local secretary laughed. 'I could have told you that was little Maddy Fayne.'

'How old is the one that played the ringmaster?'

'About seventeen or eighteen, but still at school. He's the eldest.'

'Well, well, well, this *is* extraordinary!'

Roma wrote in her notebook as the curtains swished to and fro across the smiling seven.

'So young,' was on everybody's lips, and the parents were revelling in the flow of compliments from the people behind, who did not know their connection with the actors. At last the audience let them go. They described to each other in detail their feelings and emotions, and all congratulated Vicky on her acrobatic triumph.

'It came suddenly,' she explained, 'and I just had to.'

'It was O.K., wasn't it?' said Sandra eagerly. 'They liked us.'

'But have we won? Have we beaten the Fenchester Teachers?' Nigel wrinkled his brow anxiously.

'It all depends now on Roma Seymore, whether she prefers comedy or tragedy. I think the applause was equal.'

The corridor was suddenly filled with members of the other companies.

'Come on,' they said, 'Roma wants us all on the stage. She's going to give out the results.'

They hurried into the dressing-rooms and put on their everyday clothes, washed their faces, and did their hair.

'I begin to feel less brutal,' said Nigel, as he removed his moustache with cold cream.

'Do we look tidy?' Sandra inspected them before they went on to the crowded stage. Chairs were standing in lines facing the audience, and they took places in the back row. Mrs Potter-Smith turned round to say, 'Oh, my *dears*, you don't *know* how *melancholy* you've made us feel. Everyone says that they'd have nervous breakdowns if they had to sit through your perfectly *agonizing* play again. I *do* hope you win!'

At this moment Roma came on; she had not forgotten how to make a graceful and charming entrance. First of all the mayor spoke a few halting but genial words, then the president. Then Roma rose.

'Ladies and gentlemen, I cannot tell you how much pleasure it has given me to be here tonight.'

In her perfect carrying voice she went on to pay compliments to the audience, the mayor, and the manager of the theatre.

'And now, the results! I will begin at the bottom, so that the pleasantest moments may be left till last. The company to whom I gave least points must not feel hurt, as it made a gallant effort, but has a lot to learn. I speak of the St. Michael's Ladies' Institute.' Mrs Potter-Smith's fat back heaved. 'The chief reason for its failure to reach the standard of the others lay in the choice of play. The characters were quite unsuited to the ladies' ages and shapes. Now, please don't take this as an insult. It was such a bad choice of a play that I cannot really judge the dramatic ability of the players. I must say, that had this company acted the play performed by the Blue Doors their success might have been greater. The lady who played the statue would have made a far more convincing circus-owner's wife.'

'Does she think I didn't!' wondered Sandra anxiously.

A slow flush was spreading over the back of Mrs Potter-Smith's neck.

'I alotted twenty marks to this company, ten for scenery, which was quite colourful, five for audibility, which was good on the whole, and five for keeping on when they must have sensed that the play had fallen flat.'

She went on with her criticisms, which were clever and witty, with many subtle digs that amused the audience.

The Boys' Brigade received fifty points from the hundred and St. Anne's Amateurs fifty-two. Fenchester Amateurs came next with sixty, and a good deal of praise, then the Halston Dramatic Class with sixty-five. The Blue Doors, holding hands and sucking peppermints to keep calm, expected to hear their name at any minute.

'The remaining three were so very good that I have great difficulty in sorting them out. In the end I awarded seventy to the Police Force. Their characterization was excellent, and it was a thrilling piece of action, but their articulation – oh dear!' She went on to explain their faults in this respect. 'Now, the second place goes, after much hesitation on my part . . .'

'Don't hesitate now, please,' whispered Vicky.

'. . . to the Fenchester Teachers.'

There was a gasp and a sob from the back row of chairs. Mrs Potter-Smith swung round and said vehemently to Maddy, 'If you breathe any more peppermint down my neck . . .' They did not hear the glowing appreciation that Roma gave the Fenchester Teachers, nor the applause of the audience; they were having a private gloat on their own.

'We've won!'

'We go to dramatic school!'

'We go on the stage!'

'We make the Blue Doors professional!'

'We build a theatre for Fenchester!'

'We've realized our ambitions!'

'And now – the winners. What a splendid band of young actors!' She turned and smiled at them. 'And didn't they enjoy acting? Not more than we did watching. It was an example of characterization, and the emotional parts were wonderful. I shall never forget the performance of Pearl, nor the heartrending sobs of her little brother, who, up till the time that she took off her cap, I quite believed to be a little boy. Saddler himself was gloriously brutal, and his wife was a sympathetic little portrayal, and what a sweet voice! Jennifer was a bit stiff; perhaps compared with the circus folk she should be so, but her acrobatics were splendid. This company is accomplished in many ways, for the handsome young man who played Peter played the violin equally well. The clown, though a small part, was well done, and the person who did the charming backcloth deserves special praise. There were faults, but none worth mentioning. The actors' accents were well sustained and the climax excellent. I propose we give the winners an extra clap.' She led the applause. 'Now will their producer come for the Seymore trophy?'

Smiling, she unwrapped a parcel that she was carrying, displaying the bronze figure of a woman holding out a laurel wreath. In a dream Lyn walked up to the footlights, her cheeks flushed to match the red velvet of her dress.

'Are you the producer?' she was asked by the amazed Mrs Seymore.

'Well, yes, in name,' she replied, smiling up into the friendly eyes, 'but the play produced itself.'

She took the heavy statue and turned to the applauding audience. What was she expected to do now? Why, of course — behave just as in the word-picture she had painted to the others that day at Browcliffe. She curtsied, then looking up to the familiar faces in the gallery, kissed her hand. The applause grew deafening, and gradually the people rose in their seats, still clapping. The theatre stood and cheered and stamped, while Lyn bowed and smiled for an eternity.

17

THE CURTAIN FALLS

They lay on the cliff top, baking in the sunshine. Although they had only left the blue water five minutes ago they were nearly dry. Lyn, in a semi-coma of drowsy heat, went over the remarkable events that had just ended. Or had they just begun? After the contest Roma Seymore had talked with their parents, and expressed her delight when she heard that they were to have a professional training.

'But they must come to the B.A.G. School, of course,' she cried. 'The president here is the principal of it, and I'm sure he would love to have the opportunity of training them, wouldn't you, Mr Whitfield?'

Mr Whitfield replied that he would, and when he found that Mrs Halford had been a professional, informed them that he could take Nigel and the twins at a reduced rate. Mr and Mrs Halford made an expedition to London with Nigel, to look at the school and to buy him some new clothes, and for the last week the Blue Doors had talked of nothing but the B.A.G. Dramatic School. Nigel gave the most glowing descriptions of it, and could hardly wait till the autumn term began in September. The Blue Doors found themselves reverencing Nigel as he was about to depart.

'It seems like a dream.' Lyn spoke aloud, stretching herself luxuriously in the sun.

'Just what I was thinking,' said Vicky, towelling her damp curls vigorously. 'I feel as if it's still the day we came here two years ago. The time has flown and yet – so much has happened.'

'Gosh, hasn't it!' Maddy was stirred by the thought. 'The first thing that happened was Vicky teaching me to stand on my head.'

'Then you broke the window, Maddy.'

'Yes,' she agreed proudly. 'I did the most important thing in the two years. If I hadn't, we should never have found the theatre.'

'Then there was that tea-party at the Bells'.'

'And the first concert.'

'And Stratford-on-Avon.'

'And the garden fête.'

'And the pantomime.'

'And the Easter concert.'

'And the bishop's little meeting in the Corner House.'

'And the contest.'

'And me going up to London,' ended Nigel, and once more was plagued with fresh questions about the school.

'Now let's think about the future . . .' began Lyn.

'There'll be Nigel going in September.'

'We'll throw a farewell party.'

'We shall be taking G.C.E. in a year's time.'

'We'll go to dramatic school in a year next Christmas.' Sandra rolled over on her back. 'Oh, we're lucky. All our dreams have come true; all our ambitions have been realized; and all our castles in the air are now solid ones.'

'All because Nigel and the twins came,' put in Jeremy. 'Even Maddy's got her name in the paper, as she wished.'

They let their minds run over the gushing praise they had received from the *Fenshire County Times*.

'Haven't we all changed since we've been together?' remarked Nigel.

'Rather!' agreed Maddy. 'We were far too "refaned" and highbrow before you came.'

'Maddy refaned! You make me laugh,' said Bulldog.

'But it's true,' insisted Lyn. 'We didn't like jazz—'

'I don't know that I do now —' put in Jeremy.

'Go on with you! That's only a pose. We didn't like dancing particularly, and we thought far too much about being respectable to have a good time.'

'Well, you've done a lot for *us*,' said Vicky. 'We never thought or spoke seriously till we met you, and we knew nothing about things that really matter. In fact, we were nitwitted.'

'We speak,' laughed Maddy, 'as if we were paragons at the moment.'

'We've sort of cancelled out each other's faults,' remarked Nigel. 'Oh dear, I wish I hadn't to be the first to venture out into the great big world.'

'What a silly thing to say!' reproached Lyn. 'It'll be a better adventure than if you were hampered by all of us.'

'And I shall never go,' sighed Maddy. 'How sad!'

'But you'll be luckier than any of us! You'll come to the Blue Door *Professional* Theatre Company as soon as you leave school.'

A picture of the Seymore trophy on its bracket above the blue door swept across Lyn's mind. 'At least we've got something to look at after the theatre, while we're not using it,' she remarked. 'I mean the trophy.'

'Yes, it looks marvellous on that shelf, doesn't it? We must win some more.'

'My little yacht is still in the same place as two years ago,' said Nigel.

Following his gaze they looked out to where the yacht still tacked idly, a white spot against the blue.

'We'll often come here when we're professionals, won't we?' said Maddy. 'Not give it up for the more fashionable places.'

'Of course not,' they assured her. 'We shall never be really fashionable ourselves, not as we should if we took jobs in London.'

'I shan't be sorry to come back to Fenchester,' said Sandra. 'I mean, we owe it something, don't we? It gave us the theatre and nice audiences.'

'And each other,' added Vicky.

'Of course. "Each other" is the most important.' They smiled round affectionately.

'I feel friendly towards the world in general,' announced Jeremy. 'Today is a perfect day.'

'It's the kind of day that sticks in your memory.'

'It seems to be sort of between the past and the future.'

The past was clear and colourful as a tapestry as they gazed out across the sea that was shrouded and misty as the future.

THE CURTAIN FALLS

THE RUNAWAYS

Elizabeth Goudge

When the Linnets run away, fate delivers them a pony and trap – taking them to their extraordinary Uncle Ambrose and his unusual household – and the bees who protect the children from harm.

Although Uncle Ambrose makes them learn latin, the children have the freedom to roam the moors and the Devonshire village – and discover the secrets it is hiding . . .

HENRIETTA'S HOUSE

Elizabeth Goudge

One summer's day, Henrietta sets off for a picnic among the Somerset hills, with her brother and grandparents, their friends and animals.

But something wonderful is afoot that golden afternoon. Strangely, each of the horses goes a different way, carrying the occupants of the carriages into unexpected adventures in the lush woods and echoing caves. Now the familiar hills are a place of timeless magic: wishes – and fears – are mysteriously heard . . .

And Henrietta's dearest wish has always been to have a house . . .

Hodder Modern Classics

WHISTLE DOWN THE WIND

Mary Hayley Bell

'Now look. This is to be a strict secret. Not a word to a soul.'

There's something special about the stranger hiding in the barn. Brat, Swallow and Poor Baby know it is their duty to look after him.

But then the grown-ups hear about him – they're on the lookout for an escaped convict. They don't believe that the stranger could be Jesus.

It's up to the *children* to protect him from the Doubters.

HODDER MODERN CLASSICS

☐ 72265 7   HENRIETTA'S HOUSE   £3.99
              Elizabeth Goudge
☐ 68166 7   THE RUNAWAYS   £3.99
              Elizabeth Goudge
☐ 69012 7   WHISTLE DOWN THE WIND   £3.99
              Mary Hayley Bell

All Hodder Children's books are available at your local bookshop, or can be ordered direct from the publisher. Just tick the titles you would like and complete the details below. Prices and availability are subject to change without prior notice.

Please enclose a cheque or postal order made payable to *Bookpoint Ltd*, and send to: Hodder Children's Books, 39 Milton Park, Abingdon, OXON OX14 4TD, UK.
Email Address: orders@bookpoint.co.uk

If you would prefer to pay by credit card, our call centre team would be delighted to take your order by telephone. Our direct line *01235 400414* (lines open 9.00 am–6.00 pm Monday to Saturday, 24 hour message answering service). Alternatively you can send a fax on *01235 500454.*

TITLE		FIRST NAME		SURNAME	

ADDRESS	
DAYTIME TEL:	POST CODE

If you would prefer to pay by credit card, please complete:
Please debit my Visa/Access/Diner's Card/American Express (delete as applicable) card no:

Signature .... Expiry Date: ....

If you would NOT like to receive further information on our products please tick the box. ☐